THE OUTLANDISH KNIGHT

Further Titles by Richard Adams

THE OUTLANDISH KNIGHT

Richard Adams

This first world edition published in Great Britain 2000 by
SEVERN HOUSE PUBLISHERS LTD of
9–15 High Street, Sutton, Surrey SM1 1DF.
This first world edition published in the U.S.A. 2000 by
SEVERN HOUSE PUBLISHERS INC of
595 Madison Avenue, New York, N.Y. 10022.

British Library Cataloguing in Publication Data

Adams,   Richard,   1920-
The outlandish knight
1.Historical fiction
I. Title
823.9'14 [F]

ISBN 0-7278-5496-8

Typeset by Palimpsest Book Production Ltd.,
Polmont, Stirlingshire, Scotland.
Printed and bound in Great Britain by
MPG Books Ltd, Bodmin, Cornwall.

*To my sister, Katherine Sales, the historian
whom I tried in vain to emulate.*

Part One

The spring and early summer of 1485 had been marked by weather as bad as any in living memory; late frosts in May, followed by rain and high winds which had flattened great patches of the standing corn. Nor had the fruit – for the most part pears and apples – ripened as it should have, for the sun had scarcely shone between the expanses of cloud. By mid-July men everywhere had become discouraged and worked half-heartedly, as though at a game they knew they could not win. All across the land stretched the contrary weather, which showed no sign of any change for the better. Most rated it as sheer bad luck, but there were not wanting those who felt it to be divine retribution.

The bad summer, said these who claimed to know for a certainty, was doing no more than reflect the corrupt, evil state of the whole realm. It was ubiquitous punishment naturally consequent upon the whole society's wanton destruction of law and order. Men were no longer even trying to seek peace and ensure it, and this bleak sentence was the inevitable result. For years past the country had been torn apart by murderous civil wars; and these showed no sign of ending. Four years ago, the Duke of Gloster had declared himself king, but his many enemies – and in particular the Welsh lord Henry Tudor, biding his time in Normandy – were gathering against him and awaiting their opportunity to depose him by force of arms. The kingdom could provide no security for honest men to ply their trades or work in the fields. God himself could repose no confidence in this land of hardened sinners. They were getting the weather they deserved.

One morning of late July, rain was falling steadily on the village of Crenley in the eastern Cotswolds; and there were few people out and about along the street. A tranter was delivering a load of logs to the priest's woodshed. Two labourers, with spades and pickaxes, had abandoned their work on a length of blocked drain and were sheltering under a nearby ash tree; and a servant girl was running down the street as fast as she could go, her arms full of clean washing to be taken to a widow who turned an honest penny by ironing.

The only other person to be seen appeared to be in no particular haste to reach any destination and was almost idling as he made his way slowly up the street, looking about him here and there as he went. He was wearing riding-boots and from time to time he kicked at a loose stone as though angry at its temerity in coming in his way. Over one shoulder he was carrying a knapsack, while over the other was slung a well-wrapped bundle which showed itself, by size and shape, to be a lute, and hence its owner to be a travelling minstrel. This accounted for his careless bearing as he strolled through the rain. As a wayfarer, he was probably used to it.

He was a sturdy, well-built young fellow; of middling height, in his mid-twenties, his fair hair flattened by the rain. He was wearing a leather jerkin and, belted at his waist, a sword in a scabbard. He looked anything but cheerful, gazing up and down the street with a preoccupied frown that seemed to take in little of what he saw. From time to time he tossed his head impatiently, as though to break off an unwelcome train of thought.

At length he came to the horse-chestnut tree that stood in front of The Red Lion; and here he came to a stop, putting down his two bundles and leaning back against its trunk with closed eyes, as though he was weary. After a minute or two he was alerted by the footsteps of the servant girl returning from her errand. As she passed by he smiled at her and asked, "How far is it to Gloster, sweetheart, do you know?"

She did not return his smile, but only pointed to the door of the inn as she continued on her way. "They'll tell you in there."

He nodded thanks at her retreating back, went across to the door and entered. At this time of day the tap-room was empty except for the publican, old Jim Spencer, who was on his knees, mending the fire with a couple of beech logs. He returned the minstrel's greeting, got to his feet and asked, "Well, what you goin' t'ave now you be 'ere?"

"A pint of the best," answered the minstrel, and put down a crown on the table.

"Cor bugger!" cried Jim. "Us can't change the like of they! If you wants pint you'll 'ave to break 'im smaller."

"No, one for you and one for me," replied the minstrel, and sat down beside the fire.

They were soon chatting together, about the weather, the disappointing promises of a poor harvest and the grossly unfair local levies of stone-picking for road upkeep enforced by the sheriff's officers.

"Ah," said Jim, "but I reckon 'ee don't have to worry 'bout that, do 'ee? Don't come from round 'ere, near's I can tell?"

"Well, you're quite right," replied the minstrel. "I was on the road to Gloster yesterday. Left my horse tied up to a post beside the road; not gone ten minutes and come back to find horse and money stolen. Left me with a single crown in my pocket." He grinned. "Been cursing ever since."

Jim replied with appropriate sympathy, and maledictions on the thief. "An' you ain't the only one, I'll tell 'ee. Feller come in 'ere only last Wednesday, bin served just 'bout the same trick. So what do 'ee reckon to do, like? You won't be walkin' to Gloster, not if I knows anythin' 'bout it."

"No, it's not near as bad as that, thank the Lord," answered the minstrel. "I shan't find my horse again and I'm not fool enough to think I shall. No, what I want to do now is get another horse somehow. Only my business in Gloster's urgent, you see, and if I'm not there according to agreement, I'll lose one of the best bits of business come my way in a long time."

"Ah, and ee'll 'ave a right old job to get 'orse round 'ere," said Jim. "Best thing 'ee can do now is go on over to the new manor buildin' site. That'll be your best chance. You does some work for 'en, they might let you 'ave 'orse. They got a tidy few up there, I knows that."

"How far is it?"

"'Bout three-four mile. But today – Wednesdays, that is – they sends a cart to the mill regular, picks up sacks of flour an' all such things as that. You wants go down there, ask 'em give 'ee a ride back. They won't be gone yet – no, nor for 'our or two. No hurry."

"Fine," replied the minstrel. "Let me get us two more pints then, and I'll have some bread and cheese too."

Some time later he asked the way to the mill.

"Bout 'alf a mile straight on, then you comes to Mill Lane on the left. Go straight down, an' 'ee'll come to the mill."

The minstrel thanked him and set forth. The rain had stopped and a watery sun was peering here and there between the clouds. He had gone only a short way down Mill Lane when he heard from beyond the bend ahead of him sounds of jeering and laughter and a woman's voice crying in shrill protest. He broke into a run and rounded the bend.

What he found was a gang of boys, perhaps six or seven altogether, who were harrying and teasing an old woman. She was bareheaded, supporting herself on a stick and trying in vain to break free of her tormentors. The minstrel, plunging into the mêlée, laid about them with his fists, provoking plenty of swearing and protest. In half a minute the gang had made off, and the minstrel turned to help their victim, who stood weeping close by.

Putting an arm round her shoulders, he led her to the bank beside the lane, pulled off his jerkin and spread it for her to sit on. He asked no questions but spoke only such words of reassurance and comfort as came to him spontaneously. "You're all right now. I'm with you; I shan't go away. Just sit here quietly until you feel better," and so on, in a gentle, repetitive murmur not unlike birdsong.

After some five minutes or so, she had regained her self-possession and thanked him again and again. Perceiving that she felt the better for talking, he led her on to tell him about herself and her way of life.

It was the old story. She had been widowed a few years before and had come to Crenley, to which she was a stranger, because a kindly friend – a farmer for whom her husband had once worked – had told her that she was welcome to live rent-free in a cottage he owned. The Church gave her a pittance, and with this she managed as best she could. Naturally, there were not wanting malicious local people to say that she must be a witch, and the village children molested her whenever they got the chance. She wept again as she told him this, leaning on his arm as he led her gently up the lane.

He walked with her to her cottage and accompanied her inside. The living-room was scrupulously tidy and the windows were as clean as everything else. The minstrel settled her comfortably in the single armchair and, hoping he might be able to give her a little more encouragement, showed himself in no particular hurry to leave.

After they had talked for a while, the poor old woman told him how sorry she was to have nothing to offer him. "It would have been different once," she said, "before my goodman died." A little later she excused herself.

When she returned she was carrying in her arms a black cat, which showed not the least timidity at seeing the visitor, but settled down comfortably on her lap and began to purr.

"This is my best friend now," she said. "Of course, if you're old and live alone with a cat, you must be a witch, mustn't you? But I couldn't be without him. We're fond of each other, and he's a good mouser, too."

As the minstrel admired and stroked the cat, she went on. "Of course, in a way, I've only got myself to thank for folk saying I'm a witch. I can read palms, you know – 'twas my Spanish grandmother taught me long ago, when I was a girl – and when I first came here I set out to make a little extra money by reading the palm of anyone who was ready to pay a trifle for it."

She paused, bending over the cat and tickling its ears. Then she said, "It's strange, but I think it might have been all right if I *hadn't* told the truth; I mean, if I'd just made up a lot of nonsense and they could have laughed about it; but I couldn't do that. When I told the truth – whether it was past or future – people grew suspicious and sometimes unkind. They wanted to know how I did it, and of course that's something that can't be told – not in words. In the end the priest came and told me I was to stop and *he* wasn't very kind, either."

7

"Grandmother," said the minstrel, taking her hand and kissing it, "you must read my palm. As for telling anyone else, why, I'm travelling alone and I'll be clean gone tonight or tomorrow. I'm a stranger here; don't know anyone to tell even if I wanted to." As he spoke he put some coins on the table, all but his one last groat.

It was not hard to tell how much the money would mean to her. He pressed her as gently and politely as he could, stressing that this was no coxcomb frivolity on his part; he believed in and trusted her, and had so uncertain a future that to learn something of it would be more valuable to him than to ordinary folk.

At length he persuaded her, sat down beside her on a stool and offered his right hand.

"No," she said sharply, almost peremptorily, "the left, the left." It was extraordinary to see how her air of penury, helplessness and dejection melted away like mist from a window-pane, and dignity came upon her without the least incongruity. No wonder, thought the minstrel, that people had believed her to be a witch. She had authority. She was at her mystery: she was a huntress, controlling and leading her invisible pack. He looked at her dragon eyes, looked away and shivered, almost regretting that he had concurred in the business.

She remained a long time silent and unmoving, bent over his hand. As he made a slight, involuntary movement she shook her head, evidently impatient of the least interruption. He felt himself sweating. Now, he knew, he was entirely at one with her, no least part of him held back. In the little room had been herself, himself and the cat; now there was something else, something with power but with no more identity than thunder. No doubt it was this for which she had been waiting.

At length she looked up with a confused and bewildered air, very different from her earlier manner.

"You'll slay a king and be rewarded by a king," she said, as simply as if she were speaking of the weather.

"A king?" asked Raymond. "What king?"

Now that she had relaxed her concentration on his hand, he

could smile, feeling relieved, almost flippant. "I don't know any kings, granny."

She seemed not to know that he had spoken. She made no reply, but only bent forward, and as before seemed to be gathering power; almost disappearing, he thought, into her own concentration as though into a cave.

Suddenly, abruptly, all was shattered. She flung his hand to one side, trembling as though with cold – or fear – in the close little room, and turning her head to look over her shoulder as though in flight from a pursuer. The cat leapt down and ran into a corner. As she stood up, taking both his hands in her own and kissing them, he saw fresh tears gather and fall from her eyes.

"Grief," she whispered. "Grief and sorrow in a black cloud, so thick there's no seeing through it."

She had buried her face in her hands.

"Tell me," he said. "Don't be afraid to tell me."

She gave no indication that she had heard him. He went out of the room and noiselessly closed the door. Returning to the lane, he stood unmoving for some little time, praying silently for the old woman, for her daily needs, for her health and safety. Above all, he prayed that she might be granted escape from belief in this foolish soothsaying: might, through the Lord's grace, reject it and attain true peace of mind and heart.

Sure enough, the lane led him down to the mill, outside which were standing three carts being loaded with sacks of flour and oats for the manor building site. Here the foreman readily agreed to let him ride back to the building site and the minstrel lent a hand with the loading until they set off on the track running not far from the bank of the mill race.

For well over an hour they jolted along the rutted track, through thick woodland and over a few patches of rough pasture, until at length they emerged at the east end of the wide, cleared space comprising the building site itself and the rough and ready half-camp half-village which had grown up on the gentle slope beside it.

From the left bank of the river, where a few wary coots and moorhens still scuttered about among the rushes and yellow flags, the cleared slope ran upward for about two hundred yards before giving way to the normal expanse of the seemingly unending forest – spindly oaks, ashes and rowans, broken, in sandier ground, by patches of conifers, the lower boughs all hacked, torn and stripped for burning. There were treeless tracts of thick, impenetrable gorse and brambles, and still more open stretches of rank grass, grazed nearly smooth by tethered beasts. Here and there the nearer bank of the stream was trampled, and in places, along the half-mile length that could be seen before the trees closed in down to the bank, the water was turbid, though two or three women were nevertheless stooping to fill pails.

The incline was a great, artificial glade, strewn and ugly as an old battlefield and as big as a village – which it was: a village almost unplanned, a village without a church or an alehouse; a gathering of people – men and women – and dwellings of a sort set down, one might have supposed, almost at random on this wooded riverside, far beyond which could be seen the green hills of shepherd country. The people called to one another, chattered, squabbled, shouted after straying children, cleaned or sharpened implements; busied themselves, in fact, with all the bustle of daily life common among rough – and some not so rough – working folk.

Yet their dwellings were more different from one another and in many cases more ramshackle and insubstantial than those of any village. At the further end of the messy, strewn slope stood a small group of trim wooden cottages, well made of overlapping boards with shingled roofs, and nearby a sort of shed suggestive of communal use. Outside stood several piles of undressed blocks of Cotswold stone of various sizes, upon one of which a sacking-aproned man, seated on the ground with the block propped up before him, was working carefully with a mallet and chisel. Another man called to him from a nearby door; at which he turned his head a moment, nodded and resumed his work.

Elsewhere stood huts and bothies put together from logs,

branches, wood chips and long splinters, their misshapen roofs – full of slits – tilted to half-keep out the rain. There were tents, too, of torn and dirty canvas, supported on poles cut and trimmed from the forest. Some of the work, however, was well done and the surroundings relatively tidy, so that the settlement seemed to have divided itself naturally into areas of a kind of respectability on the one hand and of squalor and impermanence on the other. Paths had been trodden through the grass, the white campion and clover and these – some of them roughly made up with small stones and gravel – led either into the forest or down to a broader, rutted track parallel with the river bank, which ran westward and out of sight among the woodland.

The whole place was studded with the stumps of felled trees on which toes were continually stubbed and bodies tripped. Most – the smaller ones – had been clumsily hacked down and then, later, smoothed off after a fashion with billhooks or knives. A few bigger trees – oak and beech – had been felled by professional woodmen as close to the ground as possible, and their great stumps burnt out later by charcoal fires lit on them, bellowed and raked. There were stacks of firewood, guarded not only with jealousy but sometimes even with ferocity. Several were watched by older children day and night.

Clothes were washed in the river – tumbled and squeezed, or beaten on flat stones dragged down from the forest; for the river itself contained no stones big enough. The gap-toothed, lank-haired women knelt in the driest places they could find, sleeves rolled up, clog-toes digging in for a footing, pummelling shifts and jerkins and every now and then lifting them up to pound them down still harder. Naked children fetched and carried, were squalled at and scolded, and splashed about in the shallow water. Older ones were sent out on longer and ever longer expeditions into the forest for bundles of firewood and such logs as they could contrive to drag.

Over the whole settlement lay a stench. Except among the masons and the builders and craftsmen themselves there was

11

no authority and no hierarchy to enforce anything resembling communal order. Innate decency kept most people from fouling the river, but the forest – which stretched for unbroken miles in all directions; indeed, few were sure how far – was used without any attempt at assignment or restraint. Wild animals – except for feral dogs and cats and now and then a wild boar or a straggle of wandering wolves – had long since been frightened away from the neighbourhood. The dogs would dash in and raid for bones and skins: virtually everything else was eaten. There were two butchers, whose cows and sheep were driven in on the hoof. There was a small milking herd. The bakers' flour, yeast and other supplies came to them in the carts from the mill. The people ate well. It was not the season for wild fruit, but small birds and even a rare rabbit could sometimes be snared and roasted. The children sucked their mothers' breasts – even those aged five or more – and ate what they were grudgingly given or could get hold of.

There were many horses and, for these, solid wooden stables had been built at the upper end of the slope. They were small, shaggy animals, heavy in the head and rump, well accustomed now to dragging loads of stone from the distant quarries. At this moment, in the hot midday sunshine could be heard the cries and orders of their masters as they controlled and encouraged them. Their oats and bran were kept under lock and key – almost the only lock in the settlement.

Everywhere the flies hung, crawling on cuts and scratches, on faeces, human and animal, on tent-sides in the sun, on spittle and on such fragments of food as might lie around. The children often ate maggots, beetles and caterpillars. In this temperate climate the flies were more or less bearable. They followed the food to your lips, your lips to the mouth of the girl you had been fondling and singing with over a leather jug of beer – for there was money and there was beer, no lack. Dysentery was not uncommon; but the place was prosperous and those living and working there considered themselves fortunate for as long as the work might last.

At the top of the slope, on an area of carefully levelled ground and dominating all else, stood the root and cause

of the settlement; the half-built stone manor house. For the
past year and a half, since the first spades had been thrust
in to begin the digging of the foundations, building had
continued in all seasons and in all but the most desperate
cold or rain. Structures of oak beams, put together by ropes,
leverage, pulleys and sheer muscle, had been erected to form
the frame of the dwelling which was to grow into being; to
become the seat not of any earl or lord, but of a commoner,
the wealthy merchant Gilbert Windrush. Gilbert had made his
fortune from the Flemish wool trade, the Italian bankers and,
above all, from his successful dealings with the not-long-dead
Yorkist king, Edward IV.

The master mason, Roger of Nottingham, or Roger Nott
as he was commonly called, was a man in every way fit to
carry the burden of this project. Even in the rough jerkin and
breeches of daily work he was formidable and impressive in
appearance: tall, scowling and broad-shouldered, a big man,
some forty-four or -five years old, with a natural air of
authority and a habitual tendency to waiting silence which
often led others to come out with more than they had at first
intended. The entire concept of the building – which had never
been drawn or written down – was continually present to his
mind. His mere approach was enough to intimidate a craftsman
at work into wondering uneasily whether any fault could be
found in what he had just done or was doing. Roger, taking
his time, would walk deliberately up to the stooping man,
his slow, heavy tread perhaps shaking precarious planks and
scaffolding twenty feet above the ground, and then pause
mutely for some little while, watching the chip of the mallet
or the turn of the auger, before moving away without a
word to continue his unsmiling scrutinies elsewhere. When
he did speak in correction or rebuke, it was as a rule not to
the workman but to some accompanying subordinate, who
would be left to make the reproof or correct the error. Yet
he had been known to pick up tools in his own hands, to
grasp the reins of horses or himself take over the giving
of orders to a gang of sweating labourers gone astray in
their task.

His grim, brooding presence was not liked, yet not one of them all wished him away. Their livings – good livings – depended upon his undisputed competence; and besides, his confidence and driving purpose were infectious, filling them with a sense of the value and worthiness of what they were doing even while they hated and envied him for his high standing and relative wealth.

"Marry, would he might fall!" said one stonemason to another, standing by the stream and watching him as he picked his way along the thirty-foot drop of the half-finished west wall.

"The devils would bear him in their hands," replied the other, "lest he should hurt his foot against a stone."

The two men were working in the stonemasons' yard, carving the decoration of the cornice stones which would, when completed, be hoisted to the roof and placed together to form the southern parapet of the house; tricky, skilled work, to be done without haste, for the repetitive motifs must match in scale and symmetry and the patterning must join and correspond between one stone and the next. To spoil a stone by an error of judgement or a slip of the drafter was a fault possibly punishable by fining, unless the spoiled stone could be used somewhere else where it would not show. Nicolas of Taunton seldom or never made errors. He was an experienced journeyman, not long returned from working in France and now nearing his time to become a master mason himself; a tall, brown-haired man of thirty-two, employing a boy as his prentice. His fellow craftsman this morning was a relative newcomer, who had given his name to Roger as Geoffrey Dean. He had come to the site about a month before, without credentials and giving no account of himself except that he was 'come from Rouen', where, he claimed, he had worked for the Earl of Oxford. Roger, no fool, suspected that he might likely be an outlaw from the north (his speech seemed northern) or at all events some kind of wanted man: the land was full of such. Yet being short of skilled masons – three or four had left for the continent during the severe weather of March – he had told him he would engage him and judge him by his work. That had so far given no grounds for dissatisfaction.

The stones cut by Nicolas and his companion, finished slowly one by one, were levered on to a sledge and horse-drawn up the slope, later to be roped and heaved by hand to the height of the parapet. Thereafter their placing and mortaring in position was a circumspect business of inches, warnings and supervision by one or other of Roger Nott's lieutenants.

This morning the carts from the mill were later than usual. A consignment of charcoal was due to come with them and one of the bakers, giving way to anxiety, had set off on foot to meet them on the track which led through the forest to Crenley. The arrival of the carts was always an occasion for children to cluster round, either in the hope of getting some fragment to eat or from mere curiosity. Several of the women would gather, too. There was always the chance that there might be a pedlar or a packman trudging with the carts for safety from forest outlaws, and selling raisins, nuts, nutmeg, honey and the like. He would have a good market, for few were short of money. Roger, as has been said, was shrewd, and made sure, by regular meetings and consultation with Gilbert Windrush, both that the on-going work was to his satisfaction and that due money was always forthcoming for pay.

The distant sound of the carts approaching through the trees was now audible to the two stonemasons, who paused a moment to listen. Voices, of course, they expected to hear, together with horses' hooves and the creaking of wheels and harness, but to hear singing was unusual. Also the voice, a strong and pleasant baritone, was new to them. It was the voice of a stranger (they knew those of most of the men in the camp) and it possessed a smooth, dominant quality, as though the singer was used both to singing and to being heard with attention and without interruption.

As the carts came closer still, the words of the song carried clearly to the masons' yard and beyond.

15

"By chance he met two troublesome men,
Two troublesome men they chanced to be;
The one of them was bold Robin Hood,
And the other was Little John so free."

Here the singer was interrupted by cries of approbation and by rough applause from those with him, but these died down as he continued.

"'O pedlar, pedlar, what's in thee pack?
Come speedily and tell to me.'
'I've many a suit of the gay green cloth,
And bodice strings by two and three.'"

The leading cart came jolting and rumbling out of the coppice, the horses pushing their way through the rustling, shrivelled leafage of high summer, and disclosed the singer seated on top of a flour-sack. To the two watching masons he was, sure enough, a stranger; with a handsome, intelligent face and intensely blue eyes that looked about him at his audience as he sang. His hair, which was (unlike most people's) clean and smoothly combed, curled upon his shoulders. In his lap lay a lute, of which he was making no use as he sang.

He plainly had an appreciative audience. The bakers' lads, walking with the convoy, were jostling round the leading cart, the better to hear him. As he finished the second stanza, there were enthusiastic cries of "Bodice strings!" and "Ah! That's it, go on, then!"

"If ye've many a suit of the gay green cloth—"

But suddenly the singer broke off, jumped lightly down from the cart and made his way off the track to where Nicolas and Geoffrey were still kneeling beside their work. A shade

16

startled, they looked up at him, squatting on their haunches as he swept them an ironic, affected bow.

"God give you good morrow!"

Nicolas replied to him merely with the sideways nod of the south countryman. "Travellin', are you?"

"Ye may well suppose me travelling," replied the minstrel, whose voice, though not that of a courtier, seemed to possess no regional accent at all, rather as though it had been rinsed and laundered for court use. "It's my craft – when there's no noble household to harbour me, that is. But I'd lief lodge here a night before I pass on. In whose will does that lie?"

"Ye'd best speak to Roger Nott," replied Nicolas curtly. The stranger had given him the impression of a somewhat over-confident, unduly animated fellow, too quick and forward of speech and movement for country ways. "What's thee name?"

"Raymond – Raymond Godsell – of anywhere," he answered with a smile. "I've been four days on the paths from Ashby and that's a good eighty miles. Had a horse, but that got stolen yesterday. What's a man to expect these days? Everyone on any road's either a discharged soldier begging and stealing, a thief, a rogue or some other son of the devil. The King's peace! Who *is* the King? That's what I'd like to know. Who *is* the King?"

"Ye'd best not talk that way in Roger Nott's hearing," said Nicolas. There were mutters of corroboration from the carters and boys standing round (for the attraction of the stranger seemed to have checked the progress of the flour convoy altogether). "It's King Richard reigns over this country; and over our master, that's for sure. So ye'd best not . . ."

The stranger seemed in no way dashed.

"Who's this great master of yours, then?"

"Gilbert Windrush, wool merchant. Ah, made 'is fortune in Flanders, 'e 'as. Dare say ye might 'a come across 'e in your . . ." – Nicolas paused – ". . . craft, if that's what ye call it."

"Lord Windrush?"

"Lord? No! 'E ain't no lord, though 'e very like will be. 'E lends money to the king, like 'e done to old King Edward died

17

eight or nine year ago. That's what they calls advancement,
what 'e've got."

"Ah! Indeed." The stranger paused deliberately. Then, "Doth
he know, d'ye think, where might be the *young* King Edward
and his brother? Might he perchance know that?"

There were more mutterings. The conversation seemed
checked, blocked like a horse by a shut gate. At last Geoffrey
said, "That's none of our business. The King's the King – King
Richard. We're honest men with work to do, and we know who
d' pay us an' all."

Raymond's reply was a snatch of song:

> "'Hey go bet all over the town:
> Sceptre and crown come tumbling down.'
> – King Henry's did, eh?"

He stood smiling at Nicolas, who did not smile back.

"Ye wants a night's lodging, ye'd best go an' see Roger
Nott 'bout it."

"Certes." He held up his empty hand, turning it this way
and that, so that they could all see. Then, suddenly, he bent
forward towards the still-squatting Nicolas.

"'Twill be easy, while ye keep groats in your ear."

As he spoke, he appeared to draw the coin out of the side
of the mason's head. Having it in his hand, he held it up to
view. There were shouts of astonishment and laughter, while
Nicolas clapped his hand to his ear and looked angrily round
with the air of a man made to look a fool. Several of the lads
pressed round Raymond to look at the coin and touch it, but
after permitting a few moments of this he held it up with a
herald's gesture.

"Lightly win, lightly tine! 'Tis gone! Ay, like the true king."

And it really had gone – or at least disappeared, as he
once more turned his hand round and let it fall. Ignoring the
onlookers' cries of delight and admiration, he turned back to
Nicolas.

"Roger Nott, ye say; I must needs seek him. Where might
he be?"

"Why, ye'll catch him all over you in a minute," growled Nicolas. "Here he comes."

Roger was indeed striding towards them with his heavy, deliberate tread. The men began to stir sheepishly. Arrived within a few yards of the group, he stopped, yet did not speak. A silence fell. The horses stood still in the shafts, stamping and continually tossing their heads, tormented by the flies.

Roger put his hands on his hips and stood gazing around him. The group of carters' lads and workmen dispersed as though he had been about to lay about them with a stick. A boy took the bridle of the leading horse, the remounted carter cracked his whip and the little cortège moved on up the slope towards the bakers' quarters. Raymond, looking by contrast clean as a new candle, his lute hanging on its cord from his shoulders, remained standing beside Nicolas and Geoffrey, who had risen to their feet upon Roger Nott's arrival.

There was a pause before Nott spoke.

"Men are here to work. Them as draw them off aren't welcome. Who are you and what do ye want?"

"Nothing. I'm a singer – minstrel – what ye will. I'm journeying. I'd reckoned to spend a night here, with your good will." He did not ask Nott whether he was the man in authority: that was plain enough.

"Journeying? Where?"

"Into the west. Journeying – that's all in my craft."

"Your craft? Ye look like a knave that lives without working."

For the first time, Raymond's air of light-hearted banter and gaiety left him. His expression hardened as he stared back at the scowling man confronting him.

"Think ye so? Come, let's take three steps together, ye and I."

Without waiting for agreement he passed by Nott and began walking up the slope into the heart of the camp. There were many – especially among the women – whose heads and eyes turned to follow him, and a few of the children fell in at his heels. Nott remained standing where he was. It was not his way to follow anyone, or to accede to requests to bear company. He

could always have the fellow thrown out later. He watched his
progress up the slope.

Raymond reached the spot outside the bakery where the
horses had stopped and the men had begun unloading the
heavy sacks. It was a thankless job, involving a disagreeable
amount of stooping and heaving. A human chain had been
formed to sling the sacks from hands to hands, but there
was much cursing and dropping, no regular movement and
an obvious disinclination on the part of some to bear their
proper burden.

Into the midst of this disarray Raymond strode with an air
both of authority and of custom. As he laid his hand firmly
on one arm of the lad who was stooping to lift a sack from
the bottom of the first cart, the young fellow naturally stopped
working and stood looking at him with a puzzled expression at
being interrupted. The chain of swung sacks being broken, they
were let fall and the botched work came to a halt. The master
baker, watching, strode forward towards Raymond, cursing
and seeming about to lay hands upon him; but Raymond, easily
and with surprising strength, put him to one side. Everyone
watched expectantly.

He stood rapidly tuning his lute – a half-turn of a peg here,
a pull on a sharp string there, a quick sweep across the strings.
Then he struck it loudly, with a heavy beating of chords, and
began to sing, or rather to chant or shout, in a slow, steady
rhythm, stamping one boot in time on the ground. As he did
so he nodded to the lad in the cart to hoist up the sack once
more and pitch it to the man below. The boy took it, swung it
by both hands and heaved it to his neighbour, who repeated
the movement. Involuntarily, they found themselves swinging
their bodies to Raymond's rhythm.

At first Raymond's cries had been a mere measured shouting
– *hi* ho, *hi* ho – slow and loud, a higher note followed by a
lower. Then, gradually, as he saw that the men were beginning
to relate to his rhythm and to grasp that it gave them a united
co-ordination of movement, following the necessarily slower
stoop and rise of the men in the carts, his shout became a lilt, a
kind of simple, melodic clamour; barely a song, yet possessing

a repetition which could be recognised by the workers and bodily identified with as they swung and heaved the sacks. Despite the strain of the work, there became evident a general wish not to miss the beat of the lilt. The job became almost a kind of slow dance, in which nobody wanted to be the one to break time.

"I met her in the morning;
Won't ye go my way?
I met her in the morning;
Won't ye go my way?"

Those who had breath to spare from the lift-and-swing were trying to join in the words in all manner of wrong ways, yet Raymond's clear baritone continued to dominate, imposing on the work order and steady progress.

By this time Roger Nott had strolled up the slope, accompanied by Nicolas, Geoffrey and one or two more. Men up on the parapet and higher scaffolding had turned their heads to watch. Raymond, satisfied that the simple rhythm had taken hold and was working, had begun to amuse himself, though without altering the air. He appeared to be improvising.

"J'ai *fait* une bonne *affaire*, veux-tu *couch*er, ma belle?
Les *yeux* de bleu sont *fermés*, veux-tu *dorm*ir, ma belle?"

Roger appeared to understand this, for a kind of reluctant and unaccustomed smile came to his lips. This disappeared, however, as the singer, without breaking his rhythm, continued his chant in what appeared to be Flemish. Through all this the pleasant quality of his voice kept hold of the little crowd, carrying indeed across the camp, so that several set down their tasks to stand and listen, filled not only by curiosity but a good many by conscious pleasure.

"That's the one we bin a-lookin' for!" cried one of the men aboard the third cart as he heaved the last sack over the side. A minute later the task was at an end, the sacks were all neatly stacked and the men stood grinning and wiping the sweat from their faces.

"That was done all right," said a man at length.

"Ah, done in 'alf the time an' all," said another. "D'ye do much o' that?" he asked Raymond.

"I can. But," – and here he turned insolently towards Nott: or perhaps not so much insolently as with the air of one who feels justifiable annoyance at having been treated in a way unbefitting what he feels to be his due – "ye see, I'm a knave that lives without working."

"'E was workin' all roight, by my record," said another of the men, looking at the bulk of Roger Nott standing nearby.

Nott spoke. "You want to spend the night here, you say."

"Why, 'tis but a night on my journey. A man must sleep somewhere. Inns cost money and I've none. This is fair weather and 'tis safer sleeping here than in the forest." He paused; then smiled full in Nott's face. "I'll not hale stone; I'm a knave that lives without working, ye see; but I'll undertake to make life easier to them that serve you in that way."

Roger paused, but in the event his mind was made up for him. There were murmurs.

"By'r Lady, 'e ought to stay."

"Let 'un sing: there's few enough as can."

"Keep 'un on. 'E done that job all roight."

Roger waited a few more moments, then shrugged his shoulders. "You seem to have roused this rabble."

Raymond answered him seriously. "It's how I live. I can help to get your heavy stones up to the roof: it's as you wish. I've no mind to sleep in the open, though."

Roger turned to Nicolas. "There's room in your shed. Give him some clean straw."

Raymond, who appeared to be carrying nothing on his journey except his lute, his scabbarded sword and a bag fastened to his belt, turned to Nicolas, put a friendly hand on his shoulder and sauntered with him down the slope towards the masons' huts beside the river.

The huts, though luxurious by the standards of the camp, were plain enough inside. There were four in all, soundly walled and roofed, and floored with snugly fitting yet loose planking laid on the flattened ground. In the bone-dry weather, these made homely but sufficiently comfortable dwellings. In Nicolas's hut there were two beds made of struts and planks knocked together and topped off with concave wooden pillows, straw mattresses and a blanket each; a table, an empty iron fire-basket and a wooden cross hung on one wall. There were also two stout quarter-staffs leaning upright in one corner. The door stood open. There were no windows, the sagging door and chinks in the timbering providing sufficient ventilation for the time of year.

Nicolas cast an eye round. "That corner do you?" He was ungracious. He still had not taken to Raymond and felt that the groat removed from his ear (which he did not understand) had made him look a fool in front of too many people. If Raymond was some sort of wizard (and he seemed to have ensorcelled the labourers all right), there was no telling what he might be up to next.

"There's straw enough in the shed by the oak tree."

Without troubling himself to point out the shed to Raymond, he crossed himself before the crucifix, turned on his heel and left him. A few minutes later he was back at his work with Geoffrey on the cornice-stones.

Raymond, left to himself, unslung his lute, sat down on one of the beds and pulled off his boots. He looked into the left one, drew out a pad of soft rags, looked carefully into it again and replaced the pad. Then he put his boots on once more, stripped himself to the waist, hung his jerkin on a nail and went out to wash in the river. He was unaware of being watched.

When he had done and returned, refreshed, to the hut, he sat down, stripped as he was, on the bed and combed his wet hair, making use of a small bronze mirror which he took from

23

one pocket. Having finished, he took up his lute and began to play and sing softly to himself.

> "*Joli mois de mai,*
> *Quand reviendras-tu?*
> *Joli mois de mai,*
> *Quand reviendras-tu?*
> *Ah, j'ai vu mon amie*
> *Sous un pommier doux.*
> *Ah, ma petite amie*
> *Viens-tu près de moi.*
> *Viens-tu près de moi . . ."*

The melody – and hence the singer – paused inconclusively, half-questioningly, almost as though expecting a reply. A reply he certainly received, unsung and unexpected. He started as the sunlight at the doorway was dimmed, and looked up to see a young woman standing before him.

She was certainly worth looking at. She might have been perhaps eighteen, with a mane of shining, black hair flung loose on her back and gathered with a red ribbon at the nape of her neck. She was of middle height, slender and graceful. Her lips, slightly moist and a deep crimson, were a little parted, showing white, even teeth. She had an attractive nose, slightly upturned, a clear skin, rosy cheeks and enormous, dark eyes. In a word, she was strikingly beautiful. In that sultry place, she seemed somehow to suggest coolness and a movement in the air.

"Oi thought ye might be wantin' some food," she said. Her voice was low and pleasant. "'Tis noon and after." This last, as he had not yet spoken, seemed to come almost apologetically.

He stood up, crossed to the doorway and offered his hand, which she took in her own.

"Ye're kind. It'd be welcome."

She smiled, turned, and led the way to the next hut. He put on a clean shirt, picked up his lute and took it with him, as though chary of leaving it to itself. The room was smoky, for a fire was burning on an iron hearth in one corner and only half the smoke – or so it would seem – was finding its way out through the cowled chimney hole above. The place was more comfortably furnished than the hut he had left. There was a double bed, a well-made table with drawers, several benches, two closets and a rack for cooking pots and utensils. A pot of stew was simmering on an iron grill over the fire and the appetising smell mingled with that of the smoke.

She gestured to one of the benches beside the table.

"Sit down, sir. Cut the bread and Oi'll serve us both."

She handed him the loaf, a knife and an iron spoon, then went over to the hearth and took up a ladle hanging there.

"Ye've no call to put a 'sir' to me," he said, smiling. "Raymond I'm hight. Raymond Godsell if any has keep of it, though that's seldom enough. Is it your husband that's the master here – the big man?"

"Ah," she said. "Roger Nott – Roger of Nottingham. That's 'e."

"Isn't he coming to eat?"

She shook her head, the black hair tossing at her back.

"'E eats with the men mid-days. It's that hot, they'd take their time in the shade if 'tweren't for 'im."

"No one to join us, then? No other wives?"

"No. Nicolas ain't married and if Geoffrey's got a wife Oi never heared tell of her. Far as other women go, Roger expects me to stay to myself. It's to maintain 'is position, d'ye see."

"Then I do amiss to that." He looked her full in the face as he took a wooden bowl of stew from her. "He'll not like me here, d'ye mean?"

She gave her head a little toss. "A guest's a guest. Oi cooked it: Oi'll say who's to eat it." Then, quickly, as though to change the subject, "Oi heard ye singin': 'twas foine. Is that thee craft, then, singin'?" And, before he could reply, "What kind of craft is that? No wages, surely? D'ye sing for what folk'll give?"

25

"Well," he answered between mouthfuls. His next words came rather slowly, for he was plainly hungry. "In a manner of speaking. I've done that in my time. But what ye need in my craft's a place in a household, d'ye see: if a rich man takes a fancy to keep you for a fool, a singer – whatever he wants. I've been a chorister in my time – chorister in a bishop's household; that was when I was a boy. But a fool's better than a chorister, to my thinking. A fool's still expected to sing, ye see. That's part of the job. I can tumble a bit, show off a few dog's tricks – anything that'll keep me under the roof of a man that'll feed me."

"A household fool? Oi've 'eard tell but Oi never met one." Sitting opposite him, she laughed across the table. "Oi saw ye take the groat out of Nicolas's ear. 'Twas a good trick ye done. But how?"

"Easy," he said. "Like this." He repeated the trick, holding up his apparently empty hand, drawing the coin out of the dark clusters by her ear, showing it to her and then making it seem to vanish.

She looked up at him wide-eyed, afraid. "That's witchcraft!"

"No, it's not. Anyone can learn to do it. I could teach you. It's just craft. There are folk better at it than I am – yes, wenches, too, some of them."

"They'll live to be burned, then."

"Not them as can get kept in good households. A man and a girl make a good pair for fools." He rubbed his bread round his almost empty bowl, nodding as she offered him more.

"Then why are ye here?" she asked him. "There's no 'ousehold here, without ye mean to go to Gilbert – Gilbert Windrush. Does 'e keep a fool in's 'ouse, then?"

"He likely will – when it's finished." He jerked his thumb over his shoulder towards the top of the slope outside. "But no, it won't be me. I'm on a journey, that's all."

She frowned. "A journey? But ye said—"

"A journey for my master. At his bidding, that is."

"Who *is* your master, then?" She was little more than a child, and questioned him almost as simply and directly as one.

He shook his head. "Lord No One, that's who."

"Doan' want to tell me? Why – are ye ashamed of 'im?"

At this he looked up sharply and for a moment seemed vexed. Then he recovered himself and smiled.

"Ashamed? No, just t'other way. I'm proud to serve him. Why else would I be here now with my feet in blisters? He's only a young man, but he's worth serving."

"Who's he, then?"

"Lord Hastings. Baron Edward Hastings of Hastings, that is. He's no more than nineteen. Fine young fellow."

"'E's young, then, I reckon, to be Baron. 'S 'e been Baron long?"

"Two years. His father was murdered by Richard of Gloster."

"Murdered? What are ye sayin'?"

"Gloster's men cut off his head, that's what I'm saying." Raymond clenched a fist. "Gloster called him a traitor. Lord Hastings had come to distrust him and he'd sent to York for men to protect the true King, young Edward, d'ye see."

She looked nonplussed. "Edward?"

"The boy. The son of King Edward the Fourth. Gloster murdered Lord Hastings and anyone'll tell you that he's murdered the true King and his brother, too: the princes in the Tower. There's none that don't know that, whatever they may say openly."

She shook her head. "We're just plain folk here: we doan' know nothin' 'bout such things. What would we want to be meddlin' with all that for? We got work an' a good living here, long as Gilbert's house is buildin'. Ah, we works for Master Windrush and I never heared 'im speak agin' the King – King Richard, that is."

He smiled at her again. "Of course. I've said too much. Forget what I said or ye'll likely get *me* into trouble, too. But Lord William Hastings – him the Duke of Gloster put to death two years ago – he was always good to me. I was his fool and no one could have wished for a better master. But ye're right. It's best for folk like us to stay quiet. These are troubled times."

"Not 'ere they bain't: these are good times. Master Windrush pays us, see, and that's all as matters to us. Are ye done? Sure? There's plenty more."

He shook his head, making a pantomime of rubbing his stomach.

"Let's 'ave your bowl, then. I'll rinse 'em in the river."

He picked up the bowl. She put her hand over his to take it from him and it was at this moment that Roger Nott entered at the open doorway.

The girl started. Raymond stood up and the bowl fell to the ground. As she stooped to pick it up Roger stood still, saying nothing.

"Oi – Oi gave Raymond 'is dinner," she said. "There's plenty to spare."

But all the same, she was blushing and seemed abashed as he still stood silent. At length he said, "Raymond? Is that his name?"

Raymond was quick enough on that. "I'm Raymond Godsell, sir; I was setting up house next door, as ye gave me leave to do, when your wife out of her kind heart came in and offered me the meal. My thanks, Mistress Nott," he added to the girl.

Roger nodded, as though words would be wasted. Then he said, "I came down for some wine, Alison. The water's too foul and warm for drinking. Where's the pitcher?"

She took off the cover and handed him an unglazed pitcher, beaded with condensation. He tilted it and drank. When he paused she took it from him and offered it to Raymond, who hesitated. For a moment it looked as though Roger might be going to object. Then he shrugged his shoulders and nodded.

Raymond drank, and plainly could have drunk more, but gave the pitcher back to Alison, wiping his mouth with the back of his hand.

"Thanks, sir. That's good wine."

"If ye're done," said Roger, "ye can come back up with me and bring that thing with ye." He pointed to the lute. "They'll be raising heavy blocks this afternoon and ye can try if they'll still fancy thee chirping."

With a smile and a bow to Alison, Raymond followed him

28

out of the door. He could smell Roger's sweat and before he had gone twenty yards was sweating himself.

During the long afternoon in the sultry heat, the masons' men, stripped to the waist, raised the cornice blocks to roof height by chain dogs, pulley and tackle and then moved them with ropes and wooden rollers into a rough line along the half-finished eastern parapet. The sweat poured off them, drenching their breeches and stinging in their eyes. Raymond, having climbed to the roof by the ladders, stripped too and stood a little elevated on a thick balk of wood, for he reckoned that to sit while they worked would hardly gain their respect. Roger Nott stood close by, sometimes speaking a word of reproof to a man or merely pointing silently to something amiss; sometimes descending to the ground to oversee the hauling up of fresh blocks. Gradually the men, hitherto unaccustomed to working with a singer, picked up the rhythms of Raymond's voice and, panting though they were, followed him in the burthens.

Raymond, like most singers involved in repetitive work, improvised most of his words, and set out to raise a laugh where he could.

"O haul it up from down below.
O heave! O heave!
Now out along this stone must go.
O heave away my bravos.

"O Roger Nott's well pleased in bed.
O heave! O heave!
He'll make us work until we're dead.
O heave away my bravos."

Nott, where he stood watching the work, said nothing, though one or two cast covert glances at him. To all appearances he had heard nothing to displease him.

"A lad in the Tower was put to death.
O *heave*! O *heave*!
And no one knows who stopped his breath.
O *heave* away my bravos!

"Lord Hastings, Hastings lost his head.
O *heave*! O *heave*—"

"All right, that'll do for a bit," said Nott suddenly. "Ye can sit in the shade awhile and get thee breath back."

The men broke off, several gathering round Raymond as he sat down in the shadow of the wall, cradling his lute in his arms.

"Ye've a fine voice," said one of the men, throwing himself down beside him. "Ye done that all roight."

Raymond joked and bantered with them and at length, finding them eagerly responsive, launched into a story of a pretty girl whose husband sold barrels. One day, he told them, she was with her lover when her husband arrived home unexpectedly. But Prunella and her friend, who had just had time to get dressed, were able to convince the goodman that the young fellow had come to look at a great barrel he wished to buy. The husband willingly showed him the barrel and then, taking a light, climbed into it to scrape and clean it. Whereupon Prunella, leaning over the edge, pointed out to him a place here and a place there for his attention: and the young man, seeing his opportunity, played the stallion and completed that on which he had been engaged.

The men roared. "And did 'e buy the barrel?" asked one.

"Nay, how should I know? The tale's from Italy. 'Twas my lord gave me the book when we were in Calais. There's a hundred tales."

"What, all the like o' that?"

"Nay." Raymond shook his head impatiently. "Many beauteous – many sad. I know them all. The best in the world,

I'm told." He stood up and turned to Nott, who had heard the story with no sign of amusement. "I'm content to go on now, master, if that's your will. Sun's dropping: it'll be cooler soon."

At the end of the day's work, Nott told Nicolas and Geoffrey to take Raymond to eat with them and the rest of the unmarried men. It was a cheerful gathering, despite the overpowering sweat and the flies, for everyone was glad enough to be making money, and hungry and thirsty enough to be keen to enjoy themselves. There was beef, there were onions, great loaves of new bread with butter, and enough ale to make everyone happily tipsy.

"Here's to Master Windrush," shouted one man, lifting up his pot. "God knows the work's enough to kill a man, but leastways 'e do pay reg'lar and we've got full bellies."

"Ah, best enjoy it while 'e can," said another. "Now us can see what we be at, best part'll be done 'fore winter and men'll be going, most of 'en."

"Who'll sing?" shouted someone else. "'Ere, Robin, give us old Barleycorn. Come on!"

At this one of the men stood up, urged on by cries of "That's roight, Robin" and "Good luck to 'ee" and began the song they all knew.

"There come three kings from out the West
Their victory to try,
And they have taken a common oath
John Barleycorn should die."

And at this the beery company took up the chorus, in all keys and in none.

31

"With a right fol lol,
A right fol riddle diddle dol.
And they have taken a common oath
John Barleycorn should die."

Raymond sat listening among the others, but with a certain air of detachment – that of the professional, one might suppose, among amateurs. He did not join in the chorus, but each time took up his ale pot and drank, by way of a mask. He did not want to out-sing them. He had enjoyed his acclaim that afternoon and as he drank the strong ale his frame of mind, by nature volatile, impulsive and excitable, grew more and more aroused by the merry-making around him. Eager, whipped-up thoughts began racing through his mind.

"Where's the bloody nightingale, then?" cried someone. "'Im as was singin' 's aft'noon when we was luggin'?"

"Ah, 'ere 'e be. What's thee name, lad?"

"I'm Raymond," he told them.

"Ye wants sing, then? That's if ye bain't tired out with it."

"Ah, that's it. Go on, let 'un sing."

Raymond stood up, his eyes seeing the foetid place swimming a little as he did so. At the other end of the table he noticed Roger Nott, intent in conversation with a colourfully dressed, clean, brown-bearded man of about fifty, of a certain cultivation of manner which set him apart, as it seemed, from the grinning boors drinking to either side of them.

He plucked Nicolas's sleeve, pointing circumspectly. "Who's that?"

Nicolas looked across. "'E? Why, 'tis Master Windrush. 'E'll be come to look over the work with Roger."

"Why, does he come every even?"

"No: but most every week. 'E'll be wantin' to go over the

bloody lot with Roger: till dark, that is. Reckon they'll be on for couple of hours, soon's 'e's 'ad 'is ale." He looked at Raymond impatiently. "Ye goin' to sing or bain't ye?"

Raymond began without announcement or introduction.

"There was an old woman lived by the sea shore,
Bam balance to me.
There was an old woman lived by the sea shore,
And she had daughters one two three and four.
And I'll be true to my love if my lover be true to me."

As he settled to his task, his head cleared and his voice rang out over the slope, carrying far into the surrounding woods and across the river. The company, who were entirely unused to singing of this quality, fell almost totally quiet and listened spellbound.

"There was a young man come by to see them,
Bam balance to me.
There was a young man come by to see them,
And the eldest girl lost her heart to him.
And I'll be true to my love if my lover be true to me."

Alison, rinsing clothes in the river, laid aside the shift she had been wringing out and knelt listening as though to an annunciation. After a minute or two her tears brimmed and trickled noiselessly down her cheeks.

"He's loike a champion," she whispered to herself. "He's loike a prince from a tale. O Mary Mother, whoy did 'un 'ave to come here? What'm Oi to do? What'm Oi to do?"

"He give to the eldest a silver bowl,

33

Richard Adams

Bam balance to me.
He give to the eldest a silver bowl,
But he give to the youngest his heart and his soul.
And I'll be true to my love if my lover be true to me."

Alison actually stopped her ears, stood up and went back into
the hut. Here she flung herself down on the bed, weeping; but
when, after a minute or two, she drew out her fingers, the story
was still continuing.

"As they was a-walkin' beside the bank brim,
Bam balance to me.
As they was a-walkin' beside the bank brim,
The eldest girl pushed the youngest in.
And I'll be true to my love if my lover be true to me."

She went out of doors again and stood by the riverside,
listening to the story as it floated to her down the slope, stanza
by stanza. In her mind she seemed to see it all – the younger girl
begging for mercy, the wicked elder sister refusing her "hand or
glove, Unless you give me your own true love"; the drifting,
drowned body caught up in the mill-dam; the passing minstrel
using the dead girl's hair to string his harp before going on to
the sisters' house to be fed and invited to sing in the great hall;
and how at last the harp began to play of itself.

"And then, as clearly as ever might be,
Bam balance to me.
And then as clearly as ever might be,
'There sits my sister that drownéd me.'
And I'll be true to my love if my lover be true to me."

There was silence for a few moments, then a roar of applause
and prolonged shouts of approval. Alison stood with her hands
pressed alongside each cheek, staring into the fading daylight
and glinting water reflections. So still was she that a trout a few
yards upstream rose to a big sedge fly and sank back without
haste to its accustomed place under the bank.

34

Geoffrey Dean, sitting beside Raymond, thumped him on the back as he sat down.

"Ye done that all right. Shame ye won't be stayin'."

"Won't be stayin'?"

"Thought ye said ye was on a journey?"

"Well . . ." Raymond paused. "I am, more's the pity. One that won't let me stay, either. But I must be on one now, anyway; I must go for a piss."

"Well, mind ye go well into the wood. Place is foul enough already."

"Ah." Raymond, still receiving congratulations as he pushed his way past the men, made his way out into the early dusk, where bats were already flitting over the open incline. He went into the woods, did his business and stood for some time, meditating. Then, as though resolved, he began to make his way carefully downhill among the thick trees.

Alison had recovered herself and was sitting on a stool at her door in the welcome coolness, plying her needle. Her clear young eyes had no difficulty with the failing light.

A light, sweet snatch of melody startled her, coming from the bushes a few yards further down the river bank.

"Ah, dame d'España,
Ah, dame d'Espagne!"

She looked quickly round her. A moment later Raymond pushed his way through the bushes, came smilingly up to her and sat down at her feet. She stood up at once and moved a little away.

"Master Godsell – Raymond – ye must go – ye shouldn't be 'ere."

"Why not, by the holydom? That's my lodging, not ten yards away, and I'm minded to sit outside in the cool, same as ye are yourself."

He slapped a horsefly on his forearm. "Cursed things."

35

"Are ye done singin', then? Oi heard you from 'ere – it was just about foine."

"Why weren't you there?"

"Roger doan' like me to be out among the men."

He stood up, took two steps towards her and took her hand gently in his own. She made no resistance.

"Ye can hardly blame him. Has there been any trouble, or has he always been that way?"

"There were a man, a carpenter; Ned of Bristol – Ned the Saw, they called 'im. 'Twas last Christmas. Folk was kissin' under the mistletoe – just kindly kissin', ye know. Ned took and kissed me every dele; on the mouth an' that. 'E were holdin' my face in's two 'ands. Roger knocked 'im down – and ye can just about reckon 'ow 'ard 'e can hit 'f 'e do want; Ned hit th' back of 's 'ead on the floor – they deemed 'e'd die – never come round for three 'ours. And Roger never spoke no word, not all that toime."

"He's like a bear, isn't he? Doesn't he even talk in bed?" Raymond was laughing down into her beautiful face.

"Ye mustn't say things like that to me."

"Your pardon. It's the good ale. Let's sit down again. Come, I'll do nothing amiss, I promise you. Fool's honour!"

She hesitated, but then sat down again on her stool and picked up her work. The last of the setting sun shone out suddenly, dazzlingly between the western clouds, fiery red, reddening the grass, the walls of the hut, the water, and Alison's mass of ebony hair. Raymond lay on his stomach, plucking foxtail grasses and chewing them. She said nothing and there was silence for some little while.

At length he said, "Alison?"

She looked up but made no reply.

"Shall we have trout for supper? If I catch it will you cook it? There'll be enough for two. If Roger's still with Master Windrush we'll have it eaten and out of the way 'fore he's back."

"Catch a trout? How?"

"Say, 'Raymond, my dear one, how?'"

"Raymond, how?"

He put a finger to his lips where he lay prone on the bank, pointed to her and shook his head. She sat as still as moss on her stool. Raymond, having bared his left arm, slid noiselessly to the edge of the bank, the side of his face pressed into the grass. Stealthily as a cat his hand and then his arm slid into the water, making neither sound nor ripple. Infused with his intent concentration, she watched, fascinated, the almost imperceptible motion of his arm upstream, inch by inch. Suddenly he clutched and leapt up in one swift movement, the trout lashing and struggling as he gripped it by finger and thumb in each gill. Alison gave a little scream and jumped to her feet. He jerked the fish's head back sharply and it hung still from his hand, the beautiful red and black spots clear and vivid as jewels.

"Oi *said* witchcraft! Raymond . . ."

"Why, surely ye've seen that done before?"

"No, that Oi never."

"Ye can't have lived near a river, then. Any boy can learn to do it. Come, give me a knife and I'll gut him. Fine fellow, isn't he? Must be close on three pounds."

She grilled the trout and they ate it with salt, bread, butter and their fingers, sitting outside in the dying light and pitching head, backbone, tail and fins into the river. She plainly enjoyed it, picking the tiniest bits of flesh off the backbone and crunching the crisp skin he offered to her. She brought out the rough wine and they drank together, she matching him cup for cup. Then, leaning back on the grass, she sighed with replete pleasure.

"Oh, ye're that likely! Thank you!"

He brushed it aside, saying nothing for a while. Then:

"Alison?"

"Yes?"

"How d'ye come to be married to this man? Tell me."

At this she grew angry, thumping her little fist again and again on the ground.

"What do ye mean? 'Ow dare you? Why shouldn't Oi be married to Roger? What d'ye mean? Go away! Go on! *Go!*"
She pointed.

He said not a word, simply waiting with an expression intent as though she had not spoken. Suddenly she began to cry, sobbing deeply with the weeping of true grief – no pettish outburst. Still he said nothing and made no move.

"Why – why did ye – why did ye 'ave to come 'ere?" She broke out at last, between her sobs. "Why did ye . . . come? Why did ye 'ave to speak?"

"I was sent."

"By Lord Hastings, ye mean?"

"No; by God; to you."

"Ye mustn't – what do ye mean?"

"I love you, Alison; that's what I mean. I truly mean it."

"Doan' speak to me that way. Ye *mustn't*."

"I'm asking you again. How is it ye're married to Roger? He must be twenty-five years older than you."

She wept again, noiselessly, yet seeming hardly able to contain her grief, her head in her hands, her whole body heaving with sobs. A huge, honey-coloured moon was slowly rising downstream, its upper rim visible in the horizon haze above the nearer oak trees. At last she whispered, "He bought me, didn' 'e?"

"*Bought* you?"

"My father was workin' for Master Manley, see? At Stockcross, up in Birksheer. But 'e broke 'is leg two year back, so we 'ad next to nothin'. There be seven of us in the family. Roger was visitin' Master Manley; come to advise 'im 'bout buildin' 'is new stables. Master Manley used to feed the men 'isself mid-day. Oi was on workin' in the kitchen: used to take the dinner out to 'en; only, they ate on tables outside, see. Roger used to speak to me, told me Oi were pretty an' all o' that. He – he used to touch me."

In her grief her Berkshire burr had become still broader, so that Raymond, listening intently, at moments could scarcely follow her.

"Zo then 'e zpoke to my vather, tells 'im 'e wants marry me, 'e'd give 'im fifty pound." Even at such a time as this, she could not withhold her pride, and repeated, "Fifty pound for – for me 'and in marriage, what 'e calls it. Oi zays to dad

No Oi didn't want but 'e says Oi 'as to do what 'e zay and my mother she croies but she wouldn' interfere – she wouldn' 'ave it no different. They takes me to the old priest and 'is clerk: 'e zays Oi must marry like a good, obedient daughter, 'twas for my vather to say 'oo. Oh – Raymond – I doan' want to go on no more."

"How long ago was this?"

"Two year come noigh on Michaelmas."

"Alison, I love you. And this is no hasty bedding business, by the Holy St Mary, it's not! I swear it! I want you with me till doomsday. Listen! What's that?"

They could hear from further up the slope the sounds of folk dispersing, and then Nicolas of Taunton's voice calling, "Ah, good night, then," from no more than fifty yards away. Alison stood up, plainly petrified, wiping her eyes and smoothing her dress. She kissed him quickly on the lips, mouthed, "Go!" and pointed.

The full moon, as it topped the trees, gained from orange to clear silver and lit up the whole trodden slope, the bothies and wood-piles, the tools laid by beside unfinished work, the poles and great stones, the scaffolding and ladders and the huge, gaunt mass of the half-built house itself, its future beauty more plainly to be discerned in this gentler light which displayed its fine planes and shadowed masses as they would one day appear; yet revealed little of the gaps, the blocks still to be cemented into place, the decoration still to be completed. A nightjar bubbled in the thicket and everywhere sounded the high 'twink, twink' of the hunting bats. As the human voices died away, the gentle sounds of the night returned, seeming like the moonlight made audible; continuous, tiny noises of barely perceptible movement – leaves, water, hunting voles, shard-borne beetles – peaceful and calm.

When Nicolas and Geoffrey stumbled in at the open door of their hut they found Raymond stretched out on his straw pallet in his shirt, apparently sleeping sound as a badger in winter.

"He said he was on a journey, but he still hasn't gone."

It was the following day. Roger Nott, with Nicolas, was

inspecting the pointing on the long north wall, a couple of underlings with trowels and mortar dutifully following behind them.

"Well, master, I suppose that's 'is own affair. 'E's earned his bread so far and the men like him. At least 'e do seem to know how to keep their spirits up."

"D'ye like him yourself?" Roger turned his head and looked directly at Nicolas.

Nicolas paused. He could sense Roger's inclination and had no wish to put him out by expressing any view with which he might disagree.

"I've no reason to *mis*like him. Maybe 'e's a bit too likely for a young fellow—"

"It may be he is."

"—but then that's all in 'is craft, it may seem."

Roger stopped and pointed with the stick in his hand at a long streak in the wall, a gap from which mortaring had fallen. As the men began the job of righting it, Roger walked on until he and Nicolas were out of their earshot. Then, without looking at Nicolas, he said quietly and expressionlessly, "Does he talk in his sleep?"

Nicolas was puzzled. "Talk in 's sleep? Not that I know, master. But then I might 'a been sleeping too, mightn't I?"

There was a silence. Then, "My wife does," murmured Roger almost inaudibly.

Before Nicolas could reply he called to the building over-seer, who was among a group of men nearby, "Basil!" and stood waiting without another word until the man came up to him, touching two fingers to his forehead.

"The stables," said Roger. "That's where your men should be now. We'll leave these walls to settle a while before the coping goes on. That'll be their full load. Do you think the stables' footings are sound?"

"Ay, master, they're sound enough. They're well settled now. I was looking at them only yesterday."

"Then I want to see the rubble in, before the men do any more work on the house. Have ye got enough rubble there for filling?"

"Horses have been bringing up rubble last two-three days, master. I can have a good pile by the stable walls afore tonight, and there's walling stone enough there now."

"Then get them started." Without more words Roger strode back to the two men plying their trowels on the mortar gap, Nicolas almost running beside him to keep up.

"How many carved stones on the coping altogether?" he asked suddenly.

"Sixty-four, master. I thought you knew."

"*I* know," replied Roger. "I wanted to see whether you did. There are two ill-carved, aren't there? Ill-carved in the same way, too."

"Not badly, master. Not so's no one'd notice."

"Like me, you mean?"

Nicolas was silent, wondering whether Roger would require two fresh stones to be cut.

"Take them out," said Roger at length, "and reset them one at each end. If anyone remarks on it, you can say it was intended for ornament."

Raymond had asked Nicolas to excuse him for an hour, pleading that he had sung himself hoarse while they piled the rubble. Actually he had a slight headache from the heat and was in such a state of inward excitement and nervous tension that he hardly knew how to contain himself. He sat in his hut, on Nicolas's bed, fingering his lute and singing to himself in a murmur. He was not surprised when Alison came in. He had been awaiting her. Without a word he stood up, took her in his arms and kissed her passionately. She responded, pressing herself close to him and trembling.

He released her, but stood looking her straight in the eye with his two hands on her shoulders. "My own true love. My dearest sweetheart."

"Raymond," she said, almost in a whisper. "O Raymond, what's to be done? Oi love you, Raymond. Oi never knew—"

"Why, I'll tell you what's to be done," said he, almost briskly. "Do you truly love me, sweetheart, and want to be mine for ever? Yes?"

She nodded, eyes brimming. "Yes! O yes! But what's the use o' talkin'—"

"Then listen to me," said he. "I can't stay here. *We* can't stay here. Indeed, I've stayed too long already. I shouldn't be here at all, only for you. I've a sworn duty to Lord Hastings and I must be on my way tonight at latest."

"But where, my love?"

"To Milford Haven, that's where."

"Milford Haven? Where's that, then?"

"In Wales. In the west. And it's a good hundred and twenty miles from here, if not more. Somehow, we've got to get a horse. Even with that it'll be four-five days: perhaps too long."

"What's it ye've to do?"

"I'll tell you later," he said. "That's if you'll come with me. You will?"

She nodded gravely.

"I promise you, I'll be as good to you as ever a man was to a girl. And if all goes right, I shall be very well off at the end of this little business. I shall be well rewarded for the pains I've been at."

"But 'ow are we to get away? They'll see us."

"Tonight," he said. "It must be tonight, no later. When he's asleep."

"Why, 'e's goin' to Bourton tonight to see the stone contractor. 'E said so afore dinner today."

"So much the better. We'll each of us slip out alone at sunset and meet on the bank a half-mile upstream. Then we'll find the road to Gloster, for it's Gloster we must go to, before we can get into Wales."

"But when 'e finds me gone?"

"He won't know where. The woods are thick. Tell me, have you got money, for I've none? I was robbed when they stole my horse."

She nodded. "There be twenty pound hidden . . ."

"More than enough to buy horses, saddles, bridles and all we'll need. Bring it with you. Alison, dear heart, you're sure you've the mettle to come? You won't go back on it?"

"Oh, ah," she said. "Oi'm ready: Oi'm resolved, my dear one. Oh, it's a real relief now, that it is. Oi trust you, Raymond. Oi love you truly." She sat down on the bed and laughed happily up at him. "Sing me what ye were singin' when Oi come in. Go on!"

For a moment he seemed to hesitate; then he, too, laughed.

"Why, I was making up a new ballad. No, not new. I've heard it often, but never in English. When I was with my lord in Calais, I heard it many times in French. French I learned to understand well, but once when it was sung in the hall in Calais my lord had a guest who had a German minstrel with him, and when this man heard the French ballad he told us he knew the like in German. So Lord Hastings asked him to sing in German. The tune was different, and as for the words, well, of course I couldn't follow them, though there were plenty who could. It's an old tale in many countries across the channel, that's plain. But I never yet heard it in English, so I took a fancy to make it up. I was just going over it when you came in."

"Sing it for me now! No, better; *teach* it me. If Oi'm to be your girl and with ye always – oh, 'tis too good to be true! – Oi'll 'ave to be learnin' songs an' ballads, woan' Oi?"

"Well, I'll sing it for you, of course I will," he answered. "Only we must be very quiet. If Roger comes—"

"'E won't be back yet. Not if 'e's doin' the day like 'e always do."

"Well, it'll be best to be quiet, all the same," said he. "We mustn't draw notice. Sit beside me here on the bed and no one else'll hear us."

She pressed herself to him while he sang, very gently plucking the lute and keeping his voice as low as though he were singing a lullaby to a child.

"An outlandish knight from the north land came,
And he came wooing of me;
And he told me he'd take me to that northern land,
And there he would marry me.

"Well, go get some of your father's gold,
And some of your mother's fee,
And two of the very best stable steeds,
Where there stand thirty and three."

As he sang on she listened with the closest concentration, and after three or four stanzas began humming the air with him. At the end she asked, "But what's a parrot?"

Raymond explained.

"But they speak? They can talk?"

"They can speak very plain – words and bits of talk they've heard repeated often. But no, they don't understand what they say. They don't listen and answer. I put the parrot in myself: a joke for a fool. Lord Hastings had a parrot when we were in Calais. A Spaniard – a nobleman – gave it to him, along with a ruby ring and a lot of other things."

"Now teach me the 'ole ballad. Oi reckon it's real lovely. Oi'll be able to sing it with ye, woan' Oi, when we're together?"

She was apt, with the excitement and heightened alertness of love. In less than half an hour she had memorised the whole ballad, and sang it by herself while he struck the chords for her. She had a delightful voice, clear and sweet, though he could not test its power. Enraptured by desire, he took her once more in his arms.

"No, my love, no!" she told him quickly, perceiving his intention as his hands fondled her body. "No, we dursen't! Not yet, dearest Raymond; 'tis not safe! We were found now, that'd just about damage us and everythin', that would. Ye must be content and let be 'til we're safe away."

She pushed herself from his arms. "Look, sweetheart, take and keep this for true love's sake. 'Ere!"

From her right-hand middle finger she drew off a plain but broad ring of silver and put it in his hand. It had no ornamentation except for an initial 'A' engraved on the bezel.

"Take it," she whispered, kissing him. "'Tis all Oi got to give. Oi were give it 'fore we was married, but now you're to wear it for my sake. Can you? Will it go on your little finger?"

He pressed it hard. He could just get it on. Then he took it off and returned it to her.

"Reckon that's something else must wait till later," he said. "Nobody here better see me wearing that. I'd best get back up the top now. We've been too long already. My darling girl, I'll be upstream in the woods on the bank soon as the sun's down. I'll wait until you come. I'll be right *on* the bank: not half a mile." He pointed. "Bring the money and whatever else you'll be needing."

"Ye goin' to sing tonight, then?" Geoffrey Dean clapped Raymond on the shoulder as they both stripped to dip in the river. Work was over for the day and a dozen or more of the men were gathered on the bank, sluicing themselves and cooling off.

Raymond had been expecting this and had prepared his excuse.

"I'll come back after supper. But first I must get a needle to my clothes while there's light enough. My shirt'll be all to pieces without I set to it soon. I shan't be that long."

"Ah. Ye got some new songs?"

"Plenty; and tales. Pray God the lute strings only hold. I've no spare ones and they're well worn already."

He rubbed himself more or less dry with his hands and set about dressing as Geoffrey turned away to speak to others.

Supper that night was no less generous than usual and the men were still in good spirits – if not better, for the day after the morrow was Sunday and they were looking forward to the day's rest. Besides, there would be pay. Raymond was obliged to repeat to more than one questioner his excuse from singing, but promised to return as soon as his stitching was done.

Nicolas and Geoffrey were both in the hut after supper, attending to some sort of matters of their own and talking, as they did so, about the carving of the stones. They paid no particular attention when he went out, saying he was going into the wood to ease himself. They were so used now to seeing him carrying the lute – which he had never left to itself – that they did not remark on it.

He did not see Alison or attempt to, but walked quickly for some way up the slope and then turned westward across the camp, through the deserted carpenters' yard, past the timber stacks and so into the woods above the river upstream. He met no one.

Making his way downhill to the bank, even though it was no more than five hundred yards, was not easy in the failing light. In the virgin forest there was little room between the thin saplings and bushes. In such woodland there was no forestry; trees remained unthinned and grew in dense competition, so that few ever attained to real stature or enjoyed any open space about them. In forest land the only relatively open spaces were natural and here there was none. Raymond stumbled through beds of nettles, barked his shins on fallen logs and more than once recoiled from twigs which jabbed into his eyes. It took him nearly half an hour to reach the bank and he sat down to rest with a feeling of relief. He was also relieved to see that along the bank ran a path – narrow, disused and overgrown with the weeds of summer – but at least a path without trees, save for a few alders. It was by this path that Alison must surely come. For safety's sake he walked a few hundred yards up it, away from the camp, and then sat down to wait.

He waited for over an hour, until it was fully dark except for the rising moonlight from downstream. The woods seemed silent, for his impatience destroyed all inward tranquillity and he had no perception of the small noises of the night – even of the gentle sound of the river. He felt shut within his own tension and expectation; anxious, continually fidgeting, peering here and there yet seeing nothing. Again and again he thought he heard her coming and again and again he was disappointed, flinging himself down to listen more intently, his ear to the ground.

When at last she came it was almost silently, so that she was within a few yards of him before he realised she was there. She had not seen him and he spoke low, intending not to startle her.

"Here I am!"

"Oh, Raymond! Oh, Oi'm that glad! Oi was beginnin' to wonder—"

"You needn't have. Here, let me tie up that bundle again. That's loose. It'll come to pieces else."

He knelt, pulled the corners of the loosened cloth tight and knotted them over the clothes and other belongings she had brought. He did not ask her whether she had brought the money. He was glad to see that despite the warm, dry night she was wearing a cloak and a pair of good, serviceable boots. No doubt Roger had always seen to it that she was well off for clothes and boots.

They were both too tense and wrought-up for endearments. As he stood up she spoke to him almost sharply. "Is it far to a road?"

"I don't know. But not far, I expect. I was never this way before."

"But to Gloster? Ye said Gloster?"

"About twenty-five miles, I'd say. But we needn't walk *there*. There'll be a farm or some such where I can buy a horse tomorrow. We'll be in Gloster well before tomorrow night. It's a big place: we can vanish into Gloster, find an inn; you'll sleep in a comfortable bed. After that it's push straight on again, I'm afraid."

"Why so fast, my darlin'?"

"Come, let's be going and I'll tell you."

They began to make their way along the river path, sometimes in single file, sometimes side by side where the going was better.

"My Lord Hastings has no love for the so-called King Richard, who murdered his father. Nor have I."

"You told me."

"Do you know of Henry, Earl of Richmond? Have you heard tell of him?"

"No, that I never."

"He's been in France – in Brittany – to be safe from Richard and his wickedness. There's many would be glad to see him take the kingdom: many that would rise for him; Earl Stanley for one."

"To see 'im take the *kingdom*! To kill King Richard, you mean?"

"That's if all goes well. There've been secret messengers passing to and fro. My young lord Hastings has received messages. He knows Henry's plans. So do I, for he told me."

She said nothing, only pressing his arm as they walked together.

"My Lord Richmond will take ship from France. He'll be sailing to Wales. He means to meet King Richard in battle."

"You mean – you mean, my sweetheart, that you'll be fightin' in that battle?"

"Well, I may. But that's not the cause of our haste now. Earl Henry will land very soon. I'm carrying a letter to him from my Lord Hastings."

"What do it say?"

"Nay, I know not. But it will be a promise of support and no doubt seeking to know how he may be of help and where they should meet. That's the letter I have to deliver; upon Lord Richmond's landing, if only we can get there in time. If not, we shall have to follow him to deliver it."

"And then you'll be rewarded?"

"I shall certainly deserve it, by my reckoning. To lose horse and money and nonetheless reach the Earl. He'll be generous. I never heard ill of him." Then, impulsively, he turned and embraced her. "We'll be rich, my love! You shall have true happiness; you'll be happier than ever you've been in your life!"

Now he began again to fondle and caress her in earnest, and she responded to him eagerly, kissing his face, his ears, his neck. They sank down together on the soft, dry bank. After a while she said, "Take those great boots off, my sweetheart.

Let's both be at our ease. There's toime, b'ain't there? We've got the toime. Oh, my love – the toime! The rest of our loives! Here's your ring. Put it on! Oh, my darlin' Raymond!"

Roger Nott had indeed set out as though to go to Bourton. Many in the camp had seen him mount his horse and go. He had taken good care that they should. He had also told Nicolas and Geoffrey, in his wife's hearing, that he might well stay that night with the stone contractor and if he did, what work they were to start the men upon in the morning. He had taken his cloak and his heavy staff, kissed his wife and departed with no more words, as was his way.

He did indeed reach Bourton, but there was no meeting with the stone contractor. None had been arranged. Nott passed the time in an alehouse, speaking to no one and drinking half-heartedly at a bench apart. No one spoke to him: strangers seldom did, feeling his great size and silent manner forbidding. When he heard the church clock strike ten he went out, re-mounted and rode back to the camp site at a canter. He reached it in half an hour.

He had been expecting to find his wife gone from the cottage, and had also been expecting to learn – if he troubled himself to ask – that no one had seen Raymond or could tell where he might be. He sat down to wait for them to return from the woods, or wherever they might be disporting themselves. After a while he lit a lamp and it was then that he noticed for the first time certain evidences of disarrangement which, in his inward agitation, he had not observed before. A closet door was hanging open: and Alison's cloak was not on its usual peg. He began to look about more systematically. Her good linen dress was gone, her best shift, her stockings, her bone comb and her studded girdle. He lifted and moved the lower legs of the bed, then the flooring beneath and then the turf. The box was empty. The twenty pounds was gone.

Roger stood silently thinking for a few minutes. Then, taking up his staff, he went in search of Nicolas, whom he met coming down the slope on his way to his hut and bed. In a few words he told him what had happened, confirmed that

Raymond had not been seen for some few hours and told him
to accompany him.

"But which way, master?" asked Nicolas.

"He said he was journeying west. No reason to suppose that
was a lie."

Unknown to Raymond, there was a rough path from the
north-west corner of the building site leading through the
woods to Charlton Abbots, and up the slope to this the two
men went and along it for perhaps three hundred yards. Here
Roger paused, leaning on his staff and considering.

"They've not gone this way."

"Why not, master? Have ye seen summat?"

Roger made no reply, merely turning and retracing his steps.
They came back to the west wall of the house and walked down
the slope towards the river. At the bank Roger turned upstream
and went a short distance along the path. When he stopped
it was without a word, pointing with the end of his staff to
something on the ground. Nicolas stooped and picked it up.
It was a lace of a girl's bodice. Roger looked at it, nodded,
put it in his pocket and went on.

The clear, full moon, now almost due south across the river,
shone directly on to the bank and into the trees, making their
progress relatively easy. They did not speak; but once, when
Nicolas cracked a stick beneath his foot, Roger turned and
glanced at him with a look sufficient to make him careful
not to tread on another. He followed Roger with caution for
a good mile.

Suddenly they both stopped. What they could hear from a
little distance was a girl's voice – Alison's – singing quietly,
tranquil and assured.

> "She borrowed some of her father's gold,
> And some of her mother's fee
> And away they did go to the stable door—"

Roger began to run, and Nicolas after him, caring nothing now
for cracking sticks or the swish of branches.

The lovers were found as they had been lying, half-clothed

in each other's arms, Raymond's hand beneath Alison's head, his lute, his sword, boots and pieces of clothing strewn beside them. As Roger came up they sprang to their feet – Alison with a cry – and Raymond snatched up and drew his sword.

In seconds it was all over. Roger swung a heavy blow at Raymond with his staff. Raymond leapt to one side and as he did so drove the point of his sword into Roger's chest.

Roger recoiled two or three feet from the force of the thrust and fell to the ground unmoving. Raymond withdrew his sword and at once released a great jet of blood. Nicolas, trembling, drew back from the body where it had fallen supine on the river bank. For long seconds he stared at it, aghast, before running blindly back by the way he and Roger had come. Raymond stood listening as he stumbled through the bushes. Then, as the sound died away, he turned to the sobbing Alison, putting his arm round her shoulders.

"I should have killed him too. He's a witness. We must go at once, and fast as we can. Get dressed, my love, quickly."

She made no move. He shook her gently.

"Get dressed, Alison. Come, hurry. We must be off."

He stooped to clean his sword in the stream, sheathed it and began pulling on his own clothes as quickly as he could.

Less than five minutes later, they were gone upstream. The body of Roger Nott lay on the bank in a silence broken only by the soft babbling of the river and the intermittent calling of an owl in the wood.

All that night they walked on beside the stream. They went slowly, for Alison was in a state of shock and several times sank down, weeping and begging Raymond to let her rest. Raymond, driven by the fear of pursuit, urged her gently but firmly forward. In places the path was overgrown and hard to follow, and he carried her, stumbling over fallen branches and broken ground. At last, soon after daybreak, they found themselves clear of the woodland, looking across cornfields and pasture, on the edge of which a flock of sheep was penned by hurdles driven into the ground. Up the slope from the stream, perhaps three quarters of a mile away, stood a farmhouse, surrounded by its barns and stables. Men were emerging into the open, some rubbing their eyes and pulling on their clothes as they came. The day's work was already beginning.

Raymond and Alison, making their way up the slope beside the straggling verge of the forest, came to a grassy lane which led to the farmhouse in one direction and in the other to a rough, stony road. Close by stood a barn, in which they found a stack of mangels and another of hay.

"Make yourself comfortable here, my love," said Raymond. "I'm going up to the farmhouse to buy a horse, if I can." He cut a mangel in two and gave her his knife. "Eat some of this. It's better than nothing and you'll feel the better for it." He unslung his lute and gave it to her, smiling. "And guard this with your life till I come back. Get in the hay and sleep."

He kissed her and made his way out of the barn and up the lane towards the farmhouse. The first building he came to was a stable, outside which two men were backing a horse into the shafts of a cart. Seeing him, they paused and stood staring with silent suspicion. They were wary of strangers; and the more so of one who was plainly not of their own farming world.

Raymond greeted them with a smile and a slight bow. "Good morrow, lads. I have some business with the farmer here. Can you tell me where to find him?"

One of the men jerked his thumb over his shoulder in the direction of the farmhouse. The other, keeping hold of the horse, spat on the ground, "What sort of business is that, then?"

"I'll tell him that when I see him," replied Raymond, looking the man in the eye and speaking firmly. "Perhaps you'll be good enough to take me to him."

The man hesitated, plainly half of a mind to refuse. Then he shrugged his shoulders, gave the reins to his companion and set off across the yard. Raymond caught him up and fell in beside him. As they approached the back door of the farmhouse, scattering the hens and geese, they were met by a tall, bearded man who was plainly the farmer, not only on account of his good clothes and deliberate, unhurried manner,

but also because he was reading – or at any rate glancing over
– a sheet of paper held in one hand. Seeing Raymond and the
man with him, he put the paper in his pocket. "What's this,
then, Ezra?"

"Says he wants see you on business, farmer," answered
Ezra, and at once turned away, leaving the two of them
together.

"Good morrow, sir," said Raymond, again bowing. "I'll not
waste your time with idle talk. I'm here to ask you to be so
kind as to sell me a horse. I have ready money and I'll pay
you a fair price."

Like his men, the farmer also hesitated, taking in Raymond's
dishevelled appearance and bloodstained clothes.

"I don't deal with men I don't know," he replied at length.
"You'd best be off, and quickly."

"Sir," said Raymond, "I assure you I'm an honest man. I'm
a messenger from the household of Lord Hastings, travelling
on his urgent business into Wales. Four nights ago my horse
was stolen and I was attacked by a couple of ruffians. One of
them I killed with this sword and it's his blood you see on
my clothes. The other got away with my horse. I've walked
all night in the forest and now I find myself here. At all costs
I must get to Gloster quickly and cross into Wales with my
lord's letter. I beg you to help me if you can. I mustn't fail
my lord."

The farmer stood considering, one hand pulling at his beard.
At length he said, "Well, you're lucky; perhaps luckier than
you deserve, for all I can tell. It so happens that I have a mare
I've planned to sell. You'd better come with me, I suppose,
and have a look at her. You'll be needing a bit and bridle and
the rest?"

"I'll be more than grateful, sir," replied Raymond. "I'll tell
Lord Hastings of your kindness upon my return."

Knowing it best to keep quiet when matters were turning
out to his advantage, he said nothing more as he and the
farmer made their way to the stables, only nodding to the
ostler whom the farmer told to saddle up the mare. Raymond,
when he had looked it over, ridden it round the yard and

found nothing wrong with it, told the farmer that he was content to buy.

The farmer's price was high. This Raymond could very well tell, but he paid with no more than a touch of bargaining for the look of the thing.

As he was about to ride away, the farmer said, "You'll be hungry, I dare say."

Raymond gladly accepted the ham and eggs which the farmer's wife cooked for him, and also the bread and cheese which she offered him for his journey. Now sure of their goodwill, he shook hands with her and with the farmer, mounted for the second time and rode away down the lane.

He found Alison sound asleep in the hay and reluctantly woke her. When she had eaten most of the bread and cheese he helped her up to sit bareback in front of him. The mare remained quiet and carried them at a walk into the rough road. After a few miles they came to a broader highway, and a stone reading: 'To Gloster, 21 miles'.

Raymond, anxious not to tire the mare, dismounted and led her by the bridle for perhaps an hour. They came to a village, where he watered her at the pond and held her while she cropped the grass and Alison once more dozed in the shade. When she woke, she seemed more cheerful and talked happily to Raymond, asking him how many days he thought it would take them to reach Milford Haven.

"Four, I'd reckon," he replied. "The mare seems sound enough, but I was never in Wales and I don't know what the roads are like. We can only pray, and trust in God."

On the highway they met with a number of people; some riding to Gloster like themselves, others driving sheep or cattle and one man leading four enormous hounds, which he told Raymond a local squire was buying to guard his house and grounds at night.

They reached the outskirts of Gloster in the late afternoon. A young man driving a horse and cart, with whom they had struck up an acquaintance on the road, recommended The Green Dragon as a comfortable and inexpensive inn, where he was going himself. He invited Alison to ride with him in the cart and, evidently finding her a pleasant companion, took pains to tell her what he knew of the churches and the wealthy houses along their way. At first Alison seemed unsure of herself and embarrassed by his attention, and Raymond could see well enough the effect on her of having been married to Roger Nott. However, when she realised that Raymond obviously had no objection to her responding warmly to their friend, she allowed herself to show her natural animation, and as they came into the centre of the city could hardly ask questions fast enough. Raymond was delighted to see her in good spirits.

As soon as they had handed over the mare to the ostler and taken a room at The Green Dragon, Raymond took Alison out into the city to buy fresh clothes. The woman from whom they bought stared pointedly at the bloodstains on Alison's dress, but asked no questions and made herself pleasant enough to her customers. Nevertheless, Raymond was careful to bring away with them everything which Alison discarded and to let fall in conversation not a word about where they had come from or whither they were going.

Having bought for himself a new shirt, tunic, breeches and stockings he was equally careful to pack up his old clothing and bring it away. He had no idea whether news of Roger Nott's death might have reached Gloster. He thought it unlikely, but all the same he was fully aware that not only Nicolas, but everyone at the manor site would be talking of the murder. Alison and he must be gone into Wales tomorrow and the earlier the better. Descriptions of himself and of her might already be widespread.

Nevertheless, to make love at leisure and in comfort banished his anxieties for the time being. Knowing that she trusted him completely, he used every endeavour to convince her that all would go well with them. Within an hour, in her joy to have escaped from her unhappy marriage and to be in the arms of this handsome young man who admired and loved her, she seemed entirely to have forgotten that they were fugitives.

Raymond was a gentle, considerate lover and did all he could to give her pleasure. The experience was so new to her that, having given herself up to it completely, she became exhausted and fell asleep almost between one word and the next. Raymond, who was if anything even more weary than she, was soon sleeping beside her.

Several hours later, he woke to a sound from below almost more familiar to him than any other; a man's voice, clear and distinct, leading an audience in singing. Alison did not wake and he lay still, happy enough to listen with a professional ear as the company joined the singer in the burthen.

"My fol lol lol to my right fol lol,
Wag for the dear old day.
And what few nuts that poor girl had
She strewed them all away."

He knew the song, a mildly suggestive one, very well, and appreciated the skill with which the singer was drawing his audience into full participation.

When it finished, there was a banging of pots on tables and cries of, "Ah, well done!"

Raymond could not resist. He slipped quietly out of bed, dressed and woke Alison with a kiss. As she opened her eyes he whispered, "Don't worry; everything's all right. Just go to sleep again. I'll soon be back."

She smiled, nodded drowsily and once more closed her eyes. Raymond, picking up his lute, slipped quietly down the stairs and as unobtrusively as possible into the tap-room facing him at the bottom.

About twenty people, mostly men and a few women, were seated on the benches, their ale pots before them on the rough wooden tables. On the far side of the room a second door stood ajar at the top of another flight of stairs leading down to the cellar. As Raymond came in, he saw a pot-boy in the act of going down with two handfuls of mugs to be refilled.

At this time of year there was no fire, and the singer, a dark-haired young man not much older than himself, was standing in front of the fireplace with his lute slung before him. Seeing Raymond, he smiled at him for a moment, nodded and again began to sing.

His song was 'Green Broom', a narrative ballad which, although it had no burthen for the company, nevertheless commanded their attention from the outset. His voice struck Raymond with its true and powerful quality.

"There was an old man and he lived in the West,
And his trade was a-selling of brooms, green brooms;
He had but one son and his name it was John
And he liéd abed till 'twas noon, bright noon,
And he liéd abed till 'twas noon."

The tune was different from the one Raymond knew, although the words were familiar. After a little he realised that the singer was varying the tune verse by verse, extemporising on the spur of the moment. He had never heard this done before. If he had been asked, he would altogether have opposed the idea, but now he found himself listening with pleasure, full of curiosity, to hear what the singer would contrive next. The audience, he perceived, were not consciously aware of the changes, but like children were simply concerned with the story. Halfway through the ballad, the young man again caught his eye across the room and gave him a slow and deliberate wink, which he returned. At the end he withdrew his attention and as the applause broke out busied himself with ordering ale from the pot-boy. He was handing over the money when a hand fell on his shoulder and he turned to see the ballad singer offering him a full pot. As Raymond took it from him, the young man said, "Good luck!", tilted his own to his lips and drank deeply.

"Am I on your pitch?" he asked. "If so, I'm sorry."

"No," replied Raymond. "I thought I must be on yours. Don't you sing here regularly, then?"

"No, I shall be gone tomorrow. I only thought to pick up a shilling or two to pay for the night's lodging."

"I'm off tomorrow too," said Raymond. "I'm going into Wales."

"So am I," answered the young man. "You wouldn't be carrying a letter, by any chance, I suppose?"

"These are dangerous times," said Raymond. "No times for a man to be telling his business to strangers."

The other nodded. "Are you travelling alone?"

"No," said Raymond. "My wife's with me. I've left her upstairs, asleep. I'll wake her and we can get a meal."

Over supper, Raymond's new acquaintance showed himself ready enough to talk about himself. His name was Martin of Lincoln and he also was a singer and musician, in the household of Lord Stanley.

"If you're travelling into Wales," he said, "I dare say I wouldn't be far out if I guessed you're bound for some friend of Henry Tudor. Every Welshman's his friend, so I'm told."

"I'm no Welshman, but it's true I carry a letter," replied Raymond. "As to the contents, I know nothing."

"Nor I of mine. But I wouldn't care to give it to Richard of Gloster and stand there while he read it, would you?"

Raymond laughed and changed the subject. "Alison and I need to be away from here early tomorrow. Will you ride with us?"

"That I will. It's always better to travel in company when your journey lies through strange places. You've never been in Wales?"

"Never."

"Welshmen don't like Englishmen, I'm told, and haven't these two hundred years."

"No," said Raymond, smiling reassuringly at Alison, "but

Wales tomorrow will be a safer place than this city for two Englishmen and a girl who'd be glad to see the so-called King Richard put down. In Wales they'll find plenty who agree with them, so young Lord Hastings told me."

"But d'ye reckon there'll be enough to put King Richard down?" asked Alison. "Only 'e must 'ave plenty of earls and lords and that to fight for 'un, surely?"

"And there's many who won't, when it comes to the point," said Martin. "God must surely be with us, for He knows all the secret, wicked deeds of Richard. Who murdered the true king – the boy Edward – if not he?"

"But will your Henry Tudor 'ave enough men to fight for 'un?" persisted Alison.

Raymond put a finger quickly to his lips as the landlord came up with their reckoning. In reply to Martin, he assured them that their horses and their breakfast would be ready at five next morning.

Nicolas of Taunton stood facing Gilbert Windrush across the body of Roger Nott, which had been laid out on the table in his hut. It had not been stripped and the blood on shirt and breeches had stiffened and turned brown. The flies clustered thickly.

With Nicolas were Geoffrey Dean and two or three of the journeymen masons. Outside clustered a crowd, men and women, peering in and talking together in low voices. It had proved impossible to disperse them. Everyone in the camp had stopped work and gathered on the lane down which they knew Gilbert Windrush would come. When he arrived, to be met by Nicolas, they had followed him down to the hut.

"So after this minstrel or whatever he was had stabbed him, you ran away, did you?" asked Windrush.

"Ay, that I did, master," answered Nicolas. "I'd got no weapon at all, d'ye see?"

"It's a bad business," said Windrush. "And you say his wife's gone off with the minstrel?"

"She must 'ave, master. She weren't there when we come back for the body."

"Where have they gone, d'you suppose?"

"Can't tell, master; only the minstrel said something yesterday about 'e was going into the west."

"And he had no horse?"

"No. 'E told us 'is 'orse 'ad been stolen."

Gilbert paused, then turned to Geoffrey Dean. "Go and get a cart ready to carry the body. See that it's clean and looks decent. It must be covered, of course."

Dean nodded, and turned to push his way through the crowd. Taking two men with him, he set off towards the stables.

"Can you go on with the building work without Nott?" asked Windrush.

"No, master, not rightly we can't," replied Nicolas. "We can finish the work 'e'd set us to do, like; that's to say, the way 'e wanted it done. But after that I can't say. Roger had it all in 'is 'ead, see, and he used to tell us what to do piece by piece, as we come to it."

"Well, you'd better do as much as you can, until I can engage another master mason. But that won't be easy. It's the wrong time of year. I shan't be able to find a man as good as Nott."

"And the pay, master? Only if they're not paid, they won't stay 'ere, see."

"I'll pay them all, tell them, as soon as I've got this wretched business properly seen to. You'll take over Nott's job as best you can. You must do your best to keep them together."

Nicolas nodded. "You're right, master. You won't get another man like Nott all that easy."

"He was one of the best in England. I'm not the only man who thought so. I'd already recommended him to the King. When we were agreeing the terms of a loan, I told the King that Roger Nott was the best master mason I knew."

"You'll tell the King of this, then, master?"

"Yes, as soon as there's occasion. The King's gone to Nottingham with his army. Wherever Henry Tudor lands – if he does – the King will be ready for him. Come now, get me a meal before I go with the body. I must see the sheriff today if I can."

"And the minstrel, master?"

"Oh, they'll catch up with him all right; don't worry about that. Him *and* the woman. She'll hang with him. Come on, now!" he shouted to the crowd. "Get back to work if you want your pay."

Alison lay beside Raymond in the half-darkness of the stable, trying in vain to sleep. After leaving Gloster that morning, they had travelled steadily on and in the evening had reached Monmouth. Raymond was now full of anxiety that they might be followed and arrested, and had persuaded Martin to press on with Alison and himself into the country beyond the town before stopping for the night. At the first village inn they came to beyond Monmouth, they had asked for a night's lodging and stabling. As it happened, the landlord was short of domestic labour, his wife being away at her mother's, but he had offered them bread and cheese and clean straw in the stables. Since it was now late and both they themselves and the horses were tired, they had accepted this and made themselves reasonably comfortable, adding to the bread and cheese two or three quarts of ale. Raymond and Martin, having seen to the horses, were now sleeping soundly.

Alison lay awake. She had at last begun to reflect seriously upon her situation. She still felt more than glad to be free of Roger Nott and to have become the consort of Raymond. But what value could she put upon his protection? She had none at all except his, and however determined, however valiant he might show himself in her defence, if he were taken as the killer of Roger — which could be proved beyond any possible denial — what could he do for her then? As an adulteress, present with him when he killed Roger, she would share his fate. But if she were to leave him now — to disappear into this strange, distant country and be ready to make the best of whatever might befall — might she not still escape?

This, she knew, was temptation. Raymond did not deserve to be deserted in this way. But in the other scale was her fear of death, and it weighed heavy. She lay imagining their arrest and every ghastly eventuality, until she trembled and her bowels moved.

She got up and silently went outside. The moon, which had barely begun to wane, was shining brightly on the stable yard and the orchard beyond. Only one light showed in an upstairs window of the inn.

To relieve herself on the ground, like an animal, was repugnant. Besides, it would be noticed, and discredit all three of them. She looked about for the privy and at once saw a likely-looking shed at one end of the inn building, on the further side of the yard. She found she was right, but on going in she stumbled and almost fell. Her open hand slapped noisily against the woodwork and in the same moment the door fell wide open and struck the brickwork beside it. A dog began to bark nearby.

Alison's need was now too pressing to see to the door. She was just in time to pull up her petticoat and sit down when her bowels emptied with a rush. Miserably, she waited for the next spasm, while the dog barked on and on.

When at last she had finished and gone out into the yard, she found herself confronted by the landlord, dressed in nothing but his shirt. Supposing him to be about the same business as herself, she gave him an awkward smile and was turning to go when he took her by the shoulder.

"Needn't go yet, my dear, needn't go yet," he muttered, and tried to put his arms round her.

Alison struggled, and managed to scream once before he put his hand over her mouth and pulled her backwards against his chest.

"Indoors, indoors," he said, his mouth against her ear. "Indoors, my dear, where we can be warm and comfortable. Come along now; you've got to; yes, got to."

She threw off his arm and screamed again before he slapped her face violently. The pain was severe and she fell down, limp and unresisting. He bent, picked her up bodily and began to carry her back into the house.

As he did so, Martin came running into the yard at the far end, paused a moment to take in the situation and then rushed upon the landlord. The landlord dropped Alison, took a step forward and hit Martin full in the face.

But now Raymond also was among them, his drawn sword in his hand. As the landlord turned to meet him, he cut him across the neck and then, thrusting, pierced his arm above the elbow.

The landlord fell backwards, clutching at his throat and trying, it seemed, to speak. Alison, struggling to her feet, saw yet again the heavy flow of blood from a mortal wound.

It was only an instant's glimpse, for Raymond, wiping his sword on the landlord's shirt, took her by one arm as Martin gripped the other. Together they half-carried her back to the stable and laid her down on the straw while they dressed.

"Wait here until we get the horses," said Raymond. He laughed mirthlessly. "Always in a hurry to leave, aren't we?"

Five minutes later they were leading the horses by the bridles out on to the lane in front of the inn. Alison rode bareback as best she could, leaning forward and gripping their horse's mane. After they had gone about half a mile, Raymond led the way into the outskirts of a coppice beside the track.

"We'll stop here and saddle up. What happened, Alison? He was going to take you by force, was he?"

Still trembling and weeping, Alison told what had happened.

"It's a pity I used the sword," said Raymond. "We should have knocked him down and given him a good beating. That would have answered just as well. Still, it can't be helped now."

The two men mounted and urged the horses into a canter. With Raymond's arm about her, Alison sat silent, reflecting miserably. Twice now she had been the cause of bloodshed and death. On her account her companions' lives were in the gravest danger. And yet, so it seemed, they were not going to alter their plans; they were still making for the same destination as before.

Day dawned. The weather remained fine and very warm. All along their way, harvesting was taking place in the fields, and in accordance with custom they gave dole to the sweating sicklemen. From time to time they fell in with other travellers, but always found some excuse to leave them before nightfall, for Raymond and Martin were agreed that it would be best not to stay long in any company. At the inns where they put up they kept to themselves as much as possible and always made early starts in the morning. In this way they travelled uneventfully for three days.

Several times they had difficulty in dealing with people who spoke only Welsh. They also found it true, as Raymond had said, that many Welsh people seemed to have no love for the English. These problems, however, were unexpectedly solved at a single stroke.

It was a little after midday when they heard behind them a large number of horses approaching. As it drew closer they could hear the riders conversing. There was no cover anywhere near, and Raymond, with a word to Martin, drew in off the road and dismounted to wait while they went by.

As the horsemen rounded the nearby bend and came into view, they disclosed themselves as an armed company, several wearing breastplates and helmets. Clearly, this was some kind of cavalry force.

The first horsemen drew level with Raymond and Martin, and one called out an order, whereupon the whole band came to a halt and dismounted, holding their horses' heads. The officer who had given the order walked across to Raymond and spoke to him in Welsh.

Raymond perforce replied in English, at which the officer smiled and gestured to one of his companions, who joined him.

"We're messengers," explained Raymond, "carrying letters to Milford Haven from our masters, Lord Hastings and Lord Stanley."

"To Henry Tudor?" asked the second officer.

"Yes. We ourselves haven't read the letters, but we're in no doubt that they're assurances of support for his cause."

"You're to deliver them to him as soon as he lands, is that it?"

"Yes; though he may already have landed, of course."

"He's not yet landed, as far as we know," said the first officer. "But he's expected any day. We're on the way to Milford, too. My name's Captain Jenkyns. You're welcome to ride with us. We expect to reach Milford tomorrow."

Raymond and Martin were glad to accept. A baggage wagon, with two or three women, was following the horsemen, and in this a place was found for Alison as the company set off again, with the two Englishmen bringing up the rear. Those around them spoke hardly a word of English, but showed themselves friendly nevertheless.

They halted for the night at a village where they were evidently expected. Two large barns had been put at their disposal. Captain Jenkyns himself paid for their rather scanty rations, as well as for fodder for the horses. The women, including Alison, were given rough pallets by the villagers, while Raymond and Martin shook down among the men.

Next day, 7th August, they covered ten or eleven miles and early in the afternoon found themselves on the winding shore of Milford Haven, among a crowd of several hundred awaiting the arrival from France of Henry Tudor, Earl of Richmond, and his followers.

Alison had never seen the sea, and was happy enough, as she gazed, to humour the good-natured banter of the Welsh cavalrymen. Captain Jenkyns set off to report to Lord Rhys ap Thomas, whom he knew to be assembling a force in support of Henry.

Raymond, Alison and Martin consulted together.

"What do you mean to do after we've delivered the letters?" asked Martin.

"Well, plainly we can't ride back the way we came," replied Raymond. "In any case, as I've told Alison, I've always meant to join Henry Tudor if I can. I'm sure it's the best thing we can do, if he'll have us."

"Oh, he'll have us: no doubt of that. Sturdy young Englishmen: he must need all he can get."

Raymond nodded. At this moment a loud cry from the shore was taken up by the whole crowd. Ships were in sight; ships that could be none other than Earl Henry's.

Raymond, Martin and Alison joined those pressing forward for a better view.

There were seven ships in all, sailing together as a fleet. During the next hour, as they approached up Freshwater Bay to the south, the crowd on shore doubled in number. A priest, standing on a low wall, led those around him in prayer and then launched into a sermon, of the Welsh fervour of which Raymond and Martin understood not a word. Everywhere the Red Dragon of Wales was flying on banners large and small. A Mayor appeared, in his robes of office, attended by councillors, and three or four coaches drew up at a short distance from the quay. Over the heads of the crowd Martin caught sight of Captain Jenkyns and, leading his horse, pushed his way towards him, followed by Raymond and Alison.

The water of the harbour was deep enough for the ships to come alongside the main quay, and the two largest vessels now did so, being then secured by ropes fore and aft, while gangplanks were put in position.

As the crowd broke into cheers, a group of five or six persons – clearly, from their dress and bearing, men of rank – came forward across the deck of the nearer ship and one by one descended the gangplank. The first on shore raised his hand in greeting to the crowd and then knelt to kiss the soil of Wales, upon which there was an even louder outburst of cheering and shouted blessings. Henry Tudor – for it was indeed he – spoke a sentence or two in Latin, which the crowd took to be a prayer commending himself and his cause to God.

Raymond, edging forward, watched as Henry drew a sword and then and there conferred knighthood on three of his companions. His age Raymond guessed to be about twenty-eight or thirty. He was dressed sombrely in grey and his only ornament was a gold chain, on which hung a heraldic star. He was a little below middle height, spare and lean. Although he lacked the build and appearance of a warrior, he looked shrewd and sharp witted, and his air, as he spoke to those about him, suggested both confidence and authority.

One other man in particular made a strong impression on Raymond. He looked to be well on in middle age, much the oldest of the group, grizzled but every inch a soldier. Raymond asked Captain Jenkyns who he was.

"That's John de Vere, Earl of Oxford," replied the captain. "Very experienced in the wars. He's been fighting against the Yorkists for years. If anyone can defeat Richard, he will."

As they still stood watching, the crowd parted and a small group of horsemen rode up to Henry, dismounted and greeted him on bended knee.

"That's our man," said Jenkyns, pointing to the one nearest to them. "Rhys ap Thomas. He's the one who'll lead the Welsh."

The other ships were now brought up to the shore and moored; and from these several hundreds of rough-looking men disembarked and stood loitering on the quay.

"And those?" asked Raymond.

"They'll be the fellows Earl Henry's brought with him from France," replied Jenkyns. "Most of them are English, I'm told; fought for the Duke of Buckingham two years ago and had to run for their lives when he was beaten. But some are men who've been let out of prison to come and fight. Look like it, too, don't they?"

It was some two hours before all Earl Henry's forces were disembarked and the welcoming crowd began to disperse. As Jenkyns was on the point of assembling his cavalrymen to leave, Raymond took opportunity to speak to him again.

"Captain, I beg you, if you can, to do me one more good turn. Alison and I want to be married, but as you know, we can't speak Welsh. Can you possibly find a priest for us? We'll bless you for ever."

"Ride on with us now, to Haverfordwest," answered the captain. "There's bound to be a priest there." He kissed Alison's hand. "It's your wedding day, sweetheart. The place will be crowded out tonight, but I'll find you both a decent room, don't worry."

And so at last Raymond and Alison were married, in a little chantry chapel, by a young priest scarcely older than Raymond and with no one else present but Martin. The priest, despite his indifferent English, was warm and friendly, and took them back the short distance to his house to share a bottle of wine. Outside, the little town of Haverfordwest was full of a louder clamour than it could ever have known, as Earl Henry's followers turned it inside out in search of food and lodging. Alison, all smiles now and more than happy, was glad enough to sit and rest for an hour before Jenkyns, having snatched a few minutes from his men and horses, accompanied all three of them to an inn he had virtually commandeered. He promised to meet them again next morning. Raymond, knowing that the captain must have ordered the landlord to put them up, mollified him with an immediate payment of a guinea. After an early supper they turned in for the night.

Some three or four hours later, Raymond woke and at once realised that Alison, beside him, was also awake, and weeping. He grasped her shoulder and kissed her.

"What's the matter?"

"Oh, 'tis nothin', my love. Nothin', really."

"Come on, tell me. I promise not to mind, whatever it is. Let me help you."

"Oh, Raymond darlin', 'tis the same thing. The war, the battle – whatever 'tis goin' to be. Oi'm that much afeared as you'll be killed. Oi wish you wouldn't go."

"Neither Martin nor I can honourably keep out of it, love. We shall be all right, don't worry. Besides, when we've won, the Earl's sure to reward the people who fought for him."

"But to foight against the king! 'Tis high treason, Raymond. Oi reckon 'tis mortal sin an' all, bain't un?"

"It's anything but that. This Duke of Gloster's no king at all. He's usurped the throne and murdered those two wretched little princes he put in the Tower."

"But all the same, there's plenty as'll foight for 'en, bain't there?"

"Perhaps; but you can take it from me there's more that'll not commit themselves; that'll stand by and wait to see what happens. This Richard has made himself hated throughout the land. I'll tell you, I wouldn't like to be one of those who have to fight for *him*."

"But, come roight down to it, Oi reckon 'e'll 'ave more men that what Earl Henry's got, woan' 'un?"

"All I can do, my love, is to tell you again and again, as often as you want to hear it, that I'm utterly sure we shall defeat this cruel, wicked man. God Himself will be on our side. Now, kiss me, and let's forget about him for a while."

Next morning, as soon as they met Jenkyns, Martin said, "Captain, you'll recall that both Raymond and I have been given letters by our lords to deliver to the earl. I certainly don't want to hand mine over to anyone else. Lord Stanley expressly told me to give it to the earl myself. What ought we to do?"

Jenkyns paused, reflecting.

"The trouble is that all the men close to Earl Henry are far too busy preparing for the march into England to take petitioners up to him. We can only try our luck."

They set out on their search. They managed to speak to Sir Edward Courtenay and then to Sir Edward Poynings. Each undertook to take the letters and give them to Earl Henry, but when Martin pleaded his sworn promise to Lord Stanley, they shook their heads.

"Good heavens, man, I shan't lose your letter!" snapped Courtenay.

"I fully believe you, sir," replied Martin, "but I am bound by my promise to Lord Stanley."

Courtenay uttered a snort expressive of exasperation, and turned away.

"I fear I must leave you now," said Jenkyns. "Time presses."

He was gone almost before they could thank him.

"I believe that after all we'll have to give them to one of these lords – knights – whatever they are," said Raymond, "to give to the earl. Else they'll never reach him at all."

"No, damn it," replied Martin. "I'm not going to miss this chance of becoming known to him."

As they stood pondering, he suddenly gripped Raymond by the elbow. "This is it. Now or never. Come on!"

A servant, carrying a tray loaded with three or four bottles of wine and about a dozen horn cups, was approaching along the passage. Martin stepped in his way and stopped him.

"The earl's sent me to bring this tray to him at once."

The man answered him in Welsh.

"No, that's all right," said Martin. "Just you leave it to me."

His manner was assured and authoritative. After a moment's hesitation, the servant relinquished the tray. Martin at once turned about and set off with it down the passage, Raymond following. Round the doorway of the dining-room a small crowd were clustering, craning their necks to see inside.

"Now, masters," said Martin. "Let me pass, if you please. This wine is for the earl himself."

At this they drew back and made way for Martin and Raymond. Earl Henry was seated at the far end of the room, at a rough wooden table strewn with papers. Also seated was the Earl of Oxford. About a dozen men were standing round them, conferring and listening.

Martin walked straight up the room and set the tray down on the table. Then he dropped upon one knee at the earl's feet.

"Pardon me, my lord. I bring you this letter from Lord Stanley. When he gave it to me, he ordered that I myself was to deliver it into your hands. I have done so."

Henry looked at him sharply and then took the sealed letter.

"From Lord Thomas Stanley, you say?"

"Yes, my lord. From Lord Thomas himself. I have brought it from Lancashire."

Henry glanced up at his followers. "Pardon me, sirs. I will read it at once." He looked carefully at the seals before breaking them.

He spent perhaps two minutes in reading the letter, before handing it to the Earl of Oxford with a smile.

"Pray keep this close."

He now found Raymond at his feet.

"This, my lord, from Lord Hastings."

"The son of him that the Earl of Gloster murdered?"

70

"Ay, my lord."

Henry passed the letter unopened to Oxford.

"We will read it later, when time serves." He turned to Raymond and Martin.

"Your names?"

When they had told him, he said, "You have both done well. Now you have leave to go."

When they were once more outside in the passage, Raymond said, "Do you think he guessed about your trick with the wine?"

"Surely. Very little escapes him."

"That must have been good news from Lord Stanley. It pleased him."

"Ay. Well, let's get back to Mistress Alison, and decide to whom we'd do best to offer ourselves as soldiers. Jenkyns has been a good friend, but we can't join his company of Welshmen. There must be some fellows here who speak English, if only we can find them."

So numerous were the Welshmen that they were some time searching. At length an English sergeant advised them to present themselves to Sir Walter Rutherford – one of those who had been knighted by Earl Henry upon his landing.

"I know he's forming an English company up at Cardigan. That's a good twenty miles from here, but it would be well worth your while to go, especially if you've got horses."

They reached Cardigan in the early evening, and were directed to the Llewellyn Arms. The oak-panelled hall seemed full of Englishmen going this way and that, all intent on their own affairs. They were about to stop one of them in passing, when a door was flung open almost at Raymond's elbow and a young man came flying out, staggering as though he had been pushed or kicked, and fell to the floor. A voice behind him roared "And *don't* come back here without it!" Then the door was slammed.

Martin helped the young man up.

"That looked like a trifling disturbance, sir. Not hurt, I trust?"

"No. But one day someone's going to stick a dagger into Sir Walter. He'll do that sort of thing once too often."

71

"It's Sir Walter we've come to see. Is there someone who can take us in to him?"

"Just go in. He's not one for standing on ceremony." And with this the young man left them.

They looked at each other. Martin shrugged his shoulders. "Well, it's what we've come for."

He opened the door and went in, Raymond following.

A man, perhaps forty years of age, in a leather jacket and muddy riding boots, looked up at them from where he was sitting at a table laid for a meal. He had a wind-roughened, ruddy face and a thick, untidy mane of greying hair. Between one finger and thumb he was holding a mutton chop, which he had evidently picked up from a pewter plate in front of him, where lay four or five more. Also on the table were a goblet, a loaf of bread, a large pat of butter and a Cheddar cheese, together with salt and pepper and a wine flagon.

Raymond and Martin approached the table, bowed and stood waiting in silence. The man, paying them no attention, continued gnawing the chop to a conclusion, tossed the bone to a hound lying in the rushes on the floor and drank from the goblet, wiping his mouth with the back of his hand.

Then he looked up and said, "What do *you* want?"

"We want to join your company, sir. We're sworn enemies of the so-called King Richard."

"Been soldiering before?"

"No, sir."

"What makes you think you'd be any good to *me*?" asked Sir Walter, picking up another chop.

"We both hate Richard, sir, and we're ready to fight."

"Got weapons?"

"I'm afraid we've only got one sword between us, but we have two horses."

"Good horses?"

"Good enough, sir."

"Where have you come from?"

"We've both been bearers of letters, sir, to Earl Henry: I from Lord Stanley and my friend here from Lord Hastings.

Now that we've delivered those letters, naturally we want to join Earl Henry's army."

"H'm. Well, go and report yourselves to Ensign Rayner. Tell him I sent you."

Ensign Rayner, a young man of about their own age, seemed sure that they must have some ulterior motive.

"Why on earth are you joining Sir Walter's company?"

"Because they speak English and not Welsh."

"No other reason?"

"None."

"Are you sure you want to?"

"Quite sure."

"No one told you about Sir Walter?"

"What about him?"

"Well," – the ensign paused and shrugged – "he's a hard man to serve under; harsh and severe. And he's got a bad temper, to say the least."

"Then why are you with him?" asked Martin.

"Oh, all sorts of reasons. Now; you say you've got horses? Are they good enough for a campaign and a battle?"

"We think so."

"Well, if you find they're not, you'll just have to do without them, won't you? Only about ten or twelve other people in the company have horses. Most of our Englishmen have come over with Earl Henry: that's why they haven't got horses. As for weapons, you'll have to find them for yourselves."

"Tell me," said Raymond, "if Sir Walter's such a bully, why did the earl knight him and give him command of a company?"

"He's brave and very experienced, and he's well known as a dyed-in-the-wool Lancastrian. All he wants to do is kill Yorkists. He was with Buckingham two years ago, and after that little venture failed he joined Henry in France."

"Will he object to my wife coming with us?"

"Oh, he won't be bothered about a trifle like that. She can come with the baggage. There's at least a dozen wives with us already."

"And how many men?"

"Not as many as we'd like; not yet. But we're sure plenty more will join us on the march, both Welsh and English."

"When do we start?"

"Day after tomorrow, Sir Walter's said. From Aberystwyth we'll go straight for England. Earl Henry needs a battle as soon as possible. For one thing, he can't expect to feed the army for long. Besides, this sort of army will fall to pieces unless it gets a battle quickly. The French, the Welsh, the English – the one thing holding them together is that they all want to fight Richard and make Earl Henry king. Unless that happens soon they'll lose their spirits."

On a cloudy, showery afternoon some days later, Raymond and Martin were riding together along the Welshpool road westwards towards Newtown.

When Henry's army had set out from Cardigan, Sir Walter's force, expanded by the addition of about four hundred French, had been placed in the van. By his own driving power he had marched them to Machynlleth in five days, and thence some way along the road to Newtown. Having reached the village of Dolfach, he had received from the Earl of Oxford orders to halt and encamp, since the remainder of the army had not been able to keep up with him. Chafing to press on, he had had to content himself with sending six or seven of his horsemen – such as they were – to reconnoitre the twenty miles ahead to Newtown.

Almost none of his men had dropped out on the march from Cardigan, since Sir Walter, whose French was as fluent as his English, had vouchsafed his personal brand of encouragement to any who had tried to do so. After remaining at Dolfach for two days, he had obtained from the earl authority to renew the march. He meant to reach Newtown the following day.

On their reconnaissance the horsemen had learned that King Richard, upon receiving news of the landing of Henry's force at Milford Haven, had set out from Nottingham to encounter them. His precise whereabouts, however, was not reliably known. With this information the horsemen, having already ridden some twenty miles that day, had returned to Dolfach to report what they had learned.

Raymond and Martin, thinking that they might be able to obtain more certain information about the enemy, had gone on a few miles in the direction of Welshpool, to make further enquiries. Having ridden as far as they judged their horses could go, they decided to return to Newtown for the night and rejoin the army next day, to report what more, if anything, they had been able to find out.

Having ridden nearly thirty miles, they were now jogging westward at a gentle pace, with the prospect of a good meal and a comfortable night's sleep in Newtown. It was not often (as they had learned) that anyone could hit upon a blameless and legitimate way to modify Sir Walter's orders to his own advantage, and they felt thoroughly satisfied with themselves.

Twilight was falling when Martin, having dismounted to pass water, caught sight in the distance of two horsemen riding towards them at breakneck speed from the direction in which they had come.

"We ought to find out, Raymond, why they're riding like that. It may be something of importance to us – something Sir Walter ought to know."

"I agree. We must do our best to stop them – if we can. Look, the road's narrower further back, between those thick hedges. That's our best chance – to make them pull up there."

At the spot to which he was pointing, there was barely room between the hedges for two horsemen to wait side by side.

"Do you think they *will* stop?" asked Raymond, with some apprehension.

"They'll have to," replied Martin. "I dare say they may try to turn aside or go back. We'd better call out to them as soon as they're close enough."

The riders approached more slowly and came to a halt about thirty yards away, their horses panting and steaming in the damp evening air. They could be seen, now, to be very young, hardly more than boys, perhaps fourteen or fifteen years old. They were clearly afraid of the two men blocking their way.

"Good sirs," called out the one who looked the older of the

two, "for Our Saviour's sake let us pass. It's a matter of life and death."

"We're no enemies to you," replied Raymond. "But you must tell us who you are, what's the matter and why you've probably ruined two good horses; or that's what it looks like. You say you're in danger. How?"

The youth who had not spoken dismounted, passed his reins to his companion and came forward until he was standing at Raymond's side.

"Our families are loyal subjects of King Richard. Yesterday our two fathers heard the news of Henry Tudor's landing, and then of his army marching towards Shrewsbury. They've both gone to join King Richard at Nottingham. We wanted to go with them, but they wouldn't let us. All round Shrewsbury people are ready to rise for Henry, but our fathers wouldn't let us go to Nottingham with them. They said that if we stayed quiet at home and took care not to anger the rebels, no one would harm us, because we were only lads."

"But it wasn't so," broke in the other. "It's not three hours since our priest came to warn us. We rode away at once, but Lancastrian enemies are following us. For all we know they mean to kill us. Good sirs, pray help us, for the love of God."

Raymond, leaning forward, put a hand on the lad's shoulder. "Do you know who we are?" He shook his head. "We're the advance guard of Earl Henry's army. They're approaching Newtown now."

The young fellow turned to run back to his horse, but Martin grabbed his arm.

"Don't try to get away. It would be quite hopeless. Believe it or not, we're the only people who can help you. We may be on Henry Tudor's side, but we don't fancy killing two young chaps like you in cold blood. We'll help you get away from the people behind, but after that you'll have to trust us." As the youth hesitated, staring at him speechlessly, he added, "There's nothing else you can do. Now follow me, and be quick about it."

Still without a word, the boy remounted. Martin led the way

about two hundred yards down the road, to where a narrow, muddy track disappeared into a wood.

"Get in there, both of you – and a good long way, too. We'll deal with the people who are after you. When they've gone, we'll come back. Don't talk: just go!"

Thereupon he rejoined Raymond, who pointed in silence to the group of eight or nine horsemen galloping towards them.

"Everyone seems in a hurry today, don't they?" said Martin. "Perhaps we'll be able to help them on their way."

"To Newtown, you mean?" replied Raymond, grinning.

Martin nodded, and as the riders came up, rode forward a few yards to meet them.

They were a mixed bunch. Two, evidently the leaders, could be seen by their clothes and bearing to be young gentlemen. They were both armed with swords and daggers. Of the rest, three had the look of upper servants or possibly tenant farmers. The remaining three were rough-looking men; labourers, thought Raymond, brought along to do as they were told.

Martin spoke first. "We're part of the advance guard of Henry Tudor's army. Earl Henry himself is approaching Newtown now. May I ask whether you are for Henry or for Richard?"

"For Henry," answered the eldest-looking of the young gentlemen. "We're pursuing two runaway Yorkists. You've no objection, I hope, to our pressing on?"

"Your fugitives passed us only a very short time ago. They told us they were making for Newtown. If only we'd known they were Yorkists . . ." He shrugged. "Anyway, they're not far ahead, I can tell you that."

The young man thanked him and led the way as the group rode off down the road.

"Since you haven't so far bothered to tell me, Martin," said Raymond, rather stiffly, "can I ask what you mean to do now?"

"Why, see to our friends, what else?" replied Martin smilingly.

He turned, rode a little way into the wood and hollered. The two lads soon appeared. One was about to speak, but Martin held up his hand.

"Now listen," he said. "This is the only way you can save yourselves from being killed or captured. You must come with us and we'll tell our commander that we met you on the road as you were coming to join Earl Henry. He won't ask you any questions: he'll be only too glad of two more horses. We shan't tell anyone who you are. You'll be perfectly safe with us for as long as you feel it's the only thing to do. Then as soon as you think there's somewhere else you can go, you can ride away. Probably you won't even be missed."

The two young men frowned, clearly perplexed.

"But why are you doing this for us?" asked one of them.

"Well, don't you see, it's not your fault that you think you're Richard's subjects. With your parentage, you couldn't help it. The notion of killing two young fellows like you doesn't appeal to my friend and me. Your fathers were quite right; you ought to be living harmlessly at home. As things are, though, you probably know some friends you can go to, don't you?"

"But . . ."

There was more talk, until at length the boys were persuaded, *faute de mieux*, to fall in with Martin's scheme. As darkness fell, with more rain, they rode into Newtown and found themselves supper and lodging for the night. The two youths remained with them and did as they were told. In other circumstances they would no doubt have acted differently, but they had been desperately frightened that afternoon and, inexperienced as they were, had come to feel that Martin's was their only course in an unfamiliar world no doubt full of Lancastrians on every side.

The following morning the four of them set out together and met the advance guard on the road near Carno. As luck would have it, Sir Walter was not with them, but further back with his main body. As Martin had foreseen, no questions were asked. Ensign Rayner, when they reported themselves, merely nodded approval of their initiative in bringing in two more horsemen, very young though they were. He thought that Sir Walter had not missed them, being

content with last night's report of a clear road to Newtown.

That evening, as the main body of the army were finishing
supper and settling down for the night, Raymond and Martin,
leaving their two protégés to their own devices, joined Alison
and a friend, strolled into Newtown and found themselves a
not-unduly overcrowded tavern. The friend, Jeanne, was a
French girl who had joined the Earl of Oxford's household
two years before and had willingly crossed with it to Milford
Haven. On the march, she had been set to help with feeding the
men. The cook, a good-natured soul, had dismissed her for the
evening – the first time she had been off duty since landing –
and she was delighted to find herself in company with Martin
and Raymond.

Her English was quite good enough for this easygoing
amusement. She told them that English was spoken almost as
much as French among the Earl of Oxford's servants. When
Martin asked her which tongue the earl himself favoured, she
laughed and replied that she had hardly ever been within
earshot of him. However, she seemed to know a good deal
about the campaign and particularly about the earl's hatred
of King Richard. "'E'll nevair stop till 'e 'as killed zat bad
king," she said. "Zat is why your 'Enry Tudor put 'im to
command all 'is soldiers. 'E 'as done very much – oh, very
much fighting."

"And do you trust him?" asked Martin. "I mean, is he the
right man to lead us?"

She shrugged. "'Ow I know? What people say is 'e is great
leader, but we 'ave not *assez de soldats*. Zis bad king, 'e 'ave
trop – too many."

Raymond spoke of his time in Calais with the young
Lord Hastings. "I enjoyed living there," he said. "The people
were friendly; we had a good time. Of course there are as
many English in Calais as French. Flemings, too, and a few
Germans."

"I've been in Calais," said Jeanne. "It was few years gone
now. Zat was first time I went away from 'ome to work. I was
sad for leaving 'ome, but" – she laughed – "zen I make great

friend wis' an Englishman 'oo work zere. I would 'ave married 'im if 'e 'ad ask. But not 'appen. 'E go back to England."

"What work was he doing?" asked Martin.

"Oh, 'e was mason. Journeyman mason, you say in English. 'E work building 'ouses, churches too – all kinds of building."

"What was his name?" asked Martin.

"'E is called Nicolas – Nicolas of Taunton. Oh, what ze matter?"

Neither Alison nor Raymond had been able to check a start. It was quickly suppressed, but Jeanne had not failed to notice.

"Why, you know heem? You are surprise?"

"We knew a fellow called Nicolas when we were in Glostershire," said Raymond shortly. "Said he'd come from working in France."

He said nothing more, and it was Alison who changed the subject.

"You ought to find yourself another Englishman to marry, Jeanne," she said, "and live in England. You'd like it."

"Well, but in England is so much fighting – always fighting." Jeanne took a silk handkerchief out of her sleeve and showed them the red rose embroidered in the corner. "Zis Nicolas, it was present from 'im."

"Well, it's the right rose," said Martin. "Lord Oxford wouldn't like you to have a white one, that's for sure."

They ate roast pork and beans in the tavern, and bought two loaves to take back to the camp. "We've been able to get just about enough food while we've been in Wales," said Martin. "The Welsh are more than ready to help followers of Henry Tudor. But I'm afraid it's going to be more difficult in England. We need to win quickly."

"I happened to overhear Sir Walter talking to Ensign Rayner and a few others yesterday," said Raymond, "and he said that almost the whole of Shropshire was either owned or controlled by Sir William Stanley – that's to say, your Lord Thomas Stanley's younger brother. It seems that Earl Henry's going to meet Sir William as soon as we're well into Shropshire, and find out what the two Stanleys will be able to do for us. Sir Walter said he felt sure the Stanleys wouldn't fight for Richard on any account."

"But will they fight for us?" asked Martin.

"Sir Walter didn't say. All I heard was what I've told you."

"Of course I didn't have a chance to read the letter I took from Lord Thomas to Earl Henry," said Martin. "But I'd swear by all the saints that it was a promise of support."

"He may have written as much," replied Raymond, "but I reckon that he's going to wait and see who wins the battle before he commits himself and his men to one side or the other."

Two days later the army marched into Shrewsbury and crossed the Severn, Sir Walter still urging his vanguard company to press on until not a few were on the point of mutiny. Nevertheless, the townspeople welcomed them heartily. Raymond and Martin, riding ahead to Newport, were the first to meet the Shropshire company commanded by Sir Gilbert Talbot, and having reported it, were sent back by Sir Walter to carry the news to Earl Henry and his entourage. Henry himself heard them, but seemed more concerned to know whether they had any news of Lord Thomas Stanley or his brother. They could, of course, tell him nothing.

The following day, the 17th August, as they were riding beside Sir Walter, leading the company towards Stafford, they were suddenly ordered to pull off to one side to make way for Earl Henry himself, who rode past them with some twenty or thirty followers and disappeared up the road. Sir Walter, who rode forward a short distance with them as they passed, returned with the news that they were on their way to meet Sir William Stanley, by agreement, at Stafford. It seemed that Lord Thomas Stanley's forces were encamped at Lichfield, and he had already assured Earl Henry that he meant him no harm.

By the evening, rumours were rife throughout the army. The officers were as much in the dark as the men. Some said Lord Thomas Stanley was soon to join them. Others said, like Raymond, that he was waiting to join whichever side won the

battle. Others again said that his force would retreat before Earl
Henry until they reached King Richard and the battle began,
when they would declare themselves for Henry and fall upon
Richard's unsuspecting army, with a decisive result.

Next day Sir Walter, returning from Earl Henry's head-
quarters, told his company that they were going to march
south-east to Lichfield and make for the high road to London.
Earl Henry's object, according to Sir Walter, was to force
Richard to march south to confront them. He was said to have
ten thousand men – far more than Earl Henry, who could not
count on more than six thousand at most. Nevertheless, his
officers were told, he was determined to fight.

Raymond, Martin and the rest of Sir Walter's horsemen
rode forward to find the enemy. A good ten miles west
of Leicester, they came upon them encamped at a village
called Sutton Cheney. They returned to find their own army
not more than two or three miles away. Both the Stanleys,
with their forces, were nearby; "and the bastards still haven't
said whether they're on our damned side or the other," said
Sir Walter. During the late afternoon, he was summoned to
a meeting of Earl Henry's commanders, and told Raymond to
accompany him as his orderly.

Some twelve or fourteen leaders in all were gathered about
Henry and the Earl of Oxford. Neither of the Stanleys was
present. Addressing them, Henry said nothing about the dis-
parity in numbers between Richard and himself, but told them
that at first light next day he was going to attack with his whole
army. He had so high an opinion of his captains and their men
that he was confident of victory. The enemy's army, he said,
was falling to pieces. Already there had been many desertions.
King Richard could not count on half his people to fight for
him: his sword would break in his hand. Henry then called
upon the Earl of Oxford, whom they all knew and trusted
for a skilful and experienced soldier, to tell them the plan
of battle.

Lord Oxford began by pointing out the low hill to the
north-east. That was the enemy's main position and that
was where he meant to defeat him. A marsh lay between

themselves and the hill, and therefore they would begin by advancing obliquely to pass the marsh on their right. Then they would turn, assault the hill, drive the enemy off it and win the day. He himself would lead them, for he hoped to kill King Richard with his own hand. The Shropshire men would form the army's right wing and the Welshmen its left.

As the various commanders were dispersing to rejoin their companies, Lord Oxford stopped Sir Walter, saying that he had a particular task for him. Raymond could see that Sir Walter was much gratified, plainly supposing that he and his men had been chosen for some dare-devil role of valour. He was soon to be disappointed. Earl Henry, Lord Oxford told him, on account of his supreme importance and his lack of experience in battle, was not to be risked in the attack, but would remain in the rear, protected by a force of foot soldiers and a troop of horsemen. The horsemen, in addition to Sir Walter's few, would come from among the Welsh, and the infantry would consist of Sir Walter's own company; Sir Walter was to command the combined force.

Sir Walter's indignation was more than he could control. He spoke angrily. He demanded to be told what he had done to deserve such ignominy. This contemptible task would destroy his military reputation. He had half a mind to withdraw from the battle altogether. He demanded to discuss the business with Earl Henry.

Both the earl and Lord Oxford remained adamant. It was not, said Lord Oxford, in spite of but because of Sir Walter's standing and reputation, that he had been selected. It might well be – they all hoped as much – that his men would not be called upon to fight. But if they were, it would be because the enemy had broken through and come dangerously close to Earl Henry: the situation would be desperate. Everything would depend upon the enemy being repulsed. This was why Sir Walter had been put in charge: the earl's guard must be commanded by an exceptional leader, of outstanding reputation and courage.

Sir Walter, still growling, made his way back to his company and put the best face he could on it. Raymond, Martin and the rest of the horsemen he ordered to await the Welsh who would be coming to make up their numbers. His foot soldiers and he himself marched off to take up the position they would occupy next morning. Most of them did not feel sorry about the part they had been ordered to play; but they took good care not to let Sir Walter hear this.

Half an hour later, Raymond, Martin and the other ten or twelve of Sir Walter's horsemen, surrounded on all sides by men speaking Welsh, could not at first find an officer to whom to make themselves known. While they were looking about in perplexity, however, they saw Captain Jenkyns approaching. He greeted them warmly and told them to remain with him while he made his dispositions for the morrow. Having seen to this, he told the Englishmen to picket their horses on the north side of their position – the place nearest to the enemy – and bivouac there for the night.

When the horses had been fed and watered, and their masters had eaten their bread and cold meat, Raymond and Martin sat down on the turf, and considered the prospect about them. On their left the whole sky was aflame as the sun set without a cloud to be seen. To their front, about a mile away, the smoke rose up straight from the chimneys of the little village of Shenton. There was not a breath of wind. Beyond Shenton, on the right, lay the camps of the two Stanleys. They glimpsed men moving here and there, but at this distance could hear only a faint murmur. As they gazed, a horseman emerged from the Stanleys' assemblage and came galloping towards them along the track from the village. He rode up to them, reined in and asked for Lord Oxford. Martin obliged him, leading his horse to the earl's tent.

Raymond renewed his silent contemplation. Ahead of him lay the tract of the marsh, a uniform, melancholy solitude broken here and there only by a gaunt willow or a cluster of reed mace. A bittern boomed and as he turned his head towards the sound in the gathering dusk, a heron flew over, paused to look down, then dropped and alighted in a pool not a hundred yards away. One of the horses whinnied but the bird, unalarmed, continued its paddling and stabbing.

Raymond stood up, stretched and went to ask Jenkyns for permission to go and see Alison.

He found her among a little group of women and their men, talking together in a somewhat subdued vein. They had been told not to wander away and this, naturally, was a frustration which many resented. Raymond embraced Alison, pressing her close, and as they were standing thus, her mouth to his ear, she whispered, "Reckon Oi'm with choild, my love."

He was startled. "Are you sure?"

"No, not certain sure yet. But Oi hope" – she caught her breath – "Oh, Oi just about hope so."

"My hope's as strong as yours, believe me, love." He led her a little apart, held her by the shoulders and looked into her eyes, smiling. "That's wonderful! You couldn't have told me anything better!" He fell to kissing her eyes, her forehead and her ears. "I'm happier than I've ever been, my dearest!"

"Oi've bin that moithered, Raymond, hoping as you'd be glad—"

"Of course I'm glad."

"—and thinkin' about the battle—"

"The battle? Everything's as good as it can be. Martin and I are part of Earl Henry's personal guard. He's remaining here, at the rear. They can't risk losing him, you see. It's almost certain we shan't be in the battle at all. Lord Oxford's going to lead the army up the hill and defeat the enemy. By this time tomorrow it'll all be over."

He drew her down on the grass, saying all he could to praise and encourage her. He spoke of their baby, and gradually her spirits rose. Soon she was laughing and talking to him as happily as ever she had. When the men were called to rejoin their companies, she kissed him goodnight with no sign of apprehension.

"Just do everything they tell you," said Raymond. "I'll come back as soon as I can."

Martin had returned, and he joined him at their appointed place. In the dusk he could just make out against the sky the dark shape of the low hill which the army was to assault next morning. All around was the scent of crushed grass, mingling with the pleasant smell of the tethered horses. Owls were calling as they hunted over the marsh. Far and near, there were still lights and bustle as the various companies took up their positions for the night.

The two friends knelt together and prayed for victory next day and for their own survival. Martin had succeeded in buying a sword that afternoon, and they compared it favourably with Raymond's. Not long after, they heard Sir Walter approaching, as loud and blustering as usual. He was evidently going the round of his men and their positions. When he reached them, however, he spoke no more than a few words of encouragement before moving on. Raymond's last thoughts, as he settled to sleep, were of Alison and what she had told him. For both their sakes, he thought, I *must* survive.

When he woke, it was no more than first light; a pale sky in the east, the twitter of a lark above, and all around, far and near, voices and a quiet commotion as the army, company by company, formed up and moved forward towards the western foot of the hill. He realised that he had woken late. Martin was up and gone. He pulled on his boots, buckled his belt, adjusted sword and scabbard and ran to the picket line. His mare was the only horse remaining there. As quickly as he could, he saddled up, mounted and rode across the turf to join Martin in their position.

"You might have woken me, you wretch!"

"Oh, you looked much too comfortable: I hadn't the heart."

"God a mercy! If Sir Walter had come round—"

"But he didn't, thanks be! The rations did, though. I got them to give me yours as well as mine. Said you'd just been sent with a message, and you'd be back directly. Here, catch hold!"

Grinning, Martin handed across half a loaf, an apple and a sizeable hunk of cheese. "And I've given one of the youngsters two groats to take care of our lutes."

Raymond bit into the cheese.

"Well, I suppose I owe you thanks after all."

"Look!" Martin pointed towards the ridge, where a few camp-fires were still burning and men could be seen bustling here and there. "The enemy! First we've seen of them, isn't it?"

Raymond nodded, then turned his head aside for a few moments and bit his lip, determined not to show the apprehension and disquiet he could not help feeling.

Soon they could both see, all across the western slope of the hill, companies of the enemy coming down to take up their positions. They seemed a disconcertingly large number. Soon the whole hillside was covered, and as the sun rose in a clear sky he caught flashes and glints from sallets, halberds and the heads of pikes. He could see, too, archers crouching in the front ranks, their longbows strung and ready.

To the north, beyond the western foot of the hill, lay Sir William Stanley's camp. Whose side would he show himself to be on? thought Raymond. What had the two Stanleys agreed with Earl Henry when they had met so recently at Atherstone?

Now trumpets were sounding from Earl Henry's army massed about the foot of the hill, and the vanguard, moving forward, began to ascend the lower slope. They were met by volleys of arrows. Men began to fall, and Raymond could hear the leaders shouting encouragement as they pressed on into the attack.

At almost the same moment, King Richard's confronting forces broke ranks and charged downhill. The clamour became deafening; everywhere was uproar, shouting, the clash of weapons and the cries of the wounded. The slope became covered with groups, large and small, locked in hand-to-hand fighting. To Raymond, it seemed as though Earl Henry's forces were giving ground. The storm of combat was moving downhill. He saw a Red Dragon banner fall and disappear, trampled underfoot.

Very gradually, the downhill movement slackened and ceased. One more desperate minute of cut and thrust, to and fro, and then it was King Richard's men who were falling back. Though Raymond could not know it, the Duke of Norfolk, the Yorkist leader, fighting in their forefront, had been struck down. The damage to morale, as the news spread, ran quickly through the Yorkist ranks. Their confidence suffered a blow from which, in the event, it was not to recover. They wavered and began, step by step, to retreat.

Nevertheless, they were far from defeated. Their main body was still intact and, with the advantage of the higher ground, remained formidable. To break it would be a hard task, and Lord Oxford's men had already been badly knocked about and wearied. To sustain their advance might prove beyond them.

Though at this moment in the battle none could know it, the deciding factor was to be the rash audacity, impatience and haste of King Richard himself. As Earl Henry had predicted, his army – or so it seemed to himself – was falling to pieces; his sword was breaking in his hand. His rearguard, commanded by the Earl of Northumberland, which he now needed to reinforce the main body fighting at the top of the hill, refused to obey the King's order to advance. Worse, neither Lord Thomas Stanley nor Sir William had made the least move to join him.

In this strait, it occurred to the King that there was one offensive blow which remained open to him. He knew that Earl Henry was not personally engaged in the battle. Earlier, his reconnoitring horsemen had spotted the Lancastrian head-quarters, protected only by a small rearguard of horse and foot. If he were to smash it up and kill Henry, he would put paid to the enemy and their cause more effectively than could anything else.

Swiftly, he assembled an élite striking force. It included his household knights: Sir Richard Ratcliffe, Sir Robert Brackenbury, Sir Robert Percy, Hugh and Thomas Stafford, Sir Ralph Assheton; and about a hundred other loyal subjects. With these about him, he rode out along the northern slope of the hill (to which the battle had not spread), descended westwards and then turned, past Sir William Stanley's inactive force, towards Earl Henry's camp.

Sir Walter Rutherford, to his credit, was the first to see them coming and to realise their intention. Shouting and cursing, he roused up his horsemen and infantry to form a protective screen across King Richard's line of attack. Then he went out and stood in front of it; where everyone could see and hear him.

A minute later the whole scene dissolved in dust, clamour and confusion. His men saw Sir Walter ridden down, and immediately afterwards the enemy were upon them. Straight through the screen of infantry they drove, cutting down man after man. Richard himself killed Sir William Brandon, Henry's standard bearer, and unhorsed Sir John Cheyney, the next antagonist to come in his way.

Raymond, in the midst of the turmoil, glimpsed Martin, sword in hand, striking at one of the enemy before being unhorsed and trampled under their hooves. Trying to reach him, he was himself overborne and knocked senseless to the ground.

Men were falling fast. For a few minutes Earl Henry, his bodyguard almost destroyed, stood in the gravest danger. Then – and who could have foreseen it? – among the flying turf, the uproar and chaos, appeared an unexpected ally. Sir William Stanley's horsemen, having taken scarcely any time to prepare themselves and form up, had followed King Richard down the same track, and now fell upon his rear with fatal effect. The Yorkists found themselves outnumbered and surrounded. Those who were not unhorsed and killed were taken prisoner.

Raymond, coming dazedly to himself in the midst of the fighting, became aware that a man lying close beside him on the ground must be an enemy. As the man rose to his feet, clutching his sword, Raymond glimpsed on his helmet a coronet. In the same moment the man thrust at and felled a Lancastrian soldier, set his back against a pile of baggage and glared about him, shouting, "Treason! Treason!"

As in a dream, Raymond cloudily perceived one unconnected image after another. He was on his knees. The ground was strewn with fallen men, some struggling to get up, others unmoving. For a brief instant he glimpsed Earl Henry in the tumult; then an armoured horseman rode between them, blotting out all else. Someone lunged at him, deeply piercing his left shoulder, and a moment later followed the sharp pain.

He was prone among the hooves again, trying to crawl away from a mêlée of interlocked, cursing men. Blood was pouring down his left arm. The armoured man with the coronet was close to him, fighting with someone he could not see, and still crying "Treason!" Raymond saw that his breastplate had slipped, exposing the upper part of his shoulder at the base of the neck. Staggering, he rose to his feet and, as the man turned towards him, drove the point of his sword into the exposed place. He felt it pierce in the same moment that the man jabbed at him, lurched backwards and fell. Raymond, too, stumbled and dropped across his enemy's body, still grasping the hilt of his sword and clawing at the grass with his bloody left hand.

The man was dead. This much he knew, but little else. His face was pressed into the turf, and he could see nothing. The pain in his shoulder was agonising. He was trying to call for help, but had no breath. He was gasping, choking.

He could hear a confused uproar, but it seemed to be in his own head, and he could distinguish no words. He moved, and at once there followed a stab of even worse pain. He was being lifted and set upon his feet; his legs gave way and he would have fallen again, but supporting hands were digging into his armpits. Someone was pushing his chin up and he saw that he was surrounded by armed men, all staring at him, some grave, others smiling. Beyond, more men were approaching, some leading their horses by the bridle as they picked their way among the bodies that everywhere covered the ground.

A voice was speaking in his ear. "You've killed the King, young fellow!" Then the voice seemed to turn in another direction and to speak louder. "He's killed King Richard!"

He felt about to faint again; his head was swimming. "Lay me down!" he gasped. To faint would be better than the pain.

They carried him on their shoulders to King Henry's tent and laid him outside it on clean straw and a bolster. A cup of wine was held to his lips and he swallowed mouthful by mouthful. A man with scissors was cutting off the sleeves of his blood-stained jerkin and shirt to bare his wounded shoulder. He heard water being poured, then screamed and struggled as a cold, wet cloth was pressed into the wound, wiping and cleansing. "Hold still, lad!" He gritted his teeth and braced himself not to jerk away. "That's nasty!" said a voice. "There's plenty worse," replied another.

Someone tilted his head and he found he was looking into the face of King Henry, who was kneeling beside him. He gasped, "My lord!"

"Well done, my brave subject!" said Henry, smiling. After a pause, he asked, "Aren't you Lord Hastings' man, who brought me a letter?"

"Yes, my lord."

The King nodded, clasped his right hand for a moment, and was gone.

They bound up his shoulder. The wine was taking effect. He felt clearer headed. "My wife," he mouthed. "Want see my wife."

Alison was kneeling beside him. There were tears in her eyes, but she was smiling. She bent over and kissed his lips. "Reckon you done a roight day's work, my darlin'," she whispered.

"Dearest," he answered. "Tired. Must sleep." She nodded. He closed his eyes and slept almost at once.

When he woke, he felt intuitively that it must be well after midnight. He was still lying outside the King's tent, and Alison was asleep beside him. Both of them had been covered with horse blankets. It was a fine, clear night; the sky was full of stars from one horizon to the other. There was no wind and all around was silent, except for a distant stamping and blowing of tethered horses.

Now he remembered the voice which had told him he had killed King Richard. It must be true, he supposed, because Earl Henry had come and spoken to him. But after some moments he found that he did not want to dwell on this. The thought was like a great weight on the edge of his mind, too heavy to lift, too much to try to drag in and find a place for. He could not be bothered with it. He did not want to contend with any serious matter, to pursue anything resembling cause and effect. For one thing his shoulder was hurting too much. He wanted only to say his prayers and then to sleep again.

He had prayed for some little while, thanking God for his survival and for the gift of Alison, when the thought became conscious: Martin! It was like knocking on a door: Martin! Martin! And it was as though he called to the impatient spirit, "All right! I'm coming!" He broke off his prayer and set his muddled, feverish mind to dwell on his friend.

He recalled seeing Martin in the midst of the enemy's charge. He recollected trying to reach him, but could not remember anything after that, until finding himself surrounded by men of his own side, who had carried him away and given him wine to drink.

But – and this was like a sudden alarm making his mind leap – if Martin had been able to come and talk with him, then he would certainly have done so. So either Martin had been killed or else so badly wounded that he could not get to him.

He must go and find him – now. Later would not do; it must be now. He knew he must be ill and his shoulder was, if anything, more painful than it had been earlier; but not so painful that he could not go and find Martin.

Very carefully he turned back the blanket and rose to his feet. Alison did not stir; she was breathing slowly and deeply. Dressed only in his shirt and without shoes, he began making his way through the camp.

He had no idea where to go to find Martin, but in his state of mind this did not matter. He would simply wander about until he found him. At least, he thought, he had enough sense not to call out. If he called out, people would come; he would be overpowered and taken back to bed. He must be silent.

The short grass pricked his bare feet, but not too badly. It was all right if he went step by step. He looked about him. He was among sleeping men. There were sleeping men all around him. But he could tell that none of them was Martin.

Suddenly a drowsy, half-asleep voice from somewhere quite near called "Who you? Wha' yer doing?"

He ran then; anywhere, as long as it was away from the voice: all among the sleeping men and the short grass sharp on his feet. Here was a Red Dragon banner; these must be Welshmen. And now there seemed to be no more men. He must have run out of the camp altogether. He'd better turn back and look somewhere else. If only his shoulder would stop hurting so badly, and the throbbing pain behind his left eye.

"Wait a minute!" he said aloud to himself. "Where have I got to?"

It was an open field like the rest of the camp. But these were not sleeping men. As he stood staring, trying to puzzle it out, a quiet voice close beside him said, "Why are you here, lad?"

He turned, to see a young man much like himself, but armed with a sword and wearing at his shoulder some kind of cognisance he did not recognise. "Why are you here?" repeated this soldier, though in no unfriendly voice. "Looking for someone?" He seemed unconcerned that Raymond was wearing nothing but his shirt, or that his shoulder was bound up.

"I'm looking for Martin Lincoln," he answered.

"You mean – there?" The man gestured towards the field.

Now he could take it in – what was to be seen. These were dead men, bodies lying on the ground a few feet apart. Their faces were not covered. As well as he could make out in the gloom, all lay open-eyed, seeming to stare up at the sky.

"These are ours," said the young man.

"Are you – are you . . ." He could not find the words he wanted.

"I'm one of the guard here. There's ten of us altogether."

"But why – why . . ."

"They've got to be guarded – until they're buried; that'll be soon as there's daylight. Got to keep off foxes, wolves. Even thieves; thieves who'd rob the bodies. You say you're looking for Martin Lincoln. Do you know that he's dead?"

"I don't know," replied Raymond. "I've been looking for him in the camp. It was only by chance that I came here. He's my mate. We got separated in the fighting."

"Well, I'll come round with you, if you want to look."

"Are there many?"

"More than six hundred, they say. Here, steady; you'd better take my arm. You're wounded yourself, aren't you?"

Raymond made his way slowly to the nearest bodies, among which two or three were still in their armour. Looking down at them, Raymond started violently and drew in his breath. There lay Sir Walter Rutherford, burly and bristling as in life. There was no wound to be seen, but the face was very pale, the features somehow pinched, diminished, almost shrunken.

Raymond crossed himself. Then, trembling, he stooped and smoothed back the hair from the forehead.

"This is our captain, God rest his soul," he said to his companion, and went on to tell how Sir Walter had drawn them up to face King Richard's charge and had placed himself in the forefront as the horses came down on them. "He was hot in his temper and drove us hard, but he was a fine soldier and always fair and just."

The sentry said nothing in reply, only murmured and nodded, waiting for Raymond to move on. They had gone only a few steps further when they came upon the body of Ensign Rayner, looking even younger than in life. Beyond him lay ten or twelve men of Sir Walter's company, with most of whom Raymond had been on friendly terms. Seeing the tears which he could not hide, the sentry asked whether any of these was the friend he was looking for.

"No," he answered. "No. Just . . ." – he made a gesture towards them – " . . . just men I knew."

"Do you want to go on?" Raymond nodded, and they turned and started back along the next row.

These, as Raymond could tell by their Red Dragon cognisances, were for the most part Welshmen whom he did not recognise. He was passing each one with little more than a glance when he found himself looking down into the fixed, waxen face of Captain Jenkyns. The lips were parted as though he were about to speak, and the right arm was bent inwards from the elbow, the hand holding a paper on which was a scrawl of writing.

"A captain of cavalry," said Raymond, turning towards his guide. "He did me many a good turn. I knew him well."

He was going on to say more in praise of Jenkyns when suddenly he caught sight, a few yards away, of Martin.

Martin's face was terribly disfigured; crushed and beaten inwards as though by a hammer. His right arm had been severed and from head to foot his clothes were drenched in blood.

With a cry, Raymond fell on his knees beside the body. He clasped his hands together as though praying, but after a few moments flung them apart and, bending forward, clasped Martin in his arms. Convulsed with sobs, he heard nothing of what the sentry was trying to tell him.

He was aware only of his terrible loss. Sir Walter, Ensign Rayner, Captain Jenkyns – these now seemed as nothing. Martin, his Martin, was dead. He himself, ought to be dead; he had no right to be alive. The ugly, the horrible remains of Martin; these were all that was left, as wretched and comfortless as the charred shell of a burned house.

He became vaguely aware that he was bleeding heavily. Drops of blood were falling from his shoulder on to Martin's body. He tried to pray, yet did not know what he was praying for. Comfort for himself? Pardon and peace for the dead? The end of the world? He was still kneeling, holding Martin in his arms, when he felt hands on his shoulders and heard Alison's voice. "Come on, poor love. Ee'd best come back with me now. Can't bide here, can us?"

Hands were separating his arms from Martin, and he was lifted, set on his feet and supported where he stood. Alison was beside him. "Can 'ee walk, dearest? Let they 'old 'ee up; come on, now; there's a love."

Two men were holding him, but clumsily, hindered by the open, bloody wound in his shoulder. "We'd best carry 'im," said one of them. "Be quicker'n 'im walking."

He was lifted once more and carried, but not far. They laid him down and again washed and bound up his wound. Soon he felt himself falling into sleep, not knowing that he was holding Alison's hand or that she, too, was weeping.

This was the beginning of a time when he did not distinguish between day and night, or sleep and waking. He told himself that it was not because he could not, but because he chose not to expend valuable energy and lucidity in doing so. He had only a certain amount of energy to dispose of, and these petty distinctions were of no importance. What was important was to endure his continual headache, and a sore throat which made swallowing a misery. Sometimes he was aware that Alison was with him and he smiled at her and whispered through dry lips. But then he would drift away again, explaining that he had to go and look for Martin. Martin wasn't really dead. He, Raymond, wasn't silly; he knew that all right; the deception was a trick played on him by the enemy. When he'd found Martin he would bring him back. No one told him he was mistaken, but after a while he would become confused, not sure whether he was looking for Martin or for his own mare, which he knew he had given up to someone at Sir Walter's order. He was tormented by muddled dreams, but on waking could never remember them for more than a second or two.

Not that he was free for a single moment from an over-whelming sense of loss, which he experienced sometimes as a heavy weight pressing him down and sometimes as a kind of invisible thread tangled round his hands and feet, so that he struggled in vain to free himself until Alison came to calm him and hold him still; and that she could easily do, for to himself he seemed to have no strength at all. And here was the dilemma, for he knew that he must search for Martin but lacked the strength to do it. And all the time he was tormented by a kind of sussuration, a whispering in his ears which he experienced as rustling leaves or the sound of a distant river.

"There's a garden," he said. "There's a garden in my ear. O please, please forgive me." For he was guilty – that he knew for certain – he was guilty of being alive. Not that Martin would condemn him; no, he condemned himself.

It was many weeks – weeks of Alison's devoted nursing – before he was sufficiently recovered to go with her to meet Lord Turville at the great house on his estate in the Cotswold country, there to be told of King Henry's gratitude and of the generous settlement conferred upon him. The King had awarded him the freehold of a fine cottage upon the Turville estate. It was here that he and Alison brought up their son and dwelt peacefully together for the years that remained to him.

Part Two

I was my parents' only child. We lived in a comfortable, spacious cottage in the Cotswold country, on the estate of Lord Turville, a supporter of King Henry Tudor, both before and since his victory at Bosworth Field. John Turville, a wealthy merchant as he then was, had contributed a large sum to Earl Henry before his invasion of Wales, and had himself fought at Bosworth. In gratitude, the new King not only raised Turville to the peerage, but conferred upon him the Cotswold estate confiscated from some Yorkist lord, declared a traitor for his support of Richard.

With the rise of Lord Turville, my parents' fortunes also rose. My father, Raymond Godsell, a household minstrel and singer, had carried across the country to Henry a letter from the young Lord Hastings, assuring him of his support, and had fought upon his side at Bosworth.

In giving him the cottage on Lord Turville's estate, as well as a modest fortune, the King had shown especial favour to my father, because it was he who, in thick and confused fighting at Bosworth, when Henry himself was in grave danger, had actually given Richard the sword-thrust which killed him. My father himself had been grievously wounded in that encounter – so badly that his life was despaired of. But my mother, who had followed the army to Bosworth, nursed him for many weeks and restored him at last to health. It was her devotion which saved him, and she cared for and loved him dearly for the rest of his life.

My father had been advised to speak little or not at all of his deed at Bosworth, for there were still plenty of former adherents of Richard scattered over the land, and one of them might well be ready to avenge his former king with a dagger in the dark. At home we never spoke of the battle at all; and this for two more good reasons.

On his way to Milford Haven with Lord Hastings' letter, my

101

father had fallen in with another professional minstrel, a young man much like himself named Martin Lincoln, who was also the bearer of a letter of support to Earl Henry. Having both delivered their letters they joined the earl's army together. They fought side by side at Bosworth, where Martin was killed. My father felt the loss of his friend most deeply and seldom or never spoke of the campaign.

The second reason was that while he was on his way to Milford Haven, my father had met and fallen in love with the beautiful girl who became my mother. She was unhappily married to a surly master mason twice her age, and had gladly eloped with the handsome young minstrel. The mason pursued them and my father killed him. For this he would undoubtedly have been arrested and hanged, had he and his lover not taken the opportunity to disappear into the fog of war – the invasion, the battle and the unsettled times which followed. It was unlikely, having regard to these times, that anyone would pursue the matter, but naturally my parents felt it best not to say anything which might identify my father as the mason's killer.

My father's wound had left him with a deformed shoulder and a useless left arm, so that he could not carry out many of the tasks which normally fall to a householder and a husband. However, he did his best and was always a kindly and loving father to me.

We were a happy family and during my childhood had the good fortune to be spared from ill luck and accidents. My father derived much pleasure from passing on to me his songs and ballads, of which he knew hundreds – or so it seemed to me. Also, when I was scarcely above five, he began teaching me to play the lute – his lute – and to accompany myself in singing. I recall my delight at the revelation – for to me it seemed nothing less – that the strings needed not to go with the voice but could be more tellingly used to contrive harmony.

On a farm every man, woman and child works while there is light, and I recollect being set to scare crows when I was four. Yet somehow there was often time for play as well, and I could whip a top or jump leap-frog with the best. But from the beginning, above all else, I loved songs and stories. In winter, when darkness fell early and firelight replaced the sun, I would listen until I fell asleep in the ashes: and on summer evenings my mother and I used to lie in the grass beside the brook while my father told tales of knights, ladies and dragons, of which I could never have enough.

By the age of ten I was already a fair performer both at playing and singing and knew perhaps thirty or forty songs and ballads by heart. To learn was no labour to me, but pleasure. But merely to become acquainted with a song, to join in the burden and at length come to know all by heart; these things were not enough to satisfy me. I felt I must be able to perform it for the enjoyment of others. At first the others were no more than my parents. Yet after a while my audience grew. I remember my pride at first being asked to sing for the company – they may have numbered twenty, perhaps – when we were merrymaking after a christening.

The death of my father was a cruel blow. His health, during the years of my childhood, had never been good. In hard weather his old wound used to trouble him badly, often compelling him to take to his bed. One of his lungs had been affected, so that at times he would choke and gasp for breath, in fits that might pass off fairly soon or might last for a frighteningly long time. Even now I feel again – and not seldom – my fear upon waking in the night to hear him fighting for breath, and the misery of my mother and myself at being unable to help him in any way. Breathing the steam from herbs crushed in boiling water afforded him some relief, but never put an end to a severe attack.

I think my mother knew that one day this recurrent breathlessness would kill him. The attacks grew more frequent. It was in the small hours of a chilly, damp winter's night that we were both woken by his choking struggles, and lit the candle to see him clutching his chest and rocking to and fro. My mother held him in her arms, comforting him as she was used to do, for what seemed a long time. When he became quiet and unmoving we thought at first that the attack had passed off, and it was not until she laid him down on the bed that we realised that he was dead

– unable to draw his breath; drowned, one might say, on dry land.

I do not want to dwell on the bitter months of sorrow that followed. Our kindly neighbours did all they could to help us and to assuage our grief. Lord Turville himself visited us, and assured my mother that the money regularly paid to us would be in no way affected. Little by little my mother came to terms with our bereavement. I recall how I would come upon her silently weeping, and would sit and hold her two hands in mine until she was able to recover her composure. We would pray together daily for my father's soul. It became my habit on summer evenings to walk down to the brook, and imagine him with me as I sat and watched the swallows darting low for flies over the water.

It was some two years after my father's death that I was prenticed as a carter's boy: and a lucky lad I was held to be, for if I learned the work well, I would in all likelihood become a carter myself one day. Among farming company the carter and the shepherd – as you may know – are men of consequence: the one because he travels about, sees the world and learns the news and gossip; and the other because his master has entrusted to him the flock which, if it stays safe and healthy in his care, is like to be worth as much as all the rest of the place together.

Ralph Woods was reckoned the best of carters, because he was a steady man, who could be trusted to go and return surely, at any season and in all manner of weather; and because he cared well for his horses and never sat drunk in the cart, as does many a carter, while they brought him home of themselves. Of all men a carter must be trustworthy, for there is none to oversee him, nor to know what he may be up to when he is miles from home. I remember my first journey to Gloster, and how greatly I was astonished – almost struck fearful – by my first sight of the cathedral, with its carved, stone towers; and by the throng in the streets, the hubbub of voices in the market and the hundreds of wheels rumbling over the cobbles. Yet before long I had learned to back the horses into the shafts without help and knew well enough the roads to Cirencester, Cricklade and Chipping Norton.

Yet although Master Woods appeared to be satisfied with the way I was shaping, I got more and more into the way of inwardly reflecting upon all I had learned from my father and upon the musical aptitude I was sure I had inherited from him. Why should I not follow where my heart led and earn my living as a minstrel and singer? I asked my mother how she felt about this idea; she replied that although she would be sorry to see me go, she believed in my ability and if my heart was so much set on it she would not stand in my way. And if all did not go aright, she added, I would always be welcome to return home.

Master Woods, who after all stood to lose my labour, was somewhat more hesitant, but at length said that if the business was to be undertaken at all, it ought to be set on foot as honest trades were; I should be apprenticed to a master of acknowledged repute, who would agree to teach me.

I was delighted by their agreement and impatient to begin. Master Woods, however, took his time, enquiring here and there as he went about, while I did all I could to make myself acceptable to my future master, whoever he might be. At length, one evening of a day when, as it happened, I had not been out with the cart he told us that he had met and spoken with a master minstrel of reputation, who was ready to hear what I could do and take me into indentures if he thought me worth it. His name was Owen Fern: many spoke well of him, and he had himself said that, now he was getting on in years, he would be glad of a willing boy, ready to learn. We were to go to see him next day.

Everything took place smoothly. It was a fine, bright September day. My mother packed bread and cheese and the few necessaries I needed to take with me, wept a little on my shoulder and kissed me good-bye with many blessings; my friends wished me luck, I climbed to my place on the cart and away we went.

Master Owen Fern was waiting for us at an inn where he was lodged. To me he seemed a venerable greybeard indeed, although I suppose now that he may have been something under three score. He was wearing sandals and a loose, grey

105

gown which billowed about him. The top of his head was
bald, so that he might have been taken for some sort of monk.
His face was firm and strong, with a prominent nose and red
cheeks all criss-crossed with wrinkles. As we shook hands I
smiled and asked how he did, but he neither answered me nor
returned my smile. No doubt he thought it best not to accord
too much welcome to a boy he might have to turn away.
Having spoken for a while with Master Woods of weather,
harvest and such commonplace matters, he asked him whether
he had heard the latest news of the Spanish princess. At this I
pricked up my ears, for the very word 'princess' struck home
with me. I had learned plenty about princesses in my father's
stories and ballads.

In his sing-song Welsh voice, Master Fern told Master
Woods that the princess, daughter to the King and Queen
of Spain, was to marry our own King Henry's eldest son,
Arthur, Prince of Wales. She had already set out, it seemed,
that summer, but been driven back by contrary winds. King
Henry had thereupon sent to her aid a Devonshire master pilot,
one Stephen Brett; and with his guidance her fleet had set sail
again. She would soon arrive at one of the ports in the West
Country, thence to travel by land to London to meet the King
and the Prince.

I felt full of questions and would have liked to hear more
but, having said as much as he wished about the princess by
way of talking politely, Master Fern turned to me and asked
me to play and sing whatever I chose. I had already decided in
my own mind what I would do, given the choice, and I began
to sing 'Lord Bateman'.

"Lord Bateman was a noble lord
A noble lord of high degree.

He set his foot into a ship,
Some foreign country to go and see.

"O he sailed east and he sailed west,
Until he came to proud Turkey,
And it's there he was caught and put in prison
Until his life grew full weary.

"The Turk he had one only daughter,
The fairest creature eyes did see—"

I had reached this far when Master Fern raised his hand.

"The boy has a good, pleasing voice," said he, "and as for the lute, he seems fairly well grounded. Who taught you the lute, my boy?"

I told him it was my father, but said no more than that.

"Well," said Master Fern, "if you are ready to be taught by me and if you can be patient and work hard, I can make a lute player out of you."

There was more talk; money changed hands and Master Woods and I signed our names, though I confess that in my eagerness I read not a word of the paper which apprenticed me to Master Fern. Master Woods left with his wagon, promising that he would take the first opportunity to come and see me again and learn of my progress. Left alone with Master Fern – or Master Owen, as he told me to call him – I asked whether he would begin to teach me that very evening: but he smiled and said that for all I was so bent upon it, there was no hurry and we would start on the morrow.

I must say of Master Owen that he was an honest and conscientious teacher. He made me work hard – not that I was loth – and sometimes even forwent his own gain – some invitation to sing – because he thought it better to devote the time to teaching me. At the time, I thought this most generous; but now I see that he judged it best for his own profit to press my work forward, so that I could the sooner play and sing together with him for money. It was not only the lute that he made me learn, but also the pipe and tabor and the recorder. I had thought at the beginning that I knew a great many songs, but I soon found that compared with Master Owen I knew all too few. His knowledge of songs, stories and ballads seemed endless, and indeed it may well be that during all the months I was with him I never heard them all. What he performed best were ballads of heroes and adventure, false love or betrayal: 'The Seven Sleepers', 'Lord Randal', 'Young Hunting' or 'Robin Hood'; for these best suited his venerable and grave appearance. Yet he also knew any number of love songs, drinking songs and songs that turned upon a riddle or a jest. Some of these he had himself made up, such as this, which was one of the first he required me to learn to sing and play alone:

"My little pretty one,
My softly winning one!
Oh! thou'rt a merry one,
And playful as can be.

"With a beck thou com'st anon;
In a trice, too, thou art gone,
And I must sigh alone,
But sighs are lost upon thee.

"Art thou, my smiling one,
Art thou, my pouting one,
Art thou, my teasing one,
A goddess, elf or grace?

"With a frown thou wound'st my heart,
With a smile thou heal'st the smart,

Why play the tyrant's part
With such an innocent face?"

His plan, which I understood he had carried out successfully
with at least one former prentice, was that together we would
be able to entertain company for a good hour; until, as he said,
we could end with the company well satisfied and ourselves
with plenty still unsung.

I had supposed at first that when I was prenticed, my master
would be a man retained by some wealthy household with
its own musicians, and that accordingly I would live where
I worked. So I was something surprised when I grasped
that Master Owen Fern had never acknowledged any man
as his lord, but considered that such a state of affairs would
be beneath him; and this notwithstanding that he might in
this way have had both an easier life and a steadier source
of money.

After a while I came to perceive his reasons. First, he was
by nature ill suited to working with anyone who would not
grant him complete authority, for that he was self-willed and
impatient of suggestions or criticism. Not that I ever dared to
offer any, but as the weeks passed I sometimes heard folk
speak of him out of his hearing, and one or two jestingly
asked me how I liked working for such a tyrant, when was
my slavery due to end, and the like. But in the second place,
Master Owen was a man of great integrity and pride in his
vocation. He believed in all truth, almost as a preaching friar
might, that his songs and stories should be heard by as many
plain folk as wished to listen. This was why he was content
to go a-foot in the rain from one tavern to another, to accept
rough hospitality where it was offered and, indeed, to forgo any
notion of a wife and children, for he had no natural inclination
that way.

You may guess from this that he was a hard task-master. And
so he was, and I would often fret inwardly when he scolded me.
Yet I knew that I must either love him or leave him; and I was
borne up partly by the sheer pains he was taking and partly by
turning my mind toward all I was learning, that I would never

109

have compassed under some easier-going man. Besides, as we
came to know each other well and he became convinced that
I was settled upon the business and truly in earnest, he grew
more warm and pleasant in his manner and would sometimes
even hazard a jest; although, as the saying goes, he joked with
difficulty.

Throughout that winter, I worked steadily with him,
accompanying him wherever he went. Before the end of
the year I was able to sing in harmony with him and others
– rounds, catches and the like – and sometimes to accompany
him on the lute. At first I was nervous and afraid to sing or
play before a crowd of people, but he said that this too was
an art that could be learned only by stumbling. He began by
asking two or three, no more, to come into the room and listen
as a favour to himself; and thus I groped my way forward until
at length I became used to an audience and thought nothing of
it. Master Owen was always just and fair with the money we
earned and, if he thought I had done well, would give me a
little over my due; at which no prentice lad could grumble.
So, although I worked hard and walked a great many miles,
I still remained sure that I had chosen the right trade. I never
regretted it; even on the days when fingers seemed all thumbs
and I had to ask forgiveness of the company and tell them that
I was but learning the craft.

Of course, we used to hear a great deal of talk and gossip
as we went about so many manors and taverns. Master Owen
made it his business to enquire for news and to pass it on,
for it made us the more welcome. It was thus we learned, in
October, that the Spanish princess and her train had landed
at Plymouth amid rejoicing guns and the clamour of bells all
over the West Country. From the very first, it seemed, she
had conducted herself most royally. As her ship was warped
in to the quay she had stood in the waist with her own suite
of honour about her, while the Lord Mayor and his aldermen
knelt in the town barge bedecked with flags and ribbons in
the fine autumn sunshine. Although she was not yet sixteen,
she had a fine presence, so folks said, and had won all hearts
as she disembarked and made her way to the church to give

thanks for her safe arrival. Next day we heard how she was travelling up the land, met at Exeter by a band of courtiers from Westminster who bore a letter of greeting from the King. The nobility and gentry of Devon and Cornwall had made themselves her escort, while the common folk crowded the roadsides to cheer her. All along her way there were banners, bonfires and rich processions. As far as we could hear, she was accompanied by continuous festival and her arrival was celebrated as the greatest event for many years. Though but a young girl, she was reported both gracious and beautiful, a princess in bearing no less than in name.

When I first learned that she was only fifteen – but five months older than myself – I was astonished; and when we were alone asked Master Owen how it could come about that she had travelled halfway across the world – so it seemed to me – to be married to a prince whom she had never even seen. He told me that such marriages were by no means unusual; that it was all a matter of diplomacy and statesmanship among royalty, and nobles and gentlefolk, the true purpose being to join lands or nations together, to make alliances and ensure peace. For the matter of that, he added, her bridegroom, Prince Arthur, was no more than fourteen. This increased my surprise but, when I asked him whether they were expected to have children so young, he only shrugged his shoulders and said that it lay in God's will. This meant, I knew, that I was to ask no more. I remained puzzled; yet if I had only known, I was to become still more puzzled, throughout the next thirty-five years, by God's will for Katherine of Aragon.

The wedding took place at St Paul's Cathedral in London. All that I heard made me wish that I could have seen it. The bride, they said, had on her arrival been conducted to the Bishop of London's palace with trumpets sounding and cannon booming, through streets hung with rich draperies and covered all across with triumphal arches. Next day she and Prince Arthur were married by the Archbishop of Canterbury himself. Outside the cathedral, a conduit spouted wine and all the bells in the city were ringing. The bride and bridegroom's procession passed through cheering streets to a place named

Baynard's Castle, where a great feast was held for all the
nobility and courtiers. At Westminster there was jousting in a
tiltyard specially built for the occasion. Each champion entered
in his pavilion; a sort of walking wagon, as I understood it,
fantastically ornate. The Earl of Essex's wagon appeared as a
kind of mountain of green, with rocks, trees and herbs upon
it, and on the summit a beautiful girl was seated. A certain
Welsh lord's pavilion represented a red dragon, led by a giant
holding a tree in his hand. But what took my fancy was the
account I heard of a banquet on the day following, when the
guests had been entertained by singing boys, who sat in a castle
and were carried before their audience by lions of gold and
silver, together with a hart and an elk. After them had come
a ship bearing figures of Hope, Desire and a semblance of the
princess herself, followed by a hill with eight knights upon
it. All these marvels were made possible by means of men
within them, secretly hid and nothing of them seen but their
legs, which were disguised according to what kind of beast
they represented. The rejoicing and spectacle continued many
days and the princess, it appeared, had delighted the Court by
herself dancing for them in the Spanish style; moreover, she
had her own fool, an acrobat who had performed marvellous
feats of tumbling and then of balancing on a high platform.

It was in November, an unkindly and raw one too, that the
tavern talk became all of the prince and princess coming to live
on the Welsh Marches. Prince Arthur was Prince of Wales, and
therefore bound to attend and at least seem to head the Council
of Wales, even though he was but fourteen. He had already,
before his marriage, dwelt for a time on the border under the
guidance of several of the King's councillors. I remember how,
when I first learned this, I felt sorry for the lad and heartily
glad that I did not have to bear such a load of grandeur and
royalty as he.

It was Ludlow Castle they were bound for, and there yet
again the princess and prince received homage from all the
nobility of Wales. There was much pageantry and singing, with
banquets in the great hall. The princess, they said, was eager
to understand everything that was said or sung, and required

her gentleman usher, one Griffith ap Rhys, to stand behind her chair and whisper to her his translations into French; for none except her own household spoke Spanish.

Master Owen often enquired what songs and ballads had been sung, and if he was now and then so fortunate as to learn (for local chatter could not usually stitch so fine) he would make me the kindly ear for his dissatisfaction; for whatever they were, he was in no doubt that he could have sung them better.

One harsh evening of winter weather, while we were singing at a well-to-do, prosperous tavern in Kidderminster, a gentleman who had been moved to contribute to us more handsomely than anyone else in the company took opportunity to ask Master Owen why he himself did not go to Ludlow to sing to the prince and princess. Master Owen shrugged his shoulders and replied that no doubt there were fellows there as good as he and likely better. Upon which the gentleman took him up sharply, saying that he himself had been at the prince's court at Ludlow not three days since, and had heard nothing near the like of ourselves. At the time Master Owen passed it off as a compliment. But a little later, when he had sung the ballad of the son of the Red Dragon who would return to spread his wings in Wales and mate with the silver hind, this same gentleman became well-nigh heated, and told Master Owen before all the company that it was no more than his plain duty to go to Ludlow: and thereupon called for pen and paper and wrote a letter for us to present to the prince's Master of the Revels.

So the long and short of it was that next day we set out for Ludlow. It was not too hard a journey, for a bailiff who recognised Master Owen on the road drove us ten miles in his cart; and later, as we were approaching Ludlow, some fellow riding with a led horse said that if we could ride it we were welcome enough to go along with him. It had both saddle and bridle, though no stirrups, but we contrived well enough, got to the city and found ourselves lodging.

Next morning we made our way to the castle and asked to speak with the Master of the Revels. There were several others

113

like-minded and it was a good hour before we were called. We presented the letter and the Master – a little, sharp-nosed man with a quick eye – without even calling upon us to sing, said that we would be welcome the following evening, but we must be freshly and cleanly clad to go before the prince and princess.

When he said this I felt downcast, for I could not imagine how we could get fresh raiment before the following evening, since we had not enough money with us. But I still knew little of the resourcefulness of Master Owen. We went to an old friend of his in the city. This man, Master Long, a well-known minstrel who had made enough money to buy a house and to live only by teaching (there are always plenty of young men, and young women, too, that wish to learn the lute) welcomed Master Owen heartily and congratulated him on our success with the Revel-Master. After half an hour of talk upon old memories, famous bygone minstrels and the like, Master Owen told Master Long our case. Master Long at once told him to set his mind at rest, for that he knew a wealthy clothier who, upon his surety, would certainly be able to lend us all the finery we could need. And so it proved, and I hardly knew myself in yellow hose and a murrey-coloured doublet and matching cap with a jay's feather in it. Master Owen wore a grey robe slashed with green silk, and with his grave manner looked for all the world like any lord of the Council of Wales.

Next evening, at the time the Revel-Master had told us, we went again to the castle. As the porter let us through the postern, we could see the lights and hear the babel of voices from the great hall. This made me tremble like a colt facing rough water, for I knew that I had never sung before any such audience as this. But Master Owen told me that these nobilities were less likely to chide than a tavern audience, for that nobility always made it their business to seem gracious and generous to common folk like ourselves. "And," said he, "they will be nowhere near so discerning or severe as many you have faced, young Raymond."

We went in by a back way, and the Revel-Master put us to wait in a side room not far from the hall. There was a man there with a bear on a chain, which frightened me at first, for I had never seen a led bear before. But after a time methought the poor creature was more fearful than I or anyone there, for it showed little spirit and only lay on the floor with its head sunk dolefully between its paws. Now we could hear more clearly the voices and laughter from the hall, and I soon perceived that much of the talk was not English. Master Owen said that some was French, but that other again might be Spanish for all he could tell. As I recall that evening, more than thirty-five years ago now, when I knew not a word of Spanish nor ever expected to, I cannot but feel a kind of wry mirth at the unpredictable ways of Fortune.

Soon a page came to summon the man with the bear, and a few moments later there was a kind of sharp outcry from the hall, which must have arisen upon the bear's appearance. Soon there followed the sound of pipe and tabor, to which, Master Owen said, the bear would be dancing. I thought he must be in jest, to see whether I would believe him. But when I said as much he told me 'twas true enough. "They are cruelly trained," he added. "Perhaps one day the poor beast may contrive to slip its muzzle and bite the man."

At length the bear-leader came out and, when the Revel-Master had paid him, went away, seeming well content. Then, after a short while, we were summoned to the hall. As we entered I felt immediately daunted by the sheer size of the place – by far the biggest room I had ever been in. It was lofty, too, and the roof could not be seen above the flames of the burning torches thrust into brackets on the walls. Their resinous smell filled the air, together with the odours of trampled rushes, dogs and human sweat. The walls were hung with tapestries and in the fireplace was a great blaze of logs, before which some three couple of hounds were lying, as well as two pages, whose task, I supposed, must be to mend the fire at need. Long tables, where clusters of candles were burning, stretched down the length of the hall, and on the benches were sitting any number of gentlemen and their ladies, cracking nuts, nibbling ginger, biting into sugar-plums; all the dainties that I had ever seen and many that I had not. What with the size of the place, the multitude and the sudden sight of so much that was strange, I could not help coming to a stop and staring about me; whereupon a gentleman seated nearby threw a walnut at me, hit me on the ear and, with a shout of laughter, invited those around him to admire his marksmanship.

Master Owen took me by the sleeve, whispered a word or two of encouragement and told me to follow him up the length of the hall. At the far end was a dais, and on this stood another table, cross-ways to the rest. As we passed by the fireplace, we came near enough to this high table to see clearly those who were sitting there. Another few paces and we were face to face with the prince and princess themselves. Master Owen bowed and went down on one knee; and I did the same. As we stood up I raised my head to find the prince's eyes fixed on my own.

He wore a scarlet surcoat with yellow sleeves and all embroidered with a contrasting yellow. A gold chain round his neck had at the centre a great ruby which glowed in the candlelight. Although he was slightly built, he looked older than his fourteen years, as though he bore a load of cares which could not be forgotten even at such a time as this. His face – the Tudor face, as I now know – was pale and his blue eyes seemed somehow remote even as they gazed at me. He looked, I thought, like a boy who had learned patience in a hard school. After a moment or two he dropped his gaze and turned to speak to the girl sitting on his left.

I believe that if I had known nothing about her and had first seen her unattended in some common place, I would nonetheless have recognised that this was a princess. She was very beautiful, with an oval face of perfect symmetry. Her brown hair, shot with golden lights from the candles, was parted in the middle and fell smoothly upon her shoulders. She was smaller than the general, yet everything – arms, hands, shoulders and head – perfectly proportioned; almost, you might have thought, like some splendid artefact, had it not been for the graceful vivacity which showed in her every movement and in the sparkle of her eyes. This, I felt at once, was a dancer – a girl whose beauty lay in movement as much as in her lovely face and her royal dignity and repose. Her expression, as she turned smilingly to answer the prince, seemed full of warmth and kindness, and with the turning of her head I could see, even in the candlelight, that she had a fresh, delicate complexion. Yet for all her littleness and her dainty appearance, I felt instinctively that she possessed a disposition of firmness and integrity. This was not only a girl who knew her own quality, but one whose word, whether plighted in small matters or great, would never be broken.

The prince must have said something to her about myself, for as he finished speaking she turned her head again and looked full at me with a kind of sweet gravity. Then she smiled with an expression that said, "Rest assured. I know you feel overwrought, but my heart bids yours to be still."

And this was the first time that ever I saw the Princess Katherine of Aragon; in all the years since I have never forgotten it, and this is how I see her still; young and radiant in the warm candlelight at Ludlow Castle.

Master Owen always had an impressive presence and an air of authority able to command the attention of any audience. As he turned and looked slowly about him, the entire hall gradually became silent until not a movement could be heard. He had told me beforehand that he would begin by singing an old favourite which everyone would know – 'Barbry Allen'; and now, as he nodded to me, I played the four chords which we always used for introduction, and then, for the first stanza, played the air in unison with his voice.

"O down in London where I was raised,
Down where I got my learning
I fell in love with a pretty little girl.
Her name was Barbry Allen."

As Master Owen came to the end of the stanza, I noticed for the first time a tall young gentleman standing behind the princess's chair, dressed soberly in black velvet, with a gold chain at his neck and below his left shoulder the device of a pomegranate stitched in gold and crimson thread. He was leaning forward to whisper in the princess's ear and she, as he spoke, kept nodding slightly in comprehension. As he continued to do this at the end of each stanza, I understood that he must be translating to the princess, but whether into French or Spanish I had no idea. Master Owen had plainly noticed as well, for he now made a pause at the end of each stanza, continuing only when the gentleman looked up and gave him a slight nod.

The song ended and was warmly applauded; so much so that I felt encouraged and more at my ease. The prince smiled for the first time and clapped as heartily as any. When there was silence once more, Master Owen announced that the pair of us would now sing the duet of 'The False Knight Upon The Road'. As you may know, the False Knight meets a child and questions him again and again, but the child always has his answer pat and stands his ground until finally the knight is forced to give up and leave him safe. I have heard tell that the knight is supposed to represent the Evil One and the child Our Lord. However that may be, we always used to make a kind of play out of this song, with Master Owen at first assailing me like one sure of his prize, but then falling back a pace or two and at last being driven to flight, almost pursued by the child. We could hardly have had a better place in which to perform this song. First Master Owen, overpowering and full of menace, came down upon me like some great bird of prey almost at the princess's feet, while towards the close I gradually drove him back, down the length of the hall and finally out of the door, as we both joined in the last of the burden,

> "He stood and he stood,
> And it's well because he stood.
> 'It's ringing you to Hell,'
> Said the child as he stood."

After all these years I cannot remember exactly what it was with which we followed; only that we sang two or three more songs and ballads and it seemed as though the lords and ladies could not have enough. The hall suited Master Owen's fine, strong voice and brought out clearly all the subtlety with which he gave expression, now fierce, now tender and caressing, to what he sang. I have learned since then to judge a singer by his ability (or otherwise) to sing very softly and to sustain this where the song requires it. No one could sing softly and tenderly with such control as Master Owen. I have seen ladies weep as he mourned for his love, vanished away with the dawn or disappeared into the midnight darkness. Yet every word would be clearly audible to all.

There came a point, after we had sung perhaps half a dozen songs altogether, when the young gentleman with the pomegranate emblem came down from the dais to say that the prince wished us to cease for a while and then to sing again. This suited us well. We were led to one of the tables, where the people moved up a little to give us room opposite each other at the bench ends. A servant brought a silver dish heaped with figs, raisins and all manner of sweetmeats, and two great goblets of white wine, very sweet and heady. As soon as he had tasted it Master Owen, smiling, forbade me to drink more than two mouthfuls; and took no more himself. I said very little, being overawed by the company. But a lady sitting next to Master Owen seemed minded to make much of me, asking me all manner of questions about my home, how I came to join myself to minstrelsy and a deal more. I did my best to answer pleasantly and discreetly, but forbore to ask her anything in return, only smiling and nibbling at a piece of marchpane while she turned to speak to others. Four or five gentlemen were standing round Master Owen, busy with their praise and with questions, when the young groom in black velvet returned to say that the prince and princess now wished us to sing again. "And," he added, "the princess would be pleased to hear the young man sing alone, if he is able."

This gave me a turn in the stomach, for I had not reckoned on it. I had a mind to ask whether I might be excused, but

Master Owen would not suffer it. "It is of her kindness," said he. "She is offering you the chance to advance yourself and become better known." And he told the young gentleman that I was ready and willing.

So I stepped out before the company, carrying my lute, and bowed to the high table and then to those on either side, while Master Owen sat where he was, his chin on his hand, waiting to hear what his prentice might contrive. In the few moments I had to consider, I resolved that I must sing something I knew very well; something that would come of itself, despite my inward trembling; and there rose up in my mind the recollection of the first ballad I had learned from my father, before ever I met with Master Owen. That will do well, I thought, for the company cannot know it at all.

I remember now, just as I was about to start, that there came a great fall of logs in the fire, sending out sparks and smoke and the hounds yelping and leaping away across the rushes. I felt uneasy and put out but, when all had been mended and I turned once more towards the high table, it was to see the princess smiling directly at me, as she had before, as much as to say that such trifles were of no account between folk like herself and me: so I took up my tale.

> "An outlandish Knight from the north land came,
> And he came wooing of me."

As before, at the end of the first stanza the young gentleman bent forward to translate. After a moment the princess's face lit up with delight. She turned to the prince, and from where I was standing I could hear her say excitedly, *"Mais je la connais! Je la connais bien!"* As I continued he smiled and took her hand in his own. Her attention never faltered and I felt as though I were singing to her alone.

> "She mounted on her lilywhite horse,
> And he upon the grey,
> And away they did ride to the fair river side
> Three hours before it was day."

I was aware of one or two botches in my singing and playing, but no one else seemed to notice – though I was careful not to look at Master Owen. At the end my chief feeling was of relief. I scurried back to my seat and so had to stand up to acknowledge the applause from there.

After two more songs from Master Owen, he asked the audience for two gentlemen to come forward and end by taking part in a catch with us. There was no lack of gentlemen eager, but Master Owen wisely left them to settle it among themselves. When we had got our two, they asked that we should sing 'My lady doth chide me', that being a catch they knew well. They made no mistakes (to our relief) and after that we bowed again to the high table and took our leave. Outside, the Revel-Master congratulated us, saying he thought the prince and princess had been well pleased. Master Owen was certainly well pleased with the money we were given, which was a good deal over what he had expected.

We remained several days in Ludlow, for word spread of our performance at the castle, and we had no lack of invitations.

It was during this time that Master Owen bought a horse – a venture he had never made before – a large, patient, easy-going beast we named Robin, which carried the pair of us barely faster than we could have walked, but left our feet easy and kept us out of the mud. It was Robin that carried us back to our native Glostershire, where we continued to find plenty of work. I had now gained a deal more confidence and was beginning to enjoy the work as much as I had hoped when I began. I practised diligently and – as is the way – the knowledge that I was improving led me to work harder still. The Christmas festival we spent, by invitation, at three different manor houses and were well treated at each. It was at one of these, Windrush Hall, a fine, new place built only twenty years before, that I first made love to a girl. Her name was Sally; a merry-hearted slip of a lass a year or two older than I, who, the first evening we were there, showed me plainly enough, without speaking a word, where her pleasure lay. It was also during the three days we spent at Windrush Hall that I learned from another visiting minstrel the beautiful love song generally called 'Locks and Bolts'. I must have sung it more than a hundred times since, and always it puts me in mind of Sally in the stable hay-loft, laughing softly in the dark as she taught me my part in our duet.

"Come men and maids and listen awhile;
I'll tell you about my darling.
She's the little one I love so well;
She's almost the complete one.

"Her yellow hair like glittering gold
Comes jingling down her pillow.
She's the little one I love so well;
She's like the weeping willow."

Master Owen and I spent the last night of Christmas at my home. My mother was overjoyed to see me again, and told Master Owen that it set her mind at rest to see that I was plainly in the right mystery and turning out an honest prentice: to which Master Owen replied that he had seen worse in his time and that at least I had done him no discredit at Ludlow.

That was not a hard winter and we got through it well enough. Robin carried us into Oxfordshire and we played and sang at Banbury, Woodstock and several of the villages in those parts. As the days began to lengthen, with thrushes singing from the tops of the trees in clear, green sunsets of March, we made our way by easy stages back to Gloster itself, where we planned to take a few days' rest, to perfect our performance of some newly come-by songs and perhaps to find a few more. Gloster is a fine city for minstrelsy and my only complaint of it has ever been that it is always full of better singers than I. But that is the case also with Oxford and Canterbury. Where there are cathedrals the people in general are well disposed towards musicians and thus attract the best.

It was while we were in Gloster that we heard the news that the Prince of Wales, young Arthur, had fallen very ill at Ludlow. He had caught the sweating sickness and there was fear for his life. The boy had made himself well liked during his time on the Marches and one Mass after another was offered for him in the cathedral. But 'twas all of no avail. It was in early April that he died; fine spring weather, with daffodils blooming and the cherry trees white with blossom. They said, too, that the princess had taken the same fever, though she was expected to recover.

Everyone in Gloster was full of grief for Prince Arthur. Older people, who could remember the evil wars of thirty years before, said that the death of so gallant and forward an heir to the throne boded no good. I myself, remembering the fair-haired lad on high table at Ludlow Castle, his face already careworn and older than his years, could not but wonder whether it had not been his high office which had wasted him and rendered him defenceless against the disease. I made continual enquiries about the princess, but all I could learn was that she still remained at Ludlow, recovering her health as the spring advanced to summer.

It must have been about the middle of May when Master Owen and I set out again, planning to try our luck in Warwickshire and the Leicestershire border. I remember little of our journeyings, save that once, near a place called Atherstone, we were stopped by two rough fellows who meant to set about robbing us. It was past poor old Robin to break loose from their hold of his bridle, and things would have gone badly with us if it had not happened that just then a gentleman, riding together with two servants, came up with us, saw at once how matters lay and drew his sword. The thieves made off; and we were glad to ride in the gentleman's company as far as the outskirts of Birmingham.

There came a day, round about midsummer, when we were travelling towards Ludlow from Worcester. We had dismounted to give Robin a rest, and he was cropping the grass by the roadside while we lay on our backs listening to the skylarks. I was imagining Sally was with us, and I sang for her a stanza or two of a favourite old ballad about Robin Hood's escape from Nottingham.

> "In summer when the shaws be sheen
> And leaves be large and long,
> It is full merry in fair forest
> To hear the fowlës song.
>
> 'A merry morning,' said Little John,
> 'By Him that died on a tree.
> A merrier man than I be one
> Dwells not in Christiante.'"

As I paused, thinking that I felt full as merry as Little John, Master Owen plucked my sleeve and pointed to a cloud of dust – the white dust of summer – far down the road. As it approached, I could make out the foremost horses and their riders ambling along and from time to time turning back, as though suiting their pace to others following.

Master Owen, peering as keenly as myself, got to his feet and held out a hand to pull me up. "This will be the procession of some nobleman or great lady, boy," said he. "We'd best show our respects, before some young devil of a groom requires it with a crop across our shoulders." And with this he took off his hat and stood back a little from the road.

What I saw now, emerging from the dust cloud, were four or five gentlemen, all on horses draped in black. Two were carrying banners reversed. Behind them, also on a black horse, rode a dark, foreign-looking lady, about thirty years old and having about her a haughty air of authority. She, too, was clad in black, with a great black cockade in her hat. Such was her air of command that for some moments I supposed that she must be the chief personage in this sombre band.

But I was mistaken. Behind, haphazard in groups of two or three, came other riders. Suddenly I recognised among them the young gentleman who, in the hall at Ludlow, had whispered his translations to the princess: and a moment after, with a leap of my heart, I saw the princess herself. She was riding in a litter borne between two pairs of mules. On the uprights and along the sides were silver medallions, some stamped with the pomegranate emblem I had seen at Ludlow, others with the three feathers of the Prince of Wales.

The princess was lying half-upright, clad in a black robe and supported by black cushions. She looked pale and drawn, her face and robe streaked with highway dust, which clung to her eyebrows and to the brown hair of her forehead. I thought she looked older than her sixteen years.

I flung up my hat, crying "Long live the princess! Long live the princess!" Master Owen contented himself with a deep bow. As the litter came almost abreast of us, the princess looked directly at Master Owen and then at me, frowning as though trying to recall us to mind. Then her face lit up with recognition and she pointed towards me, crying, "Zhe Outlandeesh Knight! Zhe Outlandeesh Knight!"

I stepped forward and went down on one knee beside the litter, followed, after a little hesitation, by Master Owen. The princess took one of my hands between her own, at the same time calling to the dark woman, "Donna Elvira!" and breaking into a stream of what I guessed to be Spanish.

Donna Elvira rode back a few yards and reined in her horse on the opposite side of the litter. Several others, both men and women, gathered round but said nothing. To me they seemed in awe rather of the duenna than of the princess.

One can often perceive the general drift of talk in a foreign language, even though one knows not a word. What I quickly grasped was that the duenna was of a strong, unyielding disposition and that the princess was pressing her to agree to some proposal of her own.

At length and as though with some reluctance, Donna Elvira bowed to the princess from her seat in the saddle; and then, turning to Master Owen and myself, said coldly, in halting English, "Her Royal Highness wish you to accompany her to London, play and sing for her, help her to better her English. She wish you to join her household."

Master Owen bowed again and asked the duenna if she would be so kind as to spare him a few moments to speak with his apprentice aside: at which she merely raised her eyebrows and shrugged her shoulders, as though astonished that the matter should need any talk between us. Then she nodded coldly and, paying us no further attention, began once more speaking to the princess in Spanish.

When we had gone some five or six paces distant, "How do you relish this, my young squire?" asked Master Owen in a low voice.

Full of excitement I replied, "Why, it seems too good to be true! Wherein lies your hesitation, master?"

"In your youth and my age," replied he, with a crooked smile. "You see nothing but the great city of London, do you not, and yourself in a princess's household, swaggering about at Court with a pomegranate badge in your cap?"

"Well, master, I see us both as household minstrels to the princess," I answered, showing, I fear, all the impatience I felt. In all the months past I had never once lost patience with Master Owen; I knew what would happen if I did. But for the life of me I could not see why he should hesitate: I thought, too, that hesitation looked bad and might be taken ill, and besides I had a kind of superstitious fear that, if we did not catch it now, as it sat before us on the branch, so to speak, this bright bird might fly away and be seen no more.

"And do you set her fortunes high?" asked Master Owen.

"Who but the King can be of higher fortune?" I replied. "Is she not a princess?" To me there seemed no two ways about it. This was, surely, the chance of a lifetime. I could have shaken Master Owen for his stupidity.

"Aye, Princess of all the realm of Yesterday," said he. "She owns not a single foot of English soil and she has no husband. If you wished it, I could try to get you out of this misadventure, Raymond, for you are no more than a stripling. That was why I asked for time to talk. London may not be all that you imagine; and believe me, the favour of a foreign princess – and she a widow – may well prove fairy gold. Whereas here we have a fair living in our own country—"

"I would serve her barefoot over the snows of the Pyrenees!" I cried.

"You may yet find yourself doing just that," replied Master Owen dryly. "We have no more time for talk, or I would be at pains to dissuade you. But there she sits, awaiting her answer. Remember later, Raymond, that I advised you not to embark on this ship of fools, and that you would have none of it."

"But you?" said I.

"*I* cannot refuse," said he sourly. "'Twould like enough be an end of me if it became known that I had declined a princess's command – for her wish is as good as a command – and if she were to put it about at Court that I had refused her, ten to one but it would be visited on me in one way or another." He paused. "Well, perhaps it may turn out better than I fear; and if it does not, there may nevertheless come a chance for an old dog like me to slip the collar."

We went back to the princess, knelt beside her litter and told her that we were honoured to accept her royal invitation.

So this was how we entered the household of the Princess Katherine of Aragon. A young English lad – for there were four or five in her train, though only ostlers and gardeners – brought me a led horse, already saddled and bridled. It seemed that its horseman had somehow slipped away that morning – news at which Master Owen nodded sagely and looked in my face without a word. He himself rode Robin, the only horse with no black in his trappings, and we set out on the road to Worcester, where the princess and her followers were to spend that night.

We reached London about a week later, still in the same June weather. There were about fifty with the princess altogether, men and women, all Spaniards except the few boys and also Sir Richard Pole, the true head of the Council of Wales, who was riding to London not only to ensure the safety of the princess during her journey but also to speak with the King on matters concerning the Council. With him were two attendant gentlemen, but it was little enough attention they paid to me. If it pleased the girl princess to pick up a pair of strolling fellows to sing and play the lute, of what concern was it to them?

Nevertheless, there were others to whom it certainly was. On no fewer than four evenings of that week, after she had dined, the princess called for Master Owen and me to sing and play for her and some ten or twenty of her people – as many as cared to listen. I quickly found out that I had not been wrong in my first judgement of Donna Elvira Manuel, the duenna. She was the most domineering woman imaginable, not only over her husband – Don Pedro Manrique, the major domo – but also over the whole household, the chamberlain, steward and butler and the maids of honour. As for the more humble servants, the laundresses, page boys, cooks and bakers, they all lived in fear of her, for her tongue never ceased berating them. For Master Owen she had some slight respect, on account of his years and grave demeanour, but I once or twice fell foul of her over trifling matters such as dirty hands or sloven dress. The only personage immune seemed to be Don Geraldini, the princess's confessor and chaplain, to whom she was more closely attached than any other member of her household. I would always take off my cap and bow to Don Geraldini, who responded with a gesture and a murmured "Benedicite" as he passed by.

With all the expectation of a green and eager lad, it had never entered my head that the princess would not be welcomed warmly back by King Henry to his Court at Richmond. Already I saw myself and Master Owen as Court minstrels, clad in the princess's livery. I was soon undeceived. It is true that she did have an audience of the King, but she was not invited to remain at Court. Instead, she and her household were given the use of Durham House on the Strand, the vacant palace of the Bishop of Durham.

The palace was a big, rambling place; old, full of rats and having the smell of a house which has not been dwelt in for many months – or many years, for aught I could tell. There was a long garden stretching down to the river, and a boathouse with no boats in it. The only part of the palace not in need of repair was the stables, by reason that before we came they had been leased to a merchant who was bound by a condition of his lease to maintain them 'to the King's satisfaction'; this meaning in practice a half-yearly inspection by some groom of the Exchequer.

The rooms – for there were two – where Master Owen and I were lodged might have been pleasant enough, if anyone had been ready to lay out ten pounds upon them. The doors sagged, several of the floorboards were rotten, there were holes in the wainscot and the wall-hangings were tattered and mouse-nibbled. However, their state was no worse than that of the rest of the house. I remember, one day, turning into a corridor and encountering the biggest rat I have ever seen. It did not run, but confronted me with an audacity which, I confess, put me in no mind to approach it closer. Yet by the time I had come back with a stout stick, it was no longer there. Donna Elvira procured half a dozen cats, which certainly reduced the vermin, yet the palace was never wholly rid of them.

I soon set to work to learn a smattering of Spanish, for without it I would have been altogether helpless. I often used to reflect that this secluded place, behind its great gates and walls, must be very different from the court of some nobleman in Spain. All the officers of the household were Spaniards – the two chamberlains, the master of the hall, the master of the state rooms, the treasurer and the rest. Not only was all their talk in Spanish, but also their haviour, customs and observances, for not being used to which I was often rebuked until I had contrived to learn better.

In this strange life the beautiful princess herself remained my fixed star. In my heart I was devoted to her. Her royal bearing, her self-assurance and good manners to all, of whatever degree, made her seem to me like a being of a different order. To her officers she was always gracious and pleasant, while to her servants she showed a smiling, amiable kindness which in no way compromised but rather added to her dignity. Although barely out of childhood and its impulses (such as her engagement of ourselves on the road from Ludlow) she possessed such authority that when she chose to exercise it even Donna Elvira became acquiescent. She was devout, and to her the Christian faith, more than anything else, dictated her conduct. She spent much time in prayer and in conversation with Don Geraldini. Indeed, it was the unfaltering piety of her heart which enabled her to disregard – or seem to disregard – the shameful indignity of her case and the neglect with which she was treated by the King.

For Master Owen had been right enough in what he said by the roadside. My head had been turned, partly by the mere word 'princess', and partly by her beauty and her gracious treatment of me in the great hall at Ludlow. I remember now the bitter moment when I realised that Master Owen had told no more than the truth when he said she was a Princess of the realm of Yesterday. The King kept her as he might have kept some outworn piece of gear in a cupboard, in case it might one day prove to be of use. No English noblemen came knocking at the door of Durham House, and for a long time the princess never went to Court. I know of a certainty, because Donna Elvira told me, that she received no more than two new dresses in five years.

The truth was that the King, not only with Princess Katherine but in all his dealings, was meaner than a Jewish usurer. The common jest went that he would burn his fingers rather than be at the cost of a candle-snuffer. The money he gave Princess Katherine was so little that we lived worse than any Thames waterman. The rushes on the floor were changed so seldom that they stank and the wall hangings would have disgraced a cobbler's widow. More than once I went to bed supperless rather than eat the fish. No other minstrels came to the house, the reason being that there was no money to pay them. Like the apostles, we had all things in common, including our worn clothes and our hunger. I recall once entering the princess's rooms with Donna Elvira and by mischance finding her on her knees in prayer. She rose immediately, but not before I had seen the holes in her shoes.

Older and wiser hearts than mine were agreed that she was an embarrassment to the King, who could not make up his mind how to turn her to his profit. The purpose of her marriage to Prince Arthur had been to make fast the friendship of England with her father Ferdinand, King of Aragon, and her mother

Isabella, Queen of Castile. Yet these, her own parents, now declined to bring her home to Spain, seldom wrote to her and never sent her any money, even when she had been forced to run into debt simply to maintain the household in semi-starvation.

If it had not been for her fool, Enrico (an amiable fellow and the best acrobat I have ever seen), and for ourselves, the princess would have been without any amusement whatever. She passed the days partly in using her needle; not only for fine embroidery (in which she was skilled) but also in the mending of worn clothes, turning of hems and the like. Her attendant ladies, of whom there were some five or six in all, would sit working with her during the gloomy days of that first winter at Durham House. The servants were expected to mend their own clothes, but Master Owen and I, who stood a little above the servants in degree, were privileged to have our clothes mended by the ladies. I suppose not many minstrels have had their worn hose stitched by a princess, although at the time I did not greatly regard it, being more concerned with the emptiness of my belly, for I was hungry more often than not.

In summer the princess walked in the garden and down to the river. Sometimes she would spend an hour watching the traffic of the boats and of such larger vessels as had occasion to come so far upstream. When we first came, the garden was fallen away and untended; but three or four of the English lads got to work upon it, and after some two years it became a passably pleasant place, with trim box walks, beds of flowers and blackbirds singing in the trees. Halfway down the garden was a little bower, covered with roses, facing the south, and here the princess often sat, reading her devotional books or talking with her confessor, Fray Diego Fernandez of the Order of Observant Franciscans (for Don Geraldini had returned to Spain about a year after our arrival at Durham House). She wrote many letters, not only to her father, but for the first year or so to her mother in Castile. It was November of 1504 when her mother died. Naturally the princess was much distressed at the news, and Christmas of that year, with the household

131

in mourning, was even more bleak than the two which had gone before.

Our household was full of discontent and quarrelling, partly by reason of our poverty and partly because every one of the Spaniards wanted nothing in the world but to go back to Spain. The princess's ladies, in particular, felt that they were being denied what they had once had every reason to expect; namely, wealthy and fortunate marriages to Spanish noblemen. In this sorry banishment to a cold, northern country, time was passing; their bloom of beauty would fade and there would be an end of their hopes. They felt shabby and neglected – as indeed they were. Tempers were short and we lived in a continual state of discord and disputes over trifles.

In all this uncertainty, isolation and wrangling, I truly believe that without Master Owen and myself the princess might have given way to despair. Our duty was to entertain her and I myself felt as though vowed to it. On winter evenings, when dusk fell early and the few candles we could afford had been brought in and lit, we would sing for her, play the lute or the pipe, and tell stories. Sometimes, to save money, we would put out the candles and our stories would be told by firelight. Firelight, in my experience, is best for story-telling, for the day's work is done and there is nothing to distract the listeners. The princess and her ladies would mark us attentively, interrupting when they did not understand some English word or phrase; and by this means, in a year or two, the princess's command of the language became well-nigh perfect. On fine summer evenings we would sit in the garden while the sun sank in the west and the watermen ceased from work and rowed their crafts away. Naturally, as the months went by, the princess came to know our songs and stories well enough; but she had her favourites, and would usually ask us for one or another; sometimes, I think, assuming eagerness simply out of the kindness of her heart. We could no longer go looking for fresh songs in taverns, for we had no money to spend on ale; but Master Owen contrived quite a number, and very good they were. This is one of them.

The Outlandish Knight

Ah! the sighs that come from my heart,
They speak of anguish passing sore,
For since I from my love must part,
Farewell to joy for ever more.
Once on me, with sweet smiling face,
My love was wont to cast an eye:
She left upon my heart a trace
That will endure until at last I die.

Still in fancy let me behold
The form I ne'er shall meet again.
Before indiff'rence whileome pain.
Now to me life's bright sun is set
Amid the shades of endless night,
But oh! its noon I'll ne'er forget,
But ever fondly dream of past delight.

I had in those days little skill in composing songs, but I would
make up fresh stories, pondering upon them when I lay in bed
or sat among the English lads, helping to mend tackle. I even
made up some short kinds of plays; though they were never
written down, but simply enacted on the floor by Master Owen
and myself, speaking extempore to the line of the narrative.
The princess, watching while Master Owen acted the part of
an old woman or the captain of a Barbary corsair, would laugh
as though she had not a care in the world. And thus we joined
with her own stout heart to save her from melancholy.

In February of the first winter we had spent at Durham House,
King Henry's queen, Elizabeth of York, died in childbed of
her seventh child, which died also. I heard that the King felt

his loss bitterly; but whatever his inward grief, he was also troubled over the succession and the safety of the throne, for he had only one surviving son, Prince Henry. Folk said he was resolved to marry again, and then I learned from Donna Elvira that he was seriously designing to marry Princess Katherine. I can believe it, for a man of his avarice would have had his reasons. There would be no need of a long, costly courtship; a large part of the princess's dowry was still owing, and could be required upon her marriage. She was young and well able to bear children. However, as I was told, the Queen of Castile had consistently refused to countenance this project.

At midsummer the King agreed with the Spaniards that the princess should be betrothed to his son: at which many privately shook their heads, for was he not the brother of her first husband? Yet the Pope did not intervene.

With the betrothal, our fortunes mended for a time, and the princess was shown hospitality at the palaces of Richmond and Greenwich, whither she took Master Owen and myself in her train. We had new clothes for the first occasion, though I cannot tell who paid for them; the King, perhaps. This was when I first saw the princess dance in the Spanish style, which she did as exquisitely as everything she undertook.

It was after our return by water to Durham House from our visit to Greenwich that Master Owen took me aside into his room and shut the door.

"Raymond," said he, "we have served the princess now for a full twelvemonth and more; nor ever complained that we got nothing by it. None could blame us for a wish to go, now that her fortunes have mended. I mean to ask her to release us. Will you come with me now to seek her consent? We could be back in Glostershire in three days."

This fairly took me by surprise, for he had given me no earlier hint that he felt in this way. Then I realised what I had not clearly known before; that I loved and admired the princess so greatly that I would not leave her for any gain in the world. To me she was the sun and the moon. If I returned to Glostershire I would feel a sorry deserter and would altogether come down in my own estimation, whatever might jingle in my pockets. Stumbling and hesitant in my speech, I tried to tell this to Master Owen.

He heard me out in silence. Then he said, "Well, Raymond, you are not yet out of your indentures as a prentice, and if I had a mind to I could stand upon that. Yet I will not, for you are a good-hearted lad and for all I know you may have chosen the better part. You are content, are you, to hitch your fortune to that of the princess, stand or fall?"

"Why not?" said I. "Now that she will one day be our queen—"

"That's as God may dispose," replied Master Owen. "I can give you no reason, Raymond, but I have a misgiving in my heart about her future."

"Well or ill," I answered, "I could not leave her now, unless she were to bid me."

I do not know what was spoken between Master Owen and the princess: but she gave him her willing consent to go, and the next day he first set out on foot, leading Robin. It was a sunny morning and I walked with him as far as Turnham Green. There we parted; I begged him to seek opportunity to greet my mother and tell her of my choice, and so he promised, as he clambered on to Robin. We never met again.

The princess showed no inclination to engage another musician in Master Owen's place, and I, of course, was well content to have no new man put over me. With the princess now at Court, I at last had opportunity to meet other musicians, to learn new songs and ballads and to play in concert. At first I had felt fearful, knowing nothing of the skills and quality of these Court musicians, lest I should show poorly beside them. But to my delight I found that I could hold my own well enough. I made several friends among the King's household singers and players, and during all the time that I spent at Court was never out of favour among them. One in particular, John Redding, who had been born at Windsor and as a boy had been a chorister there, was in my eyes a hero, for he was and remains the finest musician I have ever known. Without saying much, I willingly made myself, in effect, his pupil, and would often spend two or three hours together with him, both singing and playing. He was a merry-hearted fellow and loved a jest, and I am bound to say that I found both his company and his teaching more agreeable than Master Owen's. Yet to be fair, this was largely because I had had, under Master Owen, a good grounding and had thoroughly learned my business. For two years I was able to enjoy the company and instruction of the best musicians in the land. This was one of the happiest times in my life and I looked for nothing better.

Yet the King's favour to Princess Katherine did not last. For some reasons of State which I never understood, he fell out with the Spaniards. The princess herself once told me that she believed that had her mother, Queen Isabella of Castile, not died, all would have been well. However that may be, it was two years almost to the day when the boy Prince Henry, acting upon his father's instruction, appeared before the Privy Council and renounced his betrothal to Princess Katherine as void and made without his consent. You may judge how pleased we of the princess's household were to find ourselves, all on a midsummer day, consigned once more to Durham House. To be plain, I came close to following Master Owen back to Gloster. Yet I would not, for it touched my conscience. Even though I had taken no oath, yet in my heart I was the princess's sworn man. To see her holding back her tears, to know that she was forced to sell most of her jewels and plate simply in order to pay for our daily household expenses: these things merely increased my devotion. And indeed it is the truth that, whatever sins I have committed in this life, I have always been loyal to Katherine of Aragon.

And this is more than some of her own Spaniards can say, for during that autumn Donna Elvira and her husband, Don Pedro Manrique, left Durham House and left the country, too. Life in that bare barn was certainly easier without her tongue and her tyranny, yet it was not long before worse was put upon us. The King, in his avarice, ordered the princess to leave Durham House altogether, saying that she and her household could be more cheaply maintained at Court. Maintained cheaply we certainly were. The princess and what remained of her household lived now in outbuildings at Greenwich, now over the stables at Richmond, or again, in a forgotten manor at Fulham where the roof did not keep out the rain. There was no money for wages or for new clothes and not always enough for food.

Looking back after thirty years I recall few details of that weary time. I think that for the princess the worst of it was uncertainty of the future. At the age of twenty, she was condemned to live in poverty in a foreign country, her mother dead, her father caring nothing for her and King Henry doing naught to give her any chance of an honourable marriage. Of her future she had no surety and save to Our Lord and His saints there was no one to whom she could turn for comfort. Small wonder that she relied increasingly upon Fray Diego.

By this time all of the Princess's household – even Maria de Salinas, her favourite among her ladies-in-waiting – were at one in their desire to return to Spain. The princess was determined not to go, partly, I think, because she felt that by such a step her royal dignity would be set at naught and partly because she had nothing to hope for in returning. Her only supporters in this were Fray Diego and myself, for I had no more wish to go to Spain than to part from the princess. So the hard months ground on, and I will admit that I came down to accepting small charities from John Redding and other friends among the musicians – now a pair of cast-off shoes, now a cake, a brace of trout or other such trifles. A man forgets his pride when his belly is empty and the wind strikes through his outworn clothes.

I like to think that during that time the princess in some sort relied on me almost as much as upon Fray Diego. Sometimes, of an evening, after I had sung for her, she would bid me sit down and tell her about my boyhood and of my mother and father. Then she would tell me of Granada, where she had been a child, the youngest of all the family, and of her two sisters and her handsome, gifted brother Prince Juan, who had married young and died at Salamanca before she was eleven years old. I believe that I came to be more closely in her confidence than any saving Fray Diego. One evening she said to me, jesting, that when she was a queen she would dub me Sir Raymond, with the title of 'The Outlandish Knight'; to which I replied that on that day I would play for her on a golden lute won in a musicians' contest at Rome.

Yet despite this friendly unbending on her part, no one ever accused me of doing aught amiss or of being guilty of unseemly behaviour towards the princess. Her whole bearing and demeanour alone made such thoughts, on anyone's part, out of entertainment. Indeed I think that the thing which she and I had in common, namely our frustration, formed no small part of our accordance, for she had no one to love among her own sort; while I, a ragged fellow without a penny, had little or no hope of success among mine. It is true that I had some kindly friends among the ladies' servant girls at Court, but it was a case of a stolen kiss and never a sweetheart, as the saying goes.

Matters came to the point at which most of the princess's household were almost in rebellion against her stubborn courage, while at Court no one dared to show her any kindness, because of the King. Yet the time came when he, at Richmond, kept close in his chamber. He was ill, and the rumour grew that he was dying. There were many who wished, if only out of prudence, to make themselves friendly with the seventeen-year-old Prince of Wales; but the King himself made this impossible. Prince Henry was kept in a seclusion as close as the wife of the Grand Turk. He was never allowed out, except for exercise, and for this he went into the park by a private door, surrounded by his tutors and those companions whom the King had appointed. He ate alone, as I heard, and spent the day in his own rooms, to which there was no entrance save through the King's.

Now one day in late March, a little after Lady Day, I was sitting in the great kitchen at Richmond, playing duets on our lutes with Master John Redding, when a stranger – though clearly from his dress and bearing some sort of groom of the Court – entered, looking about him a little uncertainly. Then, when he saw us, he approached and asked whether either of us was musician to the Princess Katherine: and when I replied that 'twas I, he stared at me and my tatters with a sort of distaste

and scorn, and then told me that he was instructed to take me
to the Prince of Wales in his chamber. I could not conceal
my surprise; whereupon he, looking at me yet more coldly,
said that the prince had heard of me as a musician and had
expressed a wish to hear me play and sing. I still felt surprised,
for I knew very well that there were many about Court more
accomplished than I; but of course I merely replied that I was
honoured.

We followed one corridor after another – he always going
in front; I suppose, so that he should not seem to be in my
company – at length coming to a part of the palace which
was strange to me. We went up a short flight of stairs
and on the landing came upon two helmeted soldiers, their
halberds leaning against the double doors they were supposed
to be guarding. The young groom raised his hand to them,
whereupon one, evidently knowing him well, half opened one
of the doors and motioned to us to enter.

I found myself in the first of a succession of rooms, one
giving upon another, their doors left open, so that one could
see directly from one to another the whole length of the suite.
I understood that we had been admitted to the King's Privy
Chamber – his personal rooms – and at first, in no little awe,
I stood still, looking about me. But my companion – if so he
could be called – summoned me on, with a finger to his lips.

In the second room stood a great bed, the deep-red curtains
close-drawn. Two grooms were sitting by. I knew that the King
must be lying in that bed. We did not tarry. In ten or twelve
noiseless paces we were beyond, my guide pausing to draw a
curtain across the doorway through which we had come. And
thus we passed some four or five rooms, the one always giving
on to another, until we came to the room at the end of the wing,
which had windows on two adjoining walls. At a desk in one
corner sat a greybearded old man, black-gowned, with white
clerical bands at his neck. He glanced up as we entered, but
merely nodded and returned to his writing.

The other person in the room sitting before a table on which
were spread several sheets of music, rose to greet us. Having
seen him once or twice before, though only from a distance in

the throng of the court, I knew myself to be in the presence of Henry Tudor, Prince of Wales.

Indeed, there could have been no mistaking him, for he had the appearance almost of a god. He was very tall – the hugest man I have ever seen – his build large in proportion, with a deep chest, great, broad shoulders and the limbs of a wrestler. Yet there was about his body withal the grace and control of a dancer: he bore his giant frame lightly and with a kind of elegance. He was a handsome young man, somewhat ruddy of complexion, full of health and smiling kindly upon all in the world – so it seemed – where he had good cause to feel blessed and happy. With his red-gold hair and expression of innocent ardour he put me in mind of the figure of a young seraph in a painting by some Italian master which the princess had sold in our penury.

I fell on one knee, while the groom set about telling His Grace that this was the Princess Katherine's musician whom he had summoned. Before he had done speaking, the prince had raised me by the hand and motioned me to seat myself on the bench beside him, at the same time dismissing the groom. He appeared unaware of my dismal array, not even glancing at the shabby old hat which I had doffed and laid on the table.

He enquired first after the princess's health and listened attentively as I replied as discreetly as I could. I said that while she was well enough and in good spirits, yet His Grace might perhaps think, if he were to honour her with a visit, that her means were somewhat straitened. I was half-afraid to go so far towards plain speaking; yet I was determined, if I could, to put in a word which might turn to the princess's gain. He nodded and said he would not forget what I had told him. Then he asked whether she was fond of music, in answer to which I told him something of our evenings with the lute. He seemed much pleased with this and, upon my telling him that she could most certainly read music and herself play the lute as well as any lady I knew, replied that he would send her some new songs and pieces which he had by him. Thereupon he asked me to play and sing whatever I liked and I, to please him rather than myself, sang a hunting song well known to all at Court.

The Outlandish Knight

"The hunt is up,
The hunt is up,
And it is well nigh day:
And Harry, our King,
Has gone hunting
To bring his deer to bay.
The East is bright
With morning light,
And darkness it is fled:
The merry horn
Wakes up the morn
To leave his idle bed."

Before I had done, the prince began to sing with me; yet it was, as 'twere, a tenor part unknown to me, which I judged him to be improvising upon the spur of the moment. This alone showed him to be both of knowledge and practice in music, so that I at once felt more at my ease and in the company of a fellow-musician as much as a prince. Later I learned that he had this trick in way of many skills: he would make a huntsman love him by telling over, simply by glance, the points and merits of his hounds; he would show a wrestler a new fall, lately come from France; or defeat a player of repute in the tennis court and then restore him to countenance with some rich gift, such as a silver bowl. In short, if ever a prince showed all the parts of a hero, it was this young man, who seemed apprised of every sport and art in fashion. This, I thought, will be such a king as has seldom been seen before: a man to make all the realm right glad to do his will.

We played and sang together for some little while. The old tutor minded his book, the sun shone bright through the great glass window, the fresh rushes smelled sweet on the floor and none called to us or interrupted us in our mystery. This is what it is to be a prince, I mused, as he took up his lute again, saying that he would sing for me a song of his own devising. Listening, I thought there could be no question of him being flattered for rubbish, as they tell that Nero was. He might well earn his living as a musician, I said to myself, and doubtless will as a king.

The song he sang is well known now, though at that time it was but newly come from his hand and so known to few. Certainly it expressed well the nature of the singer.

"Pastance with good company
I love and shall until I die
Grudge who will, but none deny,
So God be pleased this life will I
For my pastance,
Hunt, sing, and dance,
My heart is set;
All goodly sport
To my comfort.
Who shall me let?
Company with honesty
Is virtue – and vice to flee.
Company is good or ill
But every man hath his free will.
The best I sue,
The worst eschew;
My mind shall be
Virtue to use;

Vice to refuse
I shall use me."

When the clock struck, he took me by the arm and led me across the room to look at it. At that time I knew nothing of such machines, but he explained its working to me, saying it was newly devised and brought from Germany. Then he added with a laugh that it had told us 'twas time to end our music, for he must now go riding.

"But I will give you some few of these new songs," he said, "to carry to the princess. Give her my good wishes and say that I hope they will please her."

Thereupon he took up from the table three or four sheets of music, which he thrust into my hand, and with them a paper folded, perhaps the size of a glove, and sealed twice with a plain seal. He made no remark upon this and I took it with the rest. As I bowed and faltered my thanks, he pressed four silver testons into my hand, said he hoped to see me again, and before I had left was already turning aside to a closet in the further wall.

The same haughty groom was awaiting me outside. He asked me whether 'those papers', as he called them, had been given to me by the prince and I told him that they were a gift of music for the princess. At this he merely nodded and conducted me back by the way we had come, pointing my direction when he judged he had gone far enough, and leaving me without any farewell.

I returned to our lodgings in the palace and, learning that the princess was at embroidery among her ladies, did not at once go in to tell where I had been. If Prince Henry was disposed to show her favour by sending her music, I thought it best that she should learn of it privily; beyond the company of her ladies, who for all I could guess would probably gossip all abroad in their own tongue until every Spaniard in the Court knew of the matter. As I have said, it was not at that time a happy household.

The evening was fine and clear, with a throstle singing high in a birch tree. Looking out, I chanced to see the princess walking by herself, picking her way along an old, broken terrace built against one side of the house. I took the folded music and went to meet her by a side door. Seeing me approach, she smiled and said, "What, Raymond, are you come to sing to me here?" "Highness," I replied, "I am come back from Prince Henry, who sent for me this forenoon." And then, before she could utter surprise or question me, I spoke of what had happened and of how the prince had openly shown his pleasure when I told him that she loved music and the lute. The prince had sent her his good wishes, I said, and had begged her to accept a present of some songs and other music. And with that I gave her all that he had entrusted to me.

The princess took the papers and thereupon I, with my errand completed, bowed and turned to leave her. Yet I had gone but a few paces when she called after me, "Did he send—"

Looking round, I saw her holding the sealed paper apart from the rest. But then she seemed, as 'twere, to think better, for she broke off, turned aside and resumed her walking on the terrace; and thus I left her.

Beyond doubt and as I felt sure at the time, that was a letter to the princess penned by Prince Henry himself. Whether she replied to it I know no more these many years after than I did during the April days that followed. It certainly did not fall to my part to bear any reply, if reply there were. Whatever the princess might have felt in her heart, 'twould not in any case have been shown openly, matters at Court standing as they did. All knew that the King was close to death. There was a kind of hush upon the palace and indeed, as I think, upon the whole kingdom; for twice at that time I was sent by water to London upon business for the princess, and everywhere folk bore themselves gravely and mirthlessly, speaking little and asking only what news there might be from the Court. "Ah," said one old man (of whom I was buying sealing-wax), "now that 'tis more than twenty years gone, there's many to call him old dog and skin-flint, but he has changed the land. He saved it from the wars and plundering of the over-mighty lords and gave us peace and safety. God grant it so remain." I told him I wholly trusted and believed that Prince Henry would prove as good a king to his people as any with which the country had ever been blest.

'Twas on 21st April that the King died, and on the day following, the prince – now our sovereign lord King Henry VIII – came from Richmond to the Tower of London. Everywhere the people cheered him and called down upon him honour and blessing. The very sight of this tall, brave and splendid young man was enough to pour encouragement into all hearts; and he responded entirely to his subjects' delight and joyful wishes, hailing and greeting them as friends on every hand.

It was not until a few days later that our household made the journey to London, the princess having been expressly sent for by the King. His messenger – one of the lords of the Council, though I forget whom – brought her two letters; one she opened forthwith and read to the household; the other she put by to read privily. The first letter, which as I suppose had been approved by the Council, stated in formal yet plain terms that the King, having been these many years past betrothed to the Princess Katherine of Aragon, now declared yet again that deep love which he had constantly felt for her, and earnestly desired that she would come to him at his Court without delay, to the end that all might be put in train for their marriage as speedily as might be.

And now, as you may suppose, the princess felt free to show and declare her joy. Yet this she did in a fine and stately manner, first withdrawing with her confessor to give thanks to our Saviour for His great mercy and benison; she was gone the moiety of an hour. When she returned, she embraced her ladies and took the hands of every one of the household, bestowing upon them her thanks and blessing for their loyalty and good service. Nor did she speak one word touching that former discord and rancour which now had fled from us like ghosts at cockcrow. "Why, Raymond," she called to me across the room, "my outlandish knight, is your lute to be silent at such a time?" So I played, and thereupon some of the ladies fell to dancing, until the princess clapped her hands and told them not only that we had matter for much business but that it would not be thought seemly, if it were to get abroad that our household should be dancing and the King but lately dead.

Now tailors and dressmakers must be sent for, cloak-makers, shoemakers, jewellers; grooms despatched for palfreys, harness and I know not what: there came such a medley of knacks and luxuries as I had never known and many of which I could not even tell the use; all manner of linens; soaps and scents, brooches and pin-cushions and combs of ivory; towels and great basins of copper, mirrors of polished silver, yards of ribbons and laces and all kinds of things which the household had either lacked for years or never possessed. Stranger grooms and servants whom I had never seen before appeared crying, 'Your will?' as though one had rubbed the magic lamp. I recall standing, near midnight, by the light of twenty wax candles, while three fellows with their mouths full of pins pulled me this way and that as they fitted me with a costume of silk and satin in which my own dear mother would not have known me. And all the while the princess, like a fixed and constant star of joyance, gravely saw after all that needed to be done, without the least show of haste or unseemly excitement. She receives now, I thought, the reward of her constancy and courage, the reward in which only a true princess could have believed or kept her heart fixed. It is her own gracious virtue which has gained her this desert. It is because she has no peer that the King so loves her.

Yet all these fine things, as soon as ready, were laid by for the present, for we and all the land were yet in mourning for King Henry. Three weeks from the day of his death he was laid to rest in his own splendid, as yet unfinished chapel at Westminster Abbey. The princess and her ladies, all in black, attended with the lords of the Council, the nobility of the realm and the whole Court. I, together with other lesser members of her household, waited at need in Westminster should she require us. I recall how the subdued clangour of the muffled bells overcame all else. I heard that they sounded far beyond the city, for St Paul's and all the city churches remained silent as the body was borne to the Abbey.

As soon as the funeral was over the new King and the

146

princess went by water to Greenwich. During long years I have come to love the palace – the great, tidal river with its traffic of shipping, the pleached alleys and arbours of the gardens and the lawns stretching down to the waterside. Here the princess and her household were established in rooms no less splendid than those of the King himself; and if I were to set out to describe the paintings, books and tapestries with which they were filled I suppose I would never be done. I found myself – for the princess would have it nowise else – head of a consort of eight or ten minstrels and singers, all clad in her livery with the pomegranate device blazoned on the breast. Some of these players were abler than I; yet I took care to make no enemies, and 'twas not hard to keep them contented, for certainly none wanted to lose such a place as he found he had gained. As for the princess's ladies, I heard no more talk of returning to Spain. Indeed most – including Maria de Salinas – later married among the English nobility.

This, then, was the place and this the time in which I, Raymond Godsell, the carter's boy from Glostershire, found it my fortune to attend upon the Princess of Spain while the King of England paid court to her and set himself to deepen and strengthen the bond of love between them. There was no open revelry, the Court and all the land being yet in mourning; but this was no hindrance – nay, rather otherwise – to the King and the princess dallying together in the gardens as May turned to June; to her receiving him to dine, and to passing evenings privately in music and singing.

Naturally I was often in close attendance when the King and his beloved were together, and could not but overhear much of their talk. Yet I purpose to tell none of this, as not becoming a devoted servant who has been of Queen Katherine's household these thirty years and who owes to her more blessings than can ever be told. Yet of this time I will affirm – since I have often heard folk question why the King should have chosen to marry her, some saying 'twas his father's dying command and others that it was brought about by the influence of her father, the King of Aragon (as if any mortal man could thrust upon King Henry VIII a course he did not favour himself) –

147

that he truly and deeply loved her ever since the days when he had first known her as his brother's widow. This I had then every chance to know of a surety. Although not yet eighteen years of age, he had already a mature and decisive mind, and it was plain enough to all of us about him that he was as much in love as ever a young man could be with this noble, beautiful and charming girl, herself no more than twenty-three. In poverty, exile and every manner of adverse fortune she had borne herself like the princess she was. How much more did her royalty and beauty display themselves now! Yet what moved my heart more than all was the noble constancy of her spirit. To us of her household, her demeanour was unchanged; as gentle, gracious, kindly yet commanding as it had been in the days of the worn shoes and the threadbare gown. Happy to have won the heart of the prince she would love for ever, and happy in the blessings which God had bestowed upon her, she nevertheless seemed to us who knew her so well to possess her true soul in a place apart, a harbour of uprightness and honesty not to be moved by fortune one way or the other.

In June the King and the princess were married, without pomp or show, at the oratory of the Franciscan Observants hard by the palace wall. 'Twas, one might say, a smooth and considered haste on the King's part, for he wished everything to be ready for her to play her part in his midsummer coronation. In accordance with custom, they slept the night before at the Tower. Then, on a royal morning of sunshine and the lightest of south winds, the Queen was carried to Westminster in a litter of cloth of gold borne by white palfreys. Her dress was of white satin, and even now I can see the length of her hair gleaming in the sunshine as it hung down full to her waist. As for His Grace, when they came forth after the ceremony, he seemed such a King as none could have dreamed of; a prince almost transfigured, like some hero of old returned to right the troubles of the land for ever. The people cheered and rejoiced beyond all that ever was heard. Here was a new order, a new reign, a new life for every subject in the land! Total strangers were blessing and embracing one another, folk were dancing in rings in the streets; and everywhere the vintners were broaching

great barrels – for all was at the King's charge. 'Twas one
universal clamour of rejoicing on every hand, stretching as far
as eye could see or ear could hear.

The months that followed seemed a continual festival of
youth and the prime; a festival of love. Fortunes were lavished
upon pageants, shows and costumes as surely never before in
all the history of the realm. The Court was full of young nobles
and their ladies, each striving to be more gorgeously apparelled
than the rest. Masques, tournaments, hunting, dancing and
minstrelsy overbore all matters of state and press of business.
At the great assemblies, dukes, earls and the King himself
would appear disguised as monarchs of the East, as King
Arthur and his Knights of the Table Round, as Alexander and
his generals, as Julius Caesar or Prester John. As the Queen's
master minstrel I was continually called upon, sometimes upon
the whim of a moment and with no least time to prepare,
to make music for some guising or fancy devised out of
legend, Froissart or the Arabian Nights. Sometimes, even in
the midst of a banquet, the King and the chosen fellows of
his plot would disappear: and anon a band of Turks, Moors or
Russians in strange and sumptuous dress would break in upon
the company, clasping the ladies and requiring them to dance.
I recall once leading my musicians to follow Robin Hood and
his outlaws all in Kendal green (and who, forsooth, to play
Little John?) as they burst into the Queen's privy chamber
and demanded to lead the ladies in a galliard. The Queen
herself always played her part most gaily and debonair, first
pretending fear and astonishment, as though there were no
perceiving in the world who these strangers might be: and
then, upon their unmasking, counterfeiting astonishment so
well that one would have believed her surprised out of her
life and then struck on the instant into laughter and delight
passing all.

At the rich tournaments the Queen and her ladies, dressed
in brilliant colours, would sit, crying applause and waving
their favours as the King and his nobles rode into the lists
in elaborate and gorgeous costume, some panoplied all about
as castles, as forests or fountains, or guised as King Mark and

Sir Tristram or as Roland and Oliver: and when these trappings were cast off (or had fallen by seeming magic) and the tilting began in earnest, each lady would raise aloft the emblem of her pledged knight and call aloud in his encouragement. 'Twas not the custom for a knight to pledge himself to his betrothed or his own wife, it being a sort of courtly game for each to choose a lady as 'twere his mistress for the nonce, as in a tale or old romance. Yet the King himself would have none of this on his own account, always wearing the Queen's pomegranate emblem and riding directly to salute her when he had won the tilt: and this was most always, on account not only of his great height and frame, but also of his skill. Adversaries would go down by the dozen. Sometimes he would run ten or more courses in a morning, yet by the afternoon be ready for more. Then in the evening to supper, seated beside his beautiful Queen. Sometimes he would take up my lute and play and sing himself. Then he and the Court would dance and so continue until all (including my men) were wearied out but he. It was small wonder that his fame went abroad over the land as a monarch whose prowess in making such grand and stately merriment was surely the forerunner of far greater matters. Under him we would conquer France, the spirit of King Henry V and his men of Agincourt riding on our banners, and the new King Henry and his lady of Spain would unite all Europe in the mightiest empire Christendom had ever known, surpassing those of Constantine and Charlemagne.

I would have no one think that in all this the Queen showed herself naught but his mirror. Her mind was no less subtle and charged with discernment than the King's: and her knowledge of the courts and counsels of foreign countries, if anything, greater; for she spent much time in converse with the envoys and ambassadors of the European realms. The King set store by her wisdom and discussed and consulted with her often. Both greatly valued the new learning and arts coming from Italy, Spain, the Low Countries and such far-off places as I have never seen nor never shall. Fine English craftsmen worked for the Court, together with Italian and Dutch artists. Music was everywhere, and I have often spent more than one day's labour in three simply to study to keep pace with the Italians who came to Court looking to put down the English minstrels and make their fortunes. Yet even here I lacked no support and encouragement from Queen Katherine, nor from the King. 'Twas with their kindly help that I began to play the organ – on which the King himself played as well as any – and the virginals too. Yet the lute remained – fortunately for me – his favourite, and many a duet have I played with him, the Queen singing with us. "Ah, Raymond," she said to me once, "thou hast a charmed skill! Whence came it, pray?" This was clearly to invite me to speak of something inherited; yet I said no word of my father, preferring to keep all close, and to give praise only to Master Owen and the blood of the Welsh.

To get the best voices and the best masters for the children of the chapel was to the King an important matter, and of this the Queen was no less heedful than he. They would listen, judge and choose together; and I have seen them at Mass smile privily to each other, as who should say, 'Our labour has borne good fruit'.

I remember the young Sir Thomas More greeting the King and his bride with a poem he had himself written in Latin. To foster and encourage learned men was the King's delight and, although I have heard him say that he wished he himself had more learning, I also heard him stoutly maintain to the Lord Mountjoy, the Queen's chamberlain, that we must at all costs encourage our learned men, for without them we should scarcely exist at all. In this the Queen was at one with him, and of her personal largesse gave to many scholars with the most open hand. Nor was she any mean scholar herself, for the years at Durham House had given her time enough to study, and by one means or another she had always found money for books.

She possessed of herself a natural gaiety and spirit, and a delight almost equal to the King's in entertainment and magnificence. She loved jewels, fine dresses (what wonder?) and rich colours; her liveries and hangings to be splendid, her women delicate and beautiful, (she had no cause to wish them otherwise). She loved hawking, and I have been told that she rode bravely, to the admiration of all. I have been told also that 'twas often amid hunting and hawking that she and the King would confide in each other upon matters of statecraft; for the King often felt his council – the old bishops and earls – something of a fardel of gravity and sadness, lacking the warmth and merriment which his nature needed (for he was but a grown boy). In the Queen he found a confidante worthy both of his mettle and of his eager, questing mind. She was the true ambassador of Spain and in this wise did much good.

To be short and make an end of my praise, I dare swear that never in all the world has there been a king and queen so deeply in love and accord; none so much honoured and admired by their subjects, and none so full of promise to a noble realm of honest men.

In the spring following the coronation the Queen was delivered of a stillborn daughter. Her grief and the King's were shared by her household and all the Court. Yet, like a wounded soldier, she allowed herself to show little of her pain. She recovered well and her courage and good hope were matched by the King's. Such misfortune, said she, had happened before and been succeeded by families of healthy children. The King, both by example and expressed wish, desired an end to the matter and nothing more to be said. He and the Queen turned aside their thoughts and set their minds to the business of the new treaty between England and Spain, and the evil doings of the French in Italy; of which I know little, for they were heavy matters and none ever thought fit – more's the pity – to set them to the lute.

The following New Year's Day, at Richmond, a prince was born to the Queen; a fine boy, as was said on all sides. There were bells up and down the land, bonfires and great firing of guns. The whole kingdom rejoiced. Amid every sort of splendour the child was christened Henry; and the King rode to Walsingham in person to give thanks to Our Lady. I recall that at one festival the King and some of the nobles, in the generosity of their gladness, laughingly suffered the common folk to throng about them and tear the golden ornaments and lettering from their robes.

The baby died, not eight weeks old. I cannot bear to dwell upon the bitter sorrow of the King and Queen, nor upon the curse and evil which now seemed everywhere, hanging upon us in the air like plague. The Queen remained much secluded, inconsolable, yet ever seeking in prayer Our Lord, in Whose mercy and dispensation she trusted – and ever did – come what might. As for the nineteen-year-old King, heretofore a stranger to all misfortune, he seemed like a man bemused, or as though groping in some evil dream. One of the grooms of the chamber told me that he had heard him say that now his kingdom was as open and defenceless as though the French were in Calais and the Scots in Newcastle; for what would now become of the realm and of his people if he himself should die?

I say little. Yet I knew that naught could be the same again. Somehow all came slowly together, for these were a great King and his Queen, who must keep Court, command their nobility and contrive to govern the realm. The King, still half-distracted, began to place much reliance on his new almoner, Thomas Wolsey, who in heavy matters and in small came more and more to direct the public business. Both King Henry and the Queen looked now to defeat the French in a great war, wherein they would have the alliance of her father the King of Aragon. Yet those years of the war – the years after the death of the baby prince Henry – brought little glory to the King, though much to the Queen. The King sent an army to Spain, yet the men would fight neither the French nor the pestilence which smote themselves, and returned home as a pack of deserters, shamed and humiliated. In the following year the King and Master Wolsey crossed to France, after proclaiming the Queen, on Dover strand, to be both governor of the realm and captain-general of England and Wales. The King, as I heard, did little more than play at war in France, though he showed himself courageous enough in the field and took several noble prisoners, whom he sent home to the Queen as though he were a knight errant of King Arthur. Meanwhile, King James of Scotland invaded the North and took Norham Castle with a great and wieldy army of thousands. In the face of this danger the Queen showed herself steadfast as any mighty prince. She gathered together the worthiest of the nobles and captains in the South and sent them northward to join our general, the Earl of Surrey. She was the very soul of all the preparations, receiving and giving out the news from the northern border and calling upon chosen men to be ready with a second force, to defend London if need should be. She would have ridden north herself had there been need. I myself was in her train when she rode to Buckingham at the head of the gentlemen and yeomen assembled, and found myself alongside the wealthy clothier Jack o' Newbury, who had enlisted thirty bowmen at his own charge. On reaching Buckingham we heard the news that the Scots had been defeated with great slaughter and King James himself slain. "Why," said Jack o' Newbury to me, "our Queen might have given her lord a king in return for all these twopenny French nobles he hath sent her."

On our return to London the people cheered her as never before. I felt fairly buffeted by the noise as we rode through street after street to Westminster. Yet the Queen, then and ever after, always spoke of Flodden as the King's victory, the greatest honour that could be to him and all the realm.

I think – though now 'tis long years ago – that it was at this time that I first began to feel – though as 'twere but fleetingly and dismissing such thoughts from my heart as a kind of treason – that some blight, some curse, was lying far off like a black cloud on the horizon of the Queen's fortunes. It approached slowly and little by little. A few months later all the Court knew that the King had taken a mistress; Elizabeth Blount, cousin of Lord Mountjoy. This in itself was perhaps no great matter, save having regard to all that had gone before. 'Twas – and is – but the way of the world, among monarchs all over Europe; aye, noblemen too, and churls for the matter of that. They say the King of France is pox-broker to his own Court, and much honour to him, fa la.

I am no chronicler; I am set to speak only of my love for the Queen. To reflect upon what she suffered in childbed and disappointment during ten long years would bring tears to the eyes of any feeling man or woman, and I have wept for her often, both for that and for all that has followed. I can but

thank Our Blessed Lady for the happy birth of the Princess
Mary, who hath been my pupil and in some sort – so far as
is becoming a princess – my friend these twenty years.

During the years following upon the death of the prince, the
Queen by little and little surrendered to Master Wolsey her
confidential place in the King's counsel, and withdrew from
taking her former active part in matters of state. The King still
paid her honour in public. They dined together daily, danced,
called upon me for music and rode a-maying in season; yet at
bottom the anchor of the realm was lacking and all knew it –
a male heir. The Queen had more than one miscarriage. Her
sole child was the Princess Mary. She became more and more
lonely in her household. Fray Diego had disgraced himself and
returned to Spain with a bad name; and Maria de Salinas, the
last of her Spanish maids to quit her service, had married Lord
Willoughby and left the Court.

I cannot, of course, tell when the King ceased to be her
husband in all but name; but I recall that 'twas ten years
after their marriage that the Queen attended perforce the high
festivities held in honour of the birth of Henry Fitzroy, Lady
Blount's bastard that was to be Duke of Richmond, of whom
more anon. Notwithstanding, the King plainly loved his infant
daughter and still hoped for the birth of a prince. 'Twas but
very gradually that his hope died. As but a household servant,
I cannot tell more.

Yet among the common people the Queen had as many
friends as there were folk in England. Though she was no
longer the beautiful girl who had been crowned at Westminster,
they had now learned – as had we of her household long
years before – to love her for more than beauty; for her
royal bearing, her gracious demeanour to all and her endless
kindness and charity to the poor. Great numbers of the aged
and wretched were at her constant charge. Many she would
visit herself, garbed, to attract least attention, as a lay sister
of the Franciscans. In whatever town or city she might be, she
would enquire about the needy and go forth to distribute alms,
linen and clothing.

I think 'twas some three or four years after Flodden that

there took place what came to be known as the Ill May Day –
the greatest London riot of King Henry's reign – though who
knows what may yet befall? Hatred had for long been growing
against the wealth and prosperity of the foreign merchants who
thronged London, taking trade and money from honest men's
pockets under pretence of fair dealing, and stuffing their bellies
with England lads' bread and meat. On this May Day broke
out the old cry 'prentices and Clubs!'. Houses were burned,
prisons forced open, and a fine plenty of the foreigners were
set upon and beaten. Shops were ransacked and goods stolen in
quantity before soldiers and cannon could restore quiet. Some
ten or twenty prentices were hanged, while no fewer than four
hundred were led before the King with ropes round their necks.
'Twas the Queen who saved them. She knelt before the King,
her hair unbound in the manner of a suppliant, and begged for
their pardon; and this though several Spaniards had died in
the riot. The King relented and released them, though Wolsey
would have had it otherwise. I myself wrote a ballad; 'twas a
poor tune and not worth singing now, though I still like the
lines at the end.

> For which, kind Queen, with joyful heart
> She heard their mothers' thanks and praise
> And lived belovèd all her days.

The ballad is still sung. Yet, as you know, since then many
more than lauded her work over the Ill May Day have openly
shown their devout love of our good Queen. Yea, and I will
say it again: 'Love of Her Gracious Majesty Katherine, rightful
Queen of England!' Now let them come and take me!

How long after this was it – four springs, perhaps – that
it came to me that the King had become a dangerous man,
one gored in his heart and wits and capable of murder? The
lack of a male heir had become all-in-all to his mind. The
thought was never absent from him for long. The Queen, now
thirty-four years old and worn out with pregnancies, had borne
six children and would bear no more, for 'twas four years since
the last. The matter was to the King like an open wound and

'twas this wound that was seized and worried by, of all men, the Duke of Buckingham. The duke was head of the house of Stafford and came of Plantagenet blood. His father had died in the cause of King Henry VII. This Edward Stafford was second to none save the King, though a man of little prowess – neither soldier, scholar nor poet. I have always believed that the true cause of his fall was the open display of his hatred of Cardinal Wolsey. Though all hated the Cardinal – even our saintly Queen, for he showed her nothing but insolence and a kind of bullying scorn – none dared show open enmity, for that he handled all matters for the King – including his wits, as many said. Yet the duke, taking it ill – and why should he not? – to be charged one day to hold the basin for the Cardinal to wash his hands before meat, poured the water on his shoes. He had been heard to say that when the King had died without issue, Staffords would be Kings of England.

It says much, you may well think, for the authority and command of the King and the Cardinal that they were able, upon a trifling bundle of evidence that was no evidence at all, to persuade a jury of peers of the realm (in fear of their lives) to pronounce the Duke of Buckingham guilty of treason. He was beheaded. I learned much from this. I was often in the King's presence, and though daisies may 'scape the hook that cuts down nettles, it is nevertheless well for them to close their petals when rain is in the air. I merely played the lute and sang no more than was set down for it.

I have told of the Queen's delight in learning and in showing favour to scholars from foreign lands. Some of these – though myself a man of little learning – I liked well and others less, though this usually turned upon whether or not they favoured music. Indeed, although I know that I always enjoyed the Queen's trust as her loyal servant and musician, yet I believe too that it did me no small good that I stood well with Lord Mountjoy, her chamberlain (and Elizabeth Blount's brother), for he delighted in music. For Erasmus, counted the most illustrious of the scholars, I could never feel any great liking, for though I was present and heard much of his talk with the King and Queen (most of which I could not understand), I never heard any of his talk with me; the reason being that there was none, though I played in his presence often enough. He was not curious in the matter of music. Old Master Linacre was kindly to me. At the King's accession he was already fifty, yet soon afterwards he was appointed one of the royal physicians and indeed 'twas he and the Queen's own physician, Dr Vittoria, who later founded the Royal College of Physicians. He was one of the tutors of the Princess Mary, and composed for her the Latin grammar in wide use today.

It was Master Vives, the Flemish scholar, who happened to be present one morning when the King and Queen were at the virginals with the princess, she being then, I think, eight years old. The King himself was helping her over the fingering of the piece, and I was playing the lute in accord (with but trifling harmonies, the less to confuse the child) while the Queen and Master Vives were glancing through some sheets of music to be approved, when Mistress Anne Boleyn entered the chamber, curtseyed and asked the King's leave to speak to the Queen on some small matter. At this time I had known Mistress Boleyn for perhaps a year – I cannot say exactly how long. She was of excellent repute for her wit, accomplishments and the swiftness of her mind, and it was these rather than her beauty (which was not great, though to be sure none could call her ill-looking, with her mane of fine black hair and dark eyes) which had gained her a place among the Queen's maids of honour. She was daughter to the rich Thomas Boleyn of Blickling and his wife who had formerly been Elizabeth Howard, daughter of the Earl of Surrey. She had been a maid of honour for some years, both in the Low Countries and at the court of the French King Francis, and accordingly spoke those foreign tongues perfectly. Although I had seen but little of her, I liked her because she could play the lute and virginals well and was a good dancer. She was swift enough, too, with a jest and now and then did not disdain to jest even with me. She must at this time have been perhaps twenty-four or -five, but I had heard no talk of her marrying.

Now it happened that the passage which the Princess Mary was striving to compass was not easy and, truth to tell, the intervals were too wide for little fingers. So the King took her up in his arms and said, "'Tis overmuch for thee, sweeting. Mistress Anne shall play it for thee." At this the princess pouted and would have protested, but the King dandled her and said 'twas no matter, for she was a princess and if she wished might command Mistress Anne to stand on her head. So then they all fell a-laughing but me (though I allowed myself barely to smile) and Mistress Anne sat down to the virginals, they having been placed on a low table with a stool beside.

She played well; as well as any lady in the Court. But 'twas not that which I remarked at the time. I had never before seen that on her left hand was a blemish – a dwarf, false little finger – of which she had no use. In Gloster they would have called it a witch-curse. And glancing at the King, I knew that he was already ware of this. I perceived more. I knew that 'twas as though he had said to her: 'Display thy hand openly, for all to see. I care not: I fancy thee, I.'

I knew then that there must be more to follow. Yet could I or any man have dreamt what? I saw Master Vives glance at her hands, yet naturally, of his good breeding, he looked away and showed naught.

It was not long after this that the six-year-old Duke of Richmond, the King's bastard by Elizabeth Blount, was formally loaded with every honour in the land, saving a few left over for general use. (I speak in jest, but indeed so one might have thought.) First he was knighted, then at once created Earl of Nottingham and Duke of Richmond and Somerset. Following this he was declared Lord Admiral of the Realm, Knight of the Garter and First Peer of England. None doubted that all this pother imported that he was intended as heir to the throne.

The Queen, naturally, protested against this insult to herself and her daughter. (I recall that that evening she asked me to sing once again 'The Outlandish Knight', though I cannot avouch that this was in any way bearing on the matter of the bastard.) Thereupon the cardinal, seizing the opportunity provided by a commission he had received from the King to change and improve the order of the royal household, dismissed a number of the Queen's ladies whom he knew to be of her party and no lovers of himself. The Queen besought the King privily, but 'twas of no avail. I myself saw that she silently wept, though she would no doubt have said – had any dared to ask – that they were tears shed for the plaint of my music; and perhaps this may have been partly true. Yet she had but that day had tidings of further malice on the part of the cardinal; it can only have been his doing. The King had ordered that the Princess Mary should go to Ludlow and take up her duties as Princess of Wales, (as had been required of his brother Arthur twenty-five years before). This was indeed no dishonour, and the princess was furnished with a fine household and attended by her beloved governess the Countess of Salisbury. Yet the parting was naturally bitter to the Queen. There was talk of my going too, yet I begged the Queen to allow me to remain, and so it was determined.

I cannot recount now all the evil signs of dishonour and malice that Wolsey showed to the Queen – he who himself dared not drive through the City of London for the stones thrown at his carriage – but it became more and more clear that he meant her harm. I know little of his dealings or the King's with the monarchs of Europe, yet I know he meant ill to her nephew the Emperor, ill to Spain and favour to the French king. He planned also to marry the Princess Mary to some French prince. The Queen would have none of this and the cardinal's enmity grew yet more bitter. He was working for nothing less than to separate the King from the Queen, and this he planned to do by persuading the leading bishops and lawyers of the land that their marriage was no marriage nor had ever been, for that she had been married first to the King's brother Arthur (as if all did not know it). The King himself needed little persuading. If he could obtain his marriage declared null in law, he meant to marry Mistress Anne Boleyn and get a male heir.

So bishops, peers and lawyers were solemnly arrayed to dwell upon this nonsense. Was ever such stuff? For if the King and Queen had had but one healthy son – had Prince Henry only lived – there would have been none of these great questions of the King's conscience (O Lord! The King's conscience!) nor of subtle interpretation of verses from the Bible, nor of consultations of bishops and of sending messengers to the Pope. 'Twas all a game of words, yet none to say so on pain of his life. It lay in the future that for this wickedness our monasteries and our Holy Church itself were to be destroyed, His Holiness the Pope to be set at naught and good men to die, on the scaffold and at the stake. And at the heart of all, firm, meek and innocent as Our Lord Himself, stood the Queen, gentle and courageous as any saint that ever testified to holy truth. In all that she suffered, as I can witness, she never ceased to love the King and to declare him her true lord and husband. Was ever a queen so wronged?

"There is a fine jest here," said John Redding to me one day at Richmond. He was ageing now and grey, yet none – not even the King – would have dreamed of turning away so fine a minstrel. "And praise be, 'tis a bitter one for the cardinal." He looked round to make sure we were alone. "A jest which may well cost him his head, if only the Lord be our helper."

I told him I could imagine many things, but not the cardinal losing his head.

"Why," says John, "can you not conceive, man? To keep the King's favour, the cardinal must succeed in obtaining this divorce. If he cannot, he is ruined. His plan from the start has been that the King should then marry a French princess. Yet this staff must surely break in his hand, for the King will marry none but Mistress Anne. Ah! And how much love doth Mistress Anne entertain for the cardinal?"

"Many hate the cardinal," I replied. "Not only she."

"Yet they do not marry and bed with the King, nor trust to bear him children, nor hold his heart in thrall. What can Master Wolsey do? The jest will be to see him, after all he has said and done to the opposite, at the hard labour of seeking to persuade Mistress Anne of his true regard. And much will she take to that! She knows how to hate! I would give him six months to gain the divorce. *That* he will surely accomplish. 'Tis what is to follow that will make the mirth."

Yet whatever the cardinal's perplexities to come, Queen Katherine's dolour was no mirth to me, nor to all London.

Whenever she drove out, they piled flowers upon her coach and held up their children to be blest. Meanwhile, Wolsey was jeered at, cursed and railed upon wherever he appeared. The King summoned the Lord Mayor, aldermen and burgesses to the palace at Bridewell, and there spoke to them of his determination to secure for them a peaceful succession to the throne. He reminded them of the old troubles brought to an end by his father, and much more to the same effect. He told them he loved the Queen truly, and that if 'twere not for his conscience – If any man spoke of the intended marriage other than as he ought, he would learn who was master and his head would leave his shoulders.

They listened and departed, but the cheering of the Queen in the streets continued. How could the King order the people not to cheer their Queen? On the wall outside Wolsey's house some man drew a cardinal's hat hanging on a gallows.

The cardinal's business went forward slowly: he was long in starting. I learned, from the talk up and down the Court, that he had supplicated the Pope to take the matter into his own hand and resolve the case himself. And this was what the Queen also desired. Yet the Pope was no man of iron and furthermore his very city of Rome was under storm by the French. Some said that Wolsey would send to him – would himself write the judgment for the Pope to sign, and there an end. Yet that is not what followed.

The Pope may have been no lion, but fox he truly was. He ordered one of his own Italian cardinals, a certain Campeggio, to travel to England to sit in judgment with Master Wolsey. Now this Campeggio was old, and hard stricken with gout: he travelled slowly and in pain. I heard from an Italian that he was under orders to draw matters out as long as he could and to delay any conclusion, for the Pope did not want to be compelled to a decision that would gain him enemies either way. I was reminded of the tale of the mountebank who told a certain king that in a year he could teach his horse to talk, and on that account was given enough money to keep himself richly for the year. If he failed, as he agreed, he should die. A friend asked him if he had lost his wits. 'Nay,' says the mountebank. 'Do but consider! I have the money; and in a year the horse may die, or the king may die, or I may die – or the horse may talk.' The King, the Queen, Mistress Anne, the Pope himself, the cardinal: any might die.

The horse that would not talk was the Queen. From the outset she despised the whole confederacy of knaves – save old Bishop Fisher, who thought as she did and comforted her much. A queen! A queen's given word to be doubted and she to be badgered and baited to swear whether or not she had had carnal knowledge of a fourteen-year-old husband, twenty-eight years dead! She wished only for the Pope to advoke the case to Rome for his own decision, and for this (so her ladies told me) she asked Campeggio, but when he replied that that could not be (the Pope having craftily instructed him so), she had no more to say. She had already told the truth. Things might go as they would. She was no suppliant, no beggar and no defendant.

The more I learned of the matter, the more the words of Our Lord sounded in my heart. 'Everyone that is of the truth, heareth My voice.' 'Swear not at all. Let your communication be Yea, yea: Nay, nay. For whatsoever is more than these cometh of evil.' The Queen had already said that when she married the King she had been a virgin. Could any who knew her doubt that she told aught but the truth? 'The governor questioned Him in many things; but Jesus answered him nothing.' These were the words and this the example which our Queen's haviour followed. And the outcome – the outcome, too, was not unlike.

Next I learned that the Queen had been asked to resign her crown and enter a nunnery. This she dismissed with scorn, replying that she had known for thirty years her course of life and her right vocation. God had called her to the state of matrimony and there she would remain. 'Twas said that Wolsey fell on his knees to her. Much good it did him.

It was not until midsummer that the cardinals' court was convened at Blackfriars. To the surprise of many, the Queen deigned to appear. We might all have known that that wise woman had her good reasons.

It will surprise you to learn that I was present, for as you may suppose, the court was crowded as it well could be. It was Lord Mountjoy, the Queen's chamberlain, who took me in and made for me a place among the crush, saying that I should certainly attend, for that the Queen had no more loyal servant.

The court was indeed a magnificent sight. On high, the King sat enthroned under a royal canopy. A little below him were the two cardinals in their hats and scarlet robes, and a little below them, the Queen. In the body of the court were ranged the various officers and the bench of bishops, having the Archbishop of Canterbury at their head. Before them, at the bar, on either side, sat the respective counsellors of the King and Queen. Nothing like this, I dare be sworn, had ever before been seen in all the history of the land. Yet 'twas naught but flummery by the King, for all to behold (he trusted) how he should get his own way in the 'great matter' of renouncing his loyal wife.

When the crier called, "King Henry of England, come into the court!" the King answered, "Here, my lords." Next was called, "Katherine, Queen of England, come into the court!"

Thereupon the Queen stood up and, as all watched her, made her way between the cardinals, mounted the steps before the King's throne, and knelt at his feet.

"Sir," said she, "I beseech you, for all the love that hath been between us, let me have justice and right, take of me some pity and compassion, for I am a poor woman, and a stranger, born out of your dominion. I have here no assured friend and much less indifferent counsel. I flee to you, as to the head of justice within this realm. I take God and all the world to witness that I have been to you a true, humble, and obedient wife, ever comfortable to your will and pleasure, being always well pleased and contented with all things wherein you had any delight or dalliance, whether it were little or much. I loved all those whom ye loved, only for your sake, whether I had cause or no, and whether they were my friends or my enemies. This twenty years or more I have been your true wife, and by me ye have had divers children, although it hath pleased God to call them from this world. And when ye had me at the first, I take God to be my judge, I was a true maid, without touch of man. And whether this be true or no, I put it to your conscience."

Never a word said the King, and there was silence throughout the whole hall. At length it became clear that he was put down and altogether at a loss.

"Those kings that made our marriage," continued the Queen, "were wise and good; true monarchs to their people. I feel here the want of all counsel and justice, for those that seem to be my advocates are but of the Privy Council and dare not defy what they believe your will. Therefore I humbly require you to spare me the extremity of this new court. And if ye will not, to God I commit my cause."

Then she curtseyed to the King and walked slowly to the door, looking neither to right nor left and regarding none. She passed something near where I stood.

"Madam," said one of the ushers, "ye be called again."

"On, on," she said, "it maketh no matter, for it is no indifferent court to me, and therefore I will not tarry."

She was gone. I elbowed my way from the court and, having followed her out, joined my fellows of her household about her and cheered her coach as she departed. Nor were we the only ones to cheer. The cheering must surely have been heard within the court.

A month later the Italian cardinal pronounced the court to be in recess. The Pope – who had had better luck against his French enemies – called the case in to Rome for his own determination, yet proceeded no further in the matter. As for Cardinal Wolsey, no lord nor commoner in the land doubted his utter ruin, though what the King would do now and how it would come about was a matter of much talk and wonder.

For my own part I believe, and ever shall, that the King himself meant to save Wolsey and did all he could to that end. 'Twas Mistress Boleyn who would have none of it – the edge of Master Redding's jest having turned out somewhat differently. The lords, most of whom had always hated Wolsey, worked with her to bring about his fall. Sir Thomas More, the new lord chancellor, attacked him in Parliament and before Christmas a Bill of Attainder was passed against him in the Lords. Yet Wolsey's friend Thomas Cromwell succeeded in defeating it in the Commons. I believe the King himself was behind this.

Yet the attacks continued. I will not relate here all I know, for my matter is my Queen. It was towards the end of the following year, the cardinal being at one of his castles near York, that the Earl of Northumberland, with another, came to arrest him for high treason. It was alleged (I know not how truly) that he had sent urging the Pope to excommunicate the King if he did not put away Anne Boleyn. None will ever know the truth of this, for the cardinal, who was already a grievously sick man, did indeed set out for London, but died at Leicester Abbey on the journey. And thus much of him.

At Greenwich palace, the Queen's strange life continued; and, one might say, the scarcely less strange life of the King. Mistress Boleyn lodged in her own rooms, maintaining what any man might well have called her own court; and here the King spent much time. Yet he also spent time with the Queen, supping with her in her chamber once or twice a week, after which she and her ladies would embroider while I and my fellows played and sang.

All the household, of course, were awaiting the Pope's decision, which the Queen never doubted would be in her favour. And so indeed it was. It was not to be given, however, for four and a half years; and this monstrous delay was to prove fatal to the Queen and to the fortunes of all of us who loved her. But of this, naturally, we as yet knew nothing, and the Queen's bearing and manner remained calm and gentle as always. In sooth, 'twas almost as though she were feigning that there had never been any breach nor any suit. We mortals fail, neglect and desert Our Lord to His face, day by day, yet his love for us never ceases – the river of life. Such was the Queen's love for the King. She avoided Mistress Boleyn and, when she could not, ignored her. In all else she was the serene lady for whose delight I had now been playing my lute for two thirds of my life.

The Outlandish Knight

I have often reflected that had it not been for her friends among the Franciscans and for my music, she might well have found herself unable to bring about such evident self-command. Music, to those that love it, ruleth its own kingdom, be the world what it will. I knew she had need of me and trusted in me for solace, and to this end I was diligent in seeking among other minstrels of the Court for fresh and newly contrived music to cheer her heart. Such music might be melancholy or merry. Was't not King Solomon who, they say, listened to the sorrow of the nightingale till all his own was gone?

One raw November evening, a little before the Queen's usual time for supper, I was seated alone with her and two or three of her ladies, pleasantly close to a beech-log fire in her privy chamber. I had been given by Master Redding a copy of a poem lately devised by young Sir Thomas Wyatt – that same who had from his travels in Italy brought back the new form of verse they call the sonnet – an excellent device for lovers' poetry. He already had a great name for this up and down the Court. This song, however, was no sonnet, but a lover's (or a lady's) lament, for which I myself had devised what I judged a simple but pleasing air. I could see that the Queen thought so too; for I weened that I saw the faint gleam of a tear in her eye.

"And wilt thou leave me thus?
Say nay, say nay, for shame!
To save thee from the blame
Of all my grief and grame.
And wilt thou leave me thus?
Say nay! say nay! for shame!

167

"And wilt thou leave me thus,
That hath loved thee so long
In wealth and woe among?
And is thy heart so strong
As for to leave me thus?
Say nay! say nay! so long!

"And wilt thou leave me thus,
That hath given thee my heart,
Never for to depart
Neither for pain nor smart;
And wilt thou leave me thus?
Say nay! say nay! my heart!

"And wilt thou leave me thus,
And have no more pity
Of her that loveth thee?
Hélas! thy cruelty!
And wilt thou leave me thus?
Say nay! say nay! pity!"

I had barely concluded this song, to the expressed pleasure of the ladies, and was about to enter upon another, when the door was thrown open and one of the maids-in-waiting announced the King. As we rose, he strode in bravely enough and greeted the Queen with a kiss, yet I could perceive that he was not easy in spirits and I could also smell the wine that he had been drinking. (Nor was it long before he belched.) I felt sure that Mistress Boleyn had been goring him as usual to separate entirely from the Queen and order her away from Greenwich. However, he said nothing of this; only that he would be pleased if he might join the Queen for supper. If she would command Master Godsell and his fellows to play, so much the better.

"And how goes it with you, Master Godsell?" he asked heartily, clapping me on the shoulder like a brother. At such times one could not help liking him. "Do you still remember bearing a musical letter for me more than twenty years ago?"

"Very well, Your Grace," said I. "And thanks to Your Grace and my lady the Queen, I go on bravely enough."

"God give you good hap," answered he, and took his seat, while I went to gather my minstrels.

At first all seemed well enough, and we played our Italian ritornellos gaily while the King and Queen supped. Yet after a while, as we paused between pieces, I heard the Queen say to the King that she saw him less and less and that he did not sup with her or visit her as he used to, but left her to sit neglected. Then, becoming more vehement, she broke into Spanish – which I, of course, had understood very well these many years past, yet will not repeat after her; only that 'twas plain she meant to vex him and set him on. This came to two gorings in one evening, and the King and his wine proved poor friends to his patience. He spat in the rushes and replied that 'twas her own fault if she lacked comfort. She was mistress of her own household; she could go where she pleased and live as she pleased. He was not her husband, and many learned doctors had told him so.

"Doctors!" stormed the Queen in Spanish, (we playing as mightily as we could and looking resolutely at naught but the music), "Doctors! Were there doctors in the bed when you took my maidenhead? Were there? You know yourself to be my husband. I came to you as much a virgin as I came from my mother's womb, and I have often heard you say so. Doctors! A king to be chaffering around Europe, fishing ragged rabbis out of their ghettos to opine against Deuteronomy at twenty crowns a man! The Pope is my judge! The Pope, I say!"

"The Pope may drown in the Tiber," bellowed the King. "Every learned doctor is for my case. I have but to wait for their opinions to be confirmed by the University at Paris. If the Pope does not decide in my favour, I shall declare him a heretic and marry whom I please. You, Master Godsell –" he suddenly rounded upon me, "– get you gone, you and your rout."

At the time I put this down to drink and choler – which was doubtless no more than the truth. Yet it showed already the drift of the King's mind. However, it was to be more than three years before he could find men and devise means wicked enough to carry out his work of spitting in the face of God. Those men were Thomas Cromwell and Thomas Cranmer. Of them anon.

But for the time being the royal lives dragged on, with the Court gossip beating about them like crows round heads on London Bridge. For myself, I was content to make it clear that I was my Queen's man. I would repeat no tittle-tattle and take part in no gossip. This was not only my own wish but my best and safest course. I tried to think of myself as a creature like a bird, whose tongue hath no use but that of song. Of course I spoke and conversed naturally with those about me, but natheless the notion of the bird kept my lips from babbling what might well have proved my downfall. I had the repute of a man whom 'twas of no use to question, for there was no bruit nor rumour which I would tell, nor none to which I would listen.

It was some eighteen months later, a little after Whitsunday, as I recall, and quite late in the evening – for the Queen was preparing to retire – that there came to her apartments a body of some thirty counsellors, led by the Dukes of Norfolk and Suffolk, with sundry lords, bishops and doctors. They had come to persuade her not to press her case at Rome. I was not present, of course, but one of her ladies told me what passed. The Duke of Norfolk, it seems, spoke but poorly and the Queen's reply was brisk and fervent. She said she had no especial reason to expect favour of the Pope, who had helped her little, but 'twas the King who had first laid the case. As for the King's self-assumed title of the Supreme Head of the Church of England, she acknowledged him lord and master in matters temporal, but for what concerned spiritual matters there was only one supreme head and judge; namely, the Pope.

Several lords fudged on, but all was of no avail. The Queen replied to each with a clear wit. "I love and have loved my lord the King," said she, "as much as any woman can love a man, but I would not have borne him company as his wife one moment against the voice of my conscience. I came to him a virgin; I am his true wife, and whatever so-called proofs my lord of Lincoln or others may allege to the contrary, I, who know better than anyone else, tell you are lies and forgeries."

I happened to be in the lobby as they departed, and myself heard Sir Henry Guildford mutter that the best thing for all who had suggested this accursed case to the King would be to be tied in a cart and sent to Rome to answer it. There seemed to be many who, from their demeanour, were of the same mind.

When in June the Court moved to Hampton Court and then to Windsor, we went with it as usual. The King still dined with the Queen on State occasions and she wore a brave face; though one evening when I came upon her weeping and asked if there were any new cause (for I enjoyed now the privilege of an old and trusted servant), she replied that she felt it much that she was kept from the Princess Mary.

In a courtyard of the palace some days later, when I had stood aside and unbonneted for the King and some half-dozen nobles to pass by, he of a sudden stepped apart (they loitering near) and beckoned to me. I went upon one knee, but he bid me rise.

"Master Godsell," said he, "a word. 'Tis time for you to be leaving the Queen."

I knew not what to say. "Your Grace," I replied in the most dismal confusion, "hath she so commanded?"

"Nay," said he, "and neither do I *command* you. But I have ever thought of you as honest, Master Godsell, and a king may give advice as well as any other man. 'Tis time."

"Your Grace," I answered, my heart knocking my ribs, "unless you or she herself were so to command me I could not leave the Queen."

"Why," growled he, "as to that, you have twangled for her like a dog these twenty-five years, and so may die like a dog for all I care."

I, being now heated, plucked up a little courage.

"By favour, Your Grace," said I, "I never yet saw the dog that twangled."

At this he burst into a great bellow of laughter and turned away, leaving me to wonder what was to befall.

It was a morning of mid-July (the year being 1531) that the

King and Mistress Boleyn set off at dawn from Windsor palace to go hunting. He did not bid the Queen farewell. They never met again.

She wrote to him and in reply was ordered to remove her household to Wolsey's old manor of the More in Hertfordshire. She replied that she would rather go to the Tower, which would fairly make plain to the folk of England how she was to be treated. But this did not take place, and to the More we went, I having a sorrowful parting from Master Redding and other friends. "Pray God you remain on live," said he. "As to that," I replied, "I will die before I desert her."

Soon another body of counsellors waited on the Queen and were sent packing as before. She was now left without a single friend at Court, save for the Imperial ambassador, Master Chapuys. Yet at home she had only to show her face in the street to be cheered. More than once tumults broke out on her behalf. I heard from Master Redding that Mistress Anne could not go out but mud and oaths were set flying after her like flocks of sparrows. As for the King, he was pursued everywhere by cries of "Take back the Queen!" "Take back thy wife!" "Herod!" and the like. Yet none was arrested or punished, the King plainly lacking the stomach to proceed. Bishop Fisher of Rochester, that was soon after to be imprisoned and to suffer death for the Queen's sake, preached in her favour and openly stood to what he had said in the pulpit.

In October we were again removed, this time to Hatfield, an old palace belonging to the Bishop of Ely, while the King and his whore travelled to Calais. Early in the following year he professed to marry her, for that, as all whispered, she was with child and the matter could be no longer delayed. The business was done very privily. At this time, too, Thomas Cranmer was created Archbishop of Canterbury, that he might cringe and grovel and perform the King's will.

Now the King's dismal hatred against the Queen, which before had but trotted and cantered, began to gallop. An act was passed in Parliament that no appeal in spiritual causes might be taken from the kingdom to Rome. Cranmer the Creep was made to declare that the Queen's marriage was no marriage, nor had ever been, and that the King was truly married to Anne Boleyn. (They had a coach, I learned, decorated in golden letters with H and A, whereat the folk shouted "Ha! Ha!" until it was seen no more.)

Now our Queen was told that she was henceforth to bear no title but that of 'Princess Dowager', while Anne Boleyn was openly declared queen. This the Queen ignored and so did all we of her household and indeed all who had to do with her.

'Twas on a hot, cloudless day of July, I recall, that Lord Mountjoy, her chamberlain, with four other gentlemen of her household, waited upon the Queen to tell her that the King now strictly forbade her to use any title but that he had commanded of 'Princess Dowager'. She was sick abed, having hurt her foot with a pin and also being in pain from a racking cough; and so received them. She told them she would have none of it and, when they showed her the written report which they intended to make to the King, struck out with her own hand every mention of 'Princess Dowager'.

So began that persecution that was intended to kill the Queen, and took twenty-eight months to do so. Our household was yet again removed, this time to the so-called palace of Buckden, a damp, drear place a little south of Huntingdon on the river Ouse; a land of fever and constant sickness from the marshes. I was riding behind the Queen's coach as we approached and first saw it. She leaned from the window and called to me gaily, "See, Raymond, Durham House!" "Pray God it be no worse, Your Grace," answered I, cursing the King in my heart; for the prospect would have daunted any man. Yet along the way the village folk were acclaiming the Queen as though she had been an angel of heaven sent to right every wrong and hardship they had ever known.

At Buckden she was treated as a prisoner. She was not allowed to go out at her own will, but only at stated hours. She could not receive visitors – though many wished to come – and she was not permitted materials for writing. Her means were so much reduced that her household was perforce halved; and several of those who remained – including myself – did so for almost nothing, out of love and loyalty. It was worse than Durham House, for that then the Queen had been young, healthy and beautiful, with hope in her heart. Hope, to her undying honour, she never lost. The hope was that the Pope would give his judgment for her and she would return to the King, against whom she entertained no anger and for whom we all prayed daily. Yet she had no way of urging the Pope, lacking even the means to write a letter, let alone to send an envoy.

The winter was more dreary than I can say, the mist, frost and wind seeming to strive to outdo one another day by day. We had barely coals and firewood (though the kindly villagers brought us what wood they could spare), and so would sit all by the one kitchen fire, Queen and servants alike. Lacking the help and company of other musicians, I took to writing much music myself and in this the Queen would join me, so that together we set many songs in Spanish and French as well as in English. There was nothing to write upon, so we wrote them on the walls and the tables, using for ink charcoal, or even mud, and washing it off as we listed.

The following summer Anne Boleyn, who was now big with her bastard, expressed to the King a desire to possess a certain rich cloth which the Queen had long ago brought with her from Spain, to be used at the baptism. She was not ashamed to ask the King to demand it of the Queen, nor he to do so. The Queen refused, and was ready to burn the cloth before ever it could be taken from her. That the King should have asked showed, me thought, to what depths he had sunk under Anne Boleyn. One of the Queen's gentlewomen fell to cursing her, whereupon the Queen said, "Hold your peace. Curse her not, but pray for her: for the time will shortly come when you will have much need to pity and lament her case."

It was near to Christmas in that same year when there came gentlemen from the King to tell the Queen that it was now determined that she should remove from Buckden to Somersham in the Isle of Ely. Plainly she was not dying fast enough for the King's satisfaction. Ely is a foul marsh surrounded by water. The gentlemen took it upon themselves to dismiss a number of her servants who refused to be sworn to the bastard Elizabeth, which had been born in September, so-called Princess of Wales. For my part, I succeeded in slipping out of the house and thus avoided their inquisition. I lodged with a friendly villager, one Master George Wedd, for the six days they remained.

They remained because the Queen declined to go with them. She locked herself in her own chamber and told them, through a hole in the wall, that if they were determined to remove her they would have to break down the doors and carry her away by force. This they could not bring themselves to do, and perforce went back to the King with the confession that they had been able to carry out only one part of their charge; whereat he was displeased.

The Queen's life at this time was passed in much prayer, in alms-giving (for she still found means, saying that there were many wretched folk poorer than we) and in abstinence. She and her gentlewomen did much needlework (though her eyes were no longer keen) in costly material sent by the Church and intended for church decoration. Nor have I seen needlework more exquisitely achieved, for she spared no pains.

There was a chamber with a window having a prospect into the chapel, and from this she was able to hear divine service. In this chamber she spent much time, and would pray at the window (whence she could see the aumbry and the reserved host), kneeling on the stones of the floor. I myself, entering to ask if she wished me to play for her at supper, have seen the stones wet with her tears. I twice besought her to allow me to place cushions there, but she would not suffer it.

For much of her time she lived in this one room, using it as kitchen, privy chamber and bedroom, for her dismissed servants had been replaced by strangers appointed by the Duke of Suffolk, and the Queen would eat only food cooked by Ann Parks that was her own chamberwoman.

'Twas in the March following the birth of the bastard that the Pope at last pronounced the Queen's marriage to be valid. Yet this, coming so late, was of no avail, for already Parliament had declared Anne Boleyn to be queen and had given her the true Queen's jointure. When two doctors of law came to Buckden to require the Queen to swear to the new Act of Succession declaring Elizabeth her father's successor and the Princess Mary illegitimate, she replied to them merely that the Pope had declared in her favour; and with this they went off down the road amid the jeers of the country folk.

In May the household was moved yet again, to a mansion twenty miles away at Kimbolton, which had once belonged to Sir Richard Wingfield. This was a more comfortable place than Buckden for a small household, and more healthy, for it seemed that much feeling had been expressed at Court that the King was treating the Queen with cruelty and seeking to compass her death. Therefore and for no other reason he showed this favour.

We had not been long at Kimbolton when we had other visitors: the Archbishop of York and the Bishop of Durham. What they had come to tell the Queen was that if she refused to swear to the new Act, she could by law be put to death. Her reply was that she was entirely ready to meet with her executioner. There was a deal of talk, and letters came from the Privy Council. But whatever was in them had no effect upon the Queen.

She was now kept entirely as a prisoner; as elsewhere was the Princess Mary, for whom the Queen grieved as deeply as would any mother. For myself, I could scarcely believe her case to be true. If 'twere an evil dream, I thought, then perchance in another dream the devil might come and bear the King away.

Soon after came the Queen's friend Master Chapuys, the Imperial ambassador, with a troop of sixty horse. The King had forbidden him to enter the Queen's dwelling, and accordingly the Queen and we of her household spoke to them from the windows. This visit gave the Queen much comfort.

I cannot bear to relate – it is sufficiently well known to all – the execution of the good Sir Thomas More and of Bishop Fisher, who had so long been the Queen's friends. Also, there were hanged, drawn and quartered four Carthusian monks that had refused to take the oath. I have no doubt that had he dared, the King would have executed the Queen. Yet he dared not, for the love the people everywhere bore her; and so he awaited her death.

Until now, I think, the Queen herself had not truly realised what evil the King's heart was able to compass. I believe that every monarch in Europe felt him accursed and, as all know, he was excommunicated by the Pope. Yet his cruelty has been successful. There have been no others who dared to defy him or refused to take the oath. Yet I myself have never taken it. They forgot me.

It was about Christmas time, most wintry and cold, when the Queen at last fell too ill to leave her bed. We all knew that she must die. Often she lay sleeping, yet at other times could not sleep for pain. At whiles I played and sang for her, yet she had not the strength even to listen for long. On New Year's Day came Master Chapuys once more, and this time was admitted to her presence. He stayed with us four days, of which I was heartily glad, for that he was a good and kindly man, well liked by all. He brought the Queen blessing and comfort, and constantly prayed with her. Then also came Lady Willoughby, that had been Maria de Salinas, the Queen's maid of honour. She declared to us all that she would not leave the Queen; nor did she, but remained with her until the end.

This holy, Christian end was granted to the Queen in the afternoon of Friday 7th January. Before this, early in the morning, she had received the sacrament and said farewell to all those of her old and loyal servants who were left in the household. When it fell to me to come to her, I knelt and took her in my arms, weeping; yet this I did only because by no other means could her lips have spoken at my ear. "God bless thee, Raymond," she whispered. "May God be with thee, my dear, dear outlandish knight."

I loved the Queen as I have loved no other, man or woman, in all my life. To me, she was like the very person of Our Lady reflected, as 'twere, in a clear mirror. She bore loss, sorrow and affliction with a strength which sprung from entire purity and nobility. Her virtue shone bright upon all who knew her. I never heard a word spoken against her and she had no enemies, saving those who set themselves against the holy will of God. Without her, I should never have known the true meaning of Christian meekness, courage, patience and charity. She was not a queen in name only, but a queen in the spirit. For witness, ask the people of this land. For me, that have so often ridden behind her down highway after highway, with the plaudits of the common folk that knew her for what she truly was, this life can no more remain the same than it did for those whom Our Lord left on his departure.

I am now in the household of Sir Henry Cavendish, and glad enough he is to have the services of a master musician of my prowess. I am looked up to by others of the craft and am as well-to-do as ever I have been. Yet while these matters are of comfort and solace they are no recompense for the loss of the Queen. I would willingly live once more in Durham House or even at Buckden, so that she were there also.

She lies in Peterborough Cathedral. Though she has no need of my prayers, I pray for her soul daily. I feel her presence always in my heart and try to live as I feel she would wish.

As for this world, what can a man say? The Queen spoke true when she told us that the time would come when we should have much need to pity and lament for Anne Boleyn. The King and his Parliament have ruined and robbed the Holy Church and are even now going about to destroy its ancient monasteries, so that no man or child is able to learn any more what is God's truth and what comes of the devil. May God have mercy on us all.

Now that my Queen has no more need of me, I mean to marry. At fifty I do not feel too old and I know a good Christian maid, kind and fair, whom I think will be willing to join with a man of comfortable means and good repute and standing. I would like to have children – a boy to play the lute and a girl to sing. The prospect makes me glad.

Take comfort, Raymond, thou outlandish knight.
Thy Queen shall bless thee. All shall go aright.

Part Three

Raymond's hope was not misplaced. The young woman to whom he proposed marriage was happy to accept him, seeing in him a man of standing and reputation as a minstrel and former loyal servant of the universally revered Queen Katherine; and also a man of some substance, for the queen, little though she had to bequeath, had remembered him generously in her will.

In 1538 their daughter Honor Mary was born, and Raymond felt himself a happy and fortunate man. It was some twelve years later that, following the advice and example of his friend John Redding, formerly a minstrel in the household of Henry VIII, he moved, with his wife and daughter, to Derbyshire, becoming a tenant of the enormously wealthy Henry Babington. The Babingtons were an old and most influential Derbyshire family, tracing their ancestry to the Norman era. A series of arranged marriages in the fifteenth century had greatly extended their estates, so that they had become one of the foremost landowners in the kingdom. Catholicism was firmly established throughout their domains; and here Raymond Godsell, living as a neighbour of two or three other minstrels, seemed justified in expecting a prosperous and happy old age. The short reigns of Edward VI and of Mary Tudor had virtually no effect on the family of Babington and their thousands of tenants.

In 1557 Raymond's nineteen-year-old daughter, Honor, being of excellent local reputation as a hard-working, trustworthy and pious girl, obtained a place as a servant in the Babington household at Dethick, where she soon came to the favourable notice of the housekeeper.

In the same year, Raymond died, aged seventy-one. He had a calm and peaceful end, with forgiveness and extreme unction ministered by a priest. What comforted him most was the knowledge that he would soon be restored to his beloved

Queen Katherine. He left his widow sufficiently well-off for her to have no need to leave their home, and here Honor would return for those few days that her employment at Dethick permitted.

Four years later Thomas Babington and his second wife, Lady Mary Darcy of Darcy, were blest by the birth of a son and heir, Anthony. Honor was appointed as his nurse, and as the baby grew to be an infant and then a healthy and promising boy, the two became deeply attached to each other. Anthony received from his 'Honsie' – as he called her – his first religious instruction, and also her patient and kindly answers to the endless questions of childhood. As the happy months went by, the two grew ever closer, the parents feeling well content to leave young Anthony in the care of so devoted and reliable an attendant.

The long stalks of the midsummer grasses swayed gently to and fro between Anthony's eyes and the sky. His head, at rest in the grass, moved with them as his eyes aligned a stalk of red sorrel with the edge of a tiny, solitary cloud. The cloud drifted, and Anthony's head tilted further to recover the alignment. A humble bee buzzed slowly across his vision and disappeared among the buttercups. He had been still for so long that a grasshopper alighted and began zipping close to his ear. The sun shone warm on his face and his bare arms, shirt-sleeves rolled up in imitation of the haymakers. The sky was intensely blue and remote; a vast, single blue.

Honsie sat on her stool nearby, back to the sun, a little humped over her needlework. He watched her; stitch, draw; stitch, draw. Slowly the rent closed under her skilful fingers. Each time she drew, her moving forearm travelled above the rosary at her waist, concealing and then revealing it again. The cross round her neck hung forward on its chain, interfering with her sight of the work, and she put it gently inside her bodice.

"Honsie?"

"Aye, Master Tony."

"Thou told me thou wast born in London. Where is London? Is it far away? How didst thou come here?"

"London's far away indeed, Master Tony; more than a hundred miles. Yes, I was born there. My father was Raymond Godsell, who at one time was musician to the Queen of England, Queen Katherine. While I was still only a lass he brought us from London to Matlock. I took service here at Dethick, and when thou wast still nothing but a babe thy mother told me I was to become thy nurse."

"London," he said thoughtfully. "London. Yet that's not the furthest of all, is it? Honsie, what's above the sky? Where does it all end?"

"Oh, bless thee, Master Tony! Why God and His holy saints live up there, with Our Lord and His Blessed Mother." She crossed herself.

Anthony considered this, looking up once more at the immense blue curving from edge to edge of the horizons of oak trees.

"Don't they ever come down?"

"Now, Master Tony, thou knowest that Our Lord came down and took upon Hisself to live as a man. And His Holy Mother was the Blessed Virgin Mary, and they were both as real as ourselves. The sun shone and the rain fell for them as it doth for us."

"Aye, but that was long ago, Honsie. I meant, don't they sometimes come down now?"

"Ah!" Honsie paused, and put her stitching hand back in her lap, folding it over the other. "Master Tony, they're here with us now, in this meadow, only we can't see them."

"Why not?"

"Why, for that we're not good enough, that's why. We're sinners, Master Tony, and that's why our sinful eyes can't see Our Lord and His Mother present in this world. But we shall see them, in heaven, when He hath redeemed us."

The grasshopper leapt above his face from one side to the other and settled itself among the foxtails.

"But – but suppose someone *wasn't* a sinner, would they see – would they . . . ?"

A pause. "Well," replied Honsie deliberately, "I don't know
– that is, I never heared tell as Our Lord ever appeared to any
man or woman. But there's some – a very few – to whom His
Blessed Mother hath appeared."

"Are there? What is she like? Did they say?"

"Ah, forsooth, I never had talk with any such folk myself,
Master Tony. They were the great saints and all such people
as that, d'ye see?" She turned for a moment to gaze at the
sun, which was beginning to decline in the west. When she
turned her head away, she put her hand for a few moments
over her eyes. "Ah, but not – not always only such. There's
been common folk too, to whom Our Lady hath appeared."

"Hath she? Who?" No reply. "Prithee, Honsie, who?"

"When I were nothin' but a damsel," replied Honsie at
length, "living back home at Matlock, there were an old
body called Goody Arkwright, and she told me once that
she'd seen Our Lady quite close, sitting at the edge of the
wood where she were gatherin' sticks. She were that frit she
ran, she said."

"But what like was Our Lady? She told thee?"

"She said as she were very beautiful, a young lass, all in
blue, blue as the sky, she said, and a little shinin' only, like
the sun on dew, but not so much."

"Did she speak?"

"No, she were quite still; only her eyes, for all they were
that gentle, seemed to look right into her, Goody Arkwright
said, like as if she couldn't hide naught from her, and that's
why she were frit. She couldn't bide."

Anthony sat up and looked about a little fearfully.

"And thou sayest she's here now?"

His fear communicated itself to Honsie, who at once laid
aside her sewing, put her arms round him and changed her
work to that of reassurance.

"Now, Master Tony, there's no call for *thee* to be frit, and
thee an innocent child not even six. Our Lady's the most
beautiful and kindly soul in all the world. She loves thee.
She's thy true Queen, Tony, the Queen of Heaven, and thou
must love her and worship her all thy days, long or short. Thou

184

must keep her ever in thy mind and pray to her for mercy and forgiveness. *Thou* – thour't one day to be a great gentleman, thee knows, and lord to us all. So thou must be her true knight. A knight to guard thy folks and worship thy Lady, the loveliest lady o' the world."

For a moment Anthony saw himself mounted on Fleetfoot, his father's favourite, and wearing armour like the suits in the great hall. His forefather had been a knight of William the Conqueror; so Honsie had told him, and his mother, before she married his father, was already a great lady, Lady Darcy of Darcy. But his own Lady, the Queen of Heaven – a thought struck him.

"But Honsie . . . ?"

"Aye?"

"I thought the Queen – the Queen's in London – the Queen—"

"Her? Elizabeth?" Honsie bit her lower lip and for a moment clenched one fist. "*She's* no queen! The Protestant Jezebel! If some brave man would but . . ." She broke off suddenly. "Master Tony, I never said yon words to thee! I was but telling thee of the great Queen Mary, that thou must always serve." Her hand took up the beads. "Come; I'll teach thee again what thou'st heard, and thou'lt mark it more truly. Take the bead – aye, yon's reet, 'twixt finger and thumb. Now, Hail, Mary, full of grace –"

"Hail, Mary, full of grace –"

"The Lord is with thee –"

"The Lord is with thee –"

The grasshopper zipped on as they stood together.

"And at the hour of our death."

"And at the hour of our death."

"Good boy."

Picking up her stool with the needlework, she gave him her other hand and began to lead him back towards the great house, gently singing:

"Through bushes and through briars
I lately took my way.
It was all to hear the small birds sing
All in the month of May.
O I overheard my own true love,
O her voice it was so clear,
'Ah, how long have I been waiting
For the coming of my dear, my dear,
The coming of my dear.'"

His father's head moved wearily, restlessly, turning from side to side in the great bed. Anthony could see the sweat standing on his forehead and hear his slow, labouring breath. His mother, seated beside him on the drawn-up bench, held his hand, which trembled in her fingers. Although it was so big, the room smelt stale and frowsty, for all the windows were shut against the cool evening air. He could hear the rooks cawing as they circled in the sunset.

"Is the boy there?" whispered his father, gazing sightlessly as his head turned yet again.

"Aye, sweetheart," replied his mother. "He is beside thee."

"Father Martin?"

"I am here, sir. This is I that touch thee. Benedicite."

His father did not look particularly old, he thought. He knew many older men: Thomas the butler, and Master Hunter that

186

kept the river and . . . He brushed these thoughts away. He knew that this was a solemn and grave time. For many days they had not let him see his father, but now he had been sent for. The mere sight of his father was enough to daunt any nine-year-old. One does not need experience to recognise the desperately ill.

"Are the girls here?"

"No, sir. Dost thou wish for them?"

"Nay."

There was silence, broken only by the rooks. Then his father's hand came slowly from the bed, groping, fingers crook't near his face. His mother put his hand into the weak grasp. It felt smooth, clean and hot.

"Anthony?"

"Yes, sir."

"Th'art my heir. Dost thou know what that means?"

"Yes, sir. I am to – to follow thee as lord of Dethick. The – the land and the people—"

"Under God, boy. Under God and Our Blessed Lord. Thou must – aah!" He broke off, sighing painfully. After a pause, he said weakly, "Speak for me, Martin. Tell the boy."

Father Martin, black-gowned and hawk-like, bent his head and spoke softly between his father's ear and Anthony's own.

"Thy father willeth that thou shouldst always rule Dethick in humility to God's holy will. What the holy Church requireth of thee, that thou must obey in all humility." He fell silent.

"Rigour," whispered his father.

"Yet thou must not shrink also from the strictness and firmness shown by Our Lord's holy example. A lord must know how to be firm in rule – even severe – as well as to show mercy."

Anthony took this in half-comprehendingly. He felt a vague, crushing weight of unspecific responsibility.

"Danger, danger," panted his father, so low that the word could scarcely be heard.

"The Church?"

His father gave the ghost of a nod.

"Thy father tells thee that the holy Church is in great danger from wicked men, traitors who deny the Lord Christ and Our

Lady. Unless thou dost guard Dethick, with thy very life if need be, they will come and destroy it – destroy God's holy Church here. Dost thou understand?"

"Aye."

"Promise—"

"Thou must promise thy father to take the shield of faith, and the sword of the Spirit, which is the Word of God."

"I promise," whispered Anthony. Pressed in as he was among the adults, the tension in the close room became unbearable. He began to cry, though almost soundlessly, trembling, drawing breath only to sob.

"Warrior," uttered his father.

"A warrior for Christ, if need be." Father Martin put a kindly hand on his shoulder. "Like the earls of the North. The child can understand no more, sir, for the present. Be thou at peace. Be assured that I myself will explain all to him, as need shall be."

"Rest, dear heart," said his mother. "I will take Anthony now. He is a good boy. He will not fail thee, even to extremity. Wilt thou?"

"Nay, madam."

Still weeping, he was led from the room. As they approached the door, it was opened from outside by Honsie. Yet she did not come in. The person who came in was Uncle Philip – Sir Philip Draycot, his father's great friend. As he entered he raised his eyebrows to Lady Babington, who held his gaze and very slightly shook her head.

The fire burned bright and clear, and every now and then a wood-knot exploded like a shot, for it was mostly pine and fir, together with the remains of an old apple-tree. Outside, the snow lay deep, a heavy, unseen presence stretching far and wide over the empty moor. The candles shone warm, each with its coloured nimbus, their reflections gleaming dully from the surface of the heavy table. The edges of the room lay in shadow, so that from the candle-lit circle Davy and Will, the servants, were only half-visible where they stood in attendance, as close to the fire as might be thought consistent with respectful servility. On one side of the room a cold draught continually stirred the arras. Anthony fidgeted with the nutcrackers lying before him on the table and wondered whether to crack another nut. They had given him half a glass of port, very full and round on the palate, and he felt his head swimming – though not more, to be sure, than a gentleman's should after dinner.

He glanced respectfully round at his companions. They were certainly a group to command deference from any devout, well-brought-up fourteen-year-old. At the end of the table, his back to the fire, sat Anthony's guardian, Uncle Philip: Sir Philip Draycot, of Leigh at Draycot-in-the-Moor, who had with kindness and understanding borne a sure hand in his upbringing and education since his father's death five years before. On his right sat his wife, Pauline, Lady Draycot, in whom Anthony delighted because of her continual good spirits and merriment. She would often tease him and positively enjoyed being teased back. Between her and himself sat Thomas, Lord Paget, a grave, furrow-browed but kindly man whose principal problem, as far as Anthony could perceive, seemed to be his wife, Nazareth, who appeared to be for ever scolding him. However, she had not joined him on this present visit to Leigh.

On Uncle Philip's left sat the dark young priest – not yet thirty, Anthony guessed – a stranger whom he had never seen before tonight and who had been introduced to him as Father James Killearn. During dinner the Father had been reserved, drinking little and, although plainly listening alertly to the conversation, not saying a great deal save to assent or corroborate. He seemed not only watchful but also in some way separate – not an uneasy guest, certainly, but nevertheless like someone unfamiliar, someone who had come from outside their circle. Anthony, though used enough to priests, could not help wondering exactly where he fitted into their company. There was an otherness about him which was puzzling.

Next to the priest sat Margery Draycot – dear, dear Margery – bright-haired, lustrous, a year older than himself and in his eyes a woman, her pretty grey and scarlet gown showing off a figure already adult. Indeed, why should not a fifteen-year-old marry? Many did. So perhaps, if just a few years could go by – to kiss her, to hold her in his arms – Anthony turned his thoughts aside as he had been taught.

Sir Philip was speaking. "The earls – the earls themselves, Father, as no doubt thou know'st, bide safe in Scotland. Yet they cost us eight hundred good Catholic lives by rope and axe, and gained no more than poor Aske's Pilgrimage of Grace forty years ago."

Father Killearn nodded, his manner implying understanding and sympathy.

"Exile, confiscation; and that Puritan villain Huntingdon set over the Queen's Council of the North. 'Tis the end of the good old North as we've known it."

"They'll fill in Trent before they're done," said Lord Paget.

"Hath Master Foljambe ever spoken to thee of the earls, Tony?" asked Sir Philip.

Henry Foljambe had married Anthony's mother not long after his father's death. He and Anthony got on well together.

"Aye, sir, often. He would have been with them but for his disability." (Master Foljambe was somewhat lame – the effect of a hunting fall.)

"There hath been no blow struck for the Church since," said Sir Philip. "No blow worth the name; and none involving the Catholic people of the land."

"But the reason for that is not far to seek," replied Lord Paget, glancing across at the priest. "We have received no help at all, Father, either from His Holiness or from King Philip of Spain. They have stood by with idle hands while the Queen, with her cunning policy of live and let live, hath let folk drift away from the true discipline of Holy Church."

"The Bull," murmured Father James with the mildest possible note of protest in his voice.

"The Bull," rejoined Sir Philip, "was ill-judged and hath done us naught but harm, Father."

"How so, sir?"

"His Holiness, I am told, is a fine man – a Dominican, ascetic and scholarly, yet neither politic nor cunning in the ways of the world. What he saw was simply that the Queen of England was a heretic: so she must be excommunicated and there an end. He did not think first to consult with the King of Spain, nor with the Emperor. He simply issued the Bull. And when was that, Tony?"

"Nearly six years ago now, sir," answered Anthony, like a good boy questioned in class. "The year before my father's death."

"Aye,'twas so. So we have a Bull which no foreign power is able to push home on behalf of the Church. It makes things worse than before. For with the Bull, an English Catholic is forced to choose between his allegiance to the Queen and his allegiance to Holy Church. I am no enemy to the Queen, heretic though she be. I have been a loyal English subject ever since Her Majesty's accession. Yet what is my case now, since His Holiness hath signed and sealed the Bull? 'Tis forced upon me: my duty to the Pope is to overthrow the Queen and thus to plunge the realm in blood. I cannot do it, yet that I cannot hath been placed upon my conscience as disobedience."

Father James cleared his throat. "There have been attempts. The Spanish ambassador—"

"The Spanish ambassador was also more harm than good," said Lord Paget. "Plotting with some Italian fellow – what was his name, Ridolfi? – fellow no one's ever heard of – and poor old Norfolk falls for the bait and gets his head cut off. Mind you, he always was a bit of a fool—"

"Anthony," said Sir Philip.

"Sir?"

"Stand him up on the bench," cried Lady Draycot. "Make him answer like a good sprack scholar. Rise up, Sir Anthony, thou outlandish knight, and do battle. Fill his glass."

"And I will deliver to thee the victor's crown, madam," answered Anthony, standing on the bench, glass in hand, and striking an attitude as Margery passed him the decanter across the table.

"Who is the rightful Queen of England?"

"Mary Stuart, sir."

191

"And where lieth she?"

"Sir, at Sheffield, in durance."

"Make him sing for us!" cried Lady Draycot. "Now that he hath the eminence, he shall sing. Sing, Anthony."

Anthony thought quickly. He was an intelligent boy with an excellent social sense of place, time and occasion and his vanity was touched. This was a chance to show off. But it must be nothing serious, nor yet nothing foolish; something short, appropriate to the snowy time and within his voice's compass. After a few moments' reflection, he began with no least trace of self-consciousness.

"There was a star in David's land,
In Beth'lem did appear:
And in King Herod's chamber
It shone both bright and clear.

"The Wise Men soon espiéd it
And told the king on high
That a princely babe was born that night
No king should e'er destroy.

"'If this be the truth,' King Herod he said,
'That thou hast told to me,
Then the roasted cock that lies in the dish
Shall crow full fences three.'

"O the cock soon thrustened and feathered well
By the might of God's own hand:
And then it crowed full fences three
In the dish where it did stand."

He sat down flushed, amid polite applause and a cock-crow from Margery, and took another mouthful of port.

"Wouldst thou fight for Queen Mary, Tony?"

"Aye, madam, and give her my hand to the throne."

Sir Philip gestured. "Enough, enough. We are no rebels nor plotters here. We do but know where allegiance lies. Yet, Tony, my boy, thou art to learn that the Pope hath at last done something for our comfort. No plotting, nor force of arms, yet a great matter for the solace of all good men of Holy Church. I trust it will speed most gradely."

"Indeed, sir?"

"Who is this?" asked Sir Philip, nodding towards the priest.

"Father Killearn, as thou didst tell me, sir."

"Aye, and whence comes he?"

"I cannot tell."

"Hast thou ever heard of Father William Allen?"

"Nay, sir."

"Father Allen is the head of a college at Rheims, in the Flemish Lowlands, for the training of priests to come to England to maintain the faith. There is no lack of priests offering service. Now the first of them are reaching us. Father Killearn is one such. He reached Leigh this afternoon from Flanders. We have never received a more welcome guest." He bowed towards the priest, who smiled. "He is Christ's own emissary, Tony."

"I wot well, sir."

"He will say Mass for us tonight. Thou, Davy, hast heard what I have been saying?"

"Aye, sir. May God bless thee, Father."

"Get thee gone, Davy. Tell all the servants. In half an hour, in the little refectory."

After Mass, still flushed with the port, Anthony felt a glow of happiness and warmth. Christ – the body and blood of Christ – was present in his own body. That flesh which had suffered on the cross and risen from the dead on Easter morning was actually within him, sanctifying and purifying every part. He was one with Christ, his sins forgiven, his future bright before him. He had never felt so happy in his life.

They were all making ready for bed. As Davy lit the candles in their sticks Margery was taking them from him and handing them to her parents and the guests. Anthony came last in order, of course, and the others were mostly turning away. Margery, as she gave him his candle, looked him full in the eyes, laughing with sheer joy, as he did himself in the circle of light surrounding them together.

One of Honsie's songs came into his mind. Where had she got it? From a wandering sailor out of the north, she'd told him. He liked the tune. He sang:

"Did she light thee up to bed, Billy Boy, Billy Boy?
Did she light thee up to bed, my Billy Boy?
Yes, she light me up to bed
With the bowing of her head,
And me Nancy kittle me fancy O me charming Billy Boy."

All the while she held his eyes, smiling. As he ceased she bent forward, kissed him quick and dry on the lips and was gone. He prayed silently, "Lord Christ, impute no sin to me, I pray. I love her and so by Thy grace will prove."

They seemed to stretch away in all directions as far as he could see, the level banks like lawns above the glassy, lolling tide. Somewhere out to sea was lying a great fleet. And all around, coming and going over the grass, were people – men and women, courtiers, priests, rough fellows, fine ladies jewelled and gowned – who nodded briefly to him, hurrying past on their own affairs. At whiles he tried to stop one of them, to speak and be spoken to: but they hastened by with "So please thee" or "There is occasion". Above all things he felt he wanted to impress them, to gain their concerted attention, to see them gathering about him with admiration and recognition. Deliberately he made his way among them, looking about him for any who might become friends, who might listen to what he knew he had to say and do. For he had something to achieve, something of the greatest importance. Yet it remained vague, a kind of shadowy weight that must be uttered and not be uttered, a treasure that he carried, money to spend that must not be spent except upon . . . The fleet was beginning to stand in to land and he walked deliberately towards it over the grass, among the busy, occupied people. A little way off, across the smooth field, he could see the lip of an edge, a vertical bank a few feet deep, forming a dry, grassy ditch that divided his field from the next. He came to the rim and looked down. In the grass, face downward, was lying the body of a woman, middle-aged, richly dressed and ornamented. She had plainly been stabbed through and through. Blood was everywhere – on her clothes, her hands, on the grass. And as he stood, horrified, the blood seemed to gather itself together and rise up to cover and smother him.

He lay struggling, then woke to find Honsie shaking him. "Master Tony! Master Tony! Come, wake up, precious boy, and get thyself fettled! Master Foljambe bids thee come to the library straight. There's tidings."

"Honsie, what tidings?"

Honsie bent towards him confidentially.

"I spoke with the messenger in the kitchen. He's the Earl of Shrewsbury's man, come from Sheffield. He brought a letter for Master Foljambe. That's all I know, Master Tony."

In less than fifteen minutes Anthony entered the library, where his mother was sitting together with her husband. He bowed and stood waiting until Master Foljambe, smiling, looked up at him over the letter he held in his hand.

"I had spoken for thee already, Tony, yet I said nothing to thee, for I did not know how the matter might speed. Now we know. Thy fortunes are good, and thou mayest well be glad at this news. Th'art to be page to Lord Shrewsbury in the household of Queen Mary at Sheffield Castle. 'Tis more than likely thou'lt find thyself page to Her Majesty, if thou makest thyself apt to learn their ways and show thyself the good lad thou art."

"To – to the queen, sir?" stammered Anthony. "I – I had not looked for it."

"Then thou mayest look for it presently." Anthony glanced across at his mother, who was clearly delighted. "Thou must be gone today, Tony. 'Tis not twenty-five miles and Morris will ride with thee. Thou canst take Linnet. Morris is saddling now. Tell Honsie to help thee pack forthwith."

"I will see to it myself," said Lady Foljambe. "Come, be well content, Tony. 'Tis a great—"

"Madam, I protest I am entirely content. Surprise—"

"Bless thy five wits! Lord Shrewsbury is well apt to be a good master. He hath—"

"Pray, madam, what like is the earl?"

"He will be, I suppose, now some fifty years old. He hath been earl these twenty years, and hath been our lord lieutenant almost as long."

"Married to Bess of Hardwick," laughed his stepfather. "That takes a strong man, no danger. I wish him joy of *her*."

"He hath been Queen Mary's gaoler these ten years about. He is a good, kindly man and I believe a true Catholic at heart, though he keeps the windy side of the law. He treats the Queen of Scots as well as he's able. Th'art to take all thine own linen, Tony, bed-sheets too, and plenty. The earl is well known to be a particular man as to expenses and no doubt the queen's housekeeper will be particular too. Remember always that the family honour lieth with thee, as well as thine own advancement."

Once he had made himself known to the guards and ridden through the gates, the lady who actually received Anthony at Sheffield Castle was Mary Seton, the only one of the queen's four Marys to have followed her into captivity: a plain, severe-seeming lady perhaps approaching forty, who made him somewhat coldly welcome, gave him cake and wine and, after sending her maid to learn whether it would be convenient, conducted him to the Earl of Shrewbury in his closet. His lordship was seated at a long table, pen in hand and abacus beside him, evidently casting up accounts. He appeared worried and preoccupied, yet he broke off, smiling, to speak kindly to Anthony, enquire after his mother and Master Foljambe, and tell him he was sure he would do very well. He desired him, he said, to attend upon the queen and do all that might be wished by herself and her ladies. She had not been well, despite the fine summer weather, and relied much on Dr Beaton, whom he, Anthony, could do a great deal to help. The housekeeper would show him his room. He was very glad to welcome him among them. Did he understand figures? he asked wryly and in jest: and when Anthony replied not very well, my lord, said that that was for the best, for they were contrary things which gave a man no peace.

It was early evening when Mary Seton conducted him down several long corridors and up a staircase to the rooms of the queen. As he followed her into the chamber, warm and bright in the declining sunlight from the western windows, he saw a group of three or four ladies sitting at the embroidery of a great cloth or quilt, all in brilliant colours, their work-boxes and materials strewn around them. The lady facing him, handsome yet drawn and pale, was wearing on her somewhat faded auburn hair a white coif, and starched ruff at her throat. Her gown was black. Although he had never seen a picture of the Queen of Scots, he knew at once that this could only be she. As he unbonneted and went down on one knee she looked keenly at him from heavy-lidded, dark eyes above a straight, intelligent nose and beautiful lips. The oval of her face seemed to him to display a deep sense of majesty, of tension and a kind of eager frailty and volatility which both aroused and attracted him. Majesty he had expected, but not this beauty. He had expected to feel abased before his queen. Instead, he felt a curious identity with her, and excitement. Whatever the queen might be, she was not going to be dull.

"Ye're Anthony Babington?"

"Aye, your Majesty."

She gave him her hand. "Ye're no' ower old to be a page?"

197

"I'm fifteen, your Majesty." Something in her manner made him add, "I don't feel too old. I feel in fine fettle."

She laughed. "God give ye good hap. *Vous parlez français?*"

"*Ah, non, altesse.*" He racked his memory. "*A peine. J'ai appris un peu d'un prêtre chez nous.*"

"*D'un prêtre? Bien alors. Mais vous n'avez jamais demeuré en France?*"

"*Non, altesse.*"

She laughed again. "'Tis no ma'er." She elided the t's. "Jane." She turned to the lady seated beside her. "Take the wee lad and show him some useful things to be doing. Och!" and she put her left hand to her right shoulder. "*Comme ça fait mal aujourd'hui.*"

As the weeks went by, and Anthony learned his work and became familiar with the people, the household and its ways, he became keenly aware of its strange nature. This consisted in an extraordinary atmosphere of transience and impermanence, a kind of nullity which seemed to characterise the household and everyone in it. The earl, in whose presence Anthony necessarily spent much time, seemed forever fretting over accounts – either those of the household or of his own estates, the troubles of which appeared to be never-ending. At length Anthony, who was shrewd for his age, came to the conclusion that the matter lay largely in his master's own character and temperament: nothing was ever going to put his affairs entirely straight; it was not in his nature. Before things could go right, something had first to be wrong. He received a flow of letters from the Privy Council and the Queen in London, but they seemed to afford him little reassurance. He was always working for change and no change brought peace.

As for the Queen of Scots, her beautiful presence was like nothing so much as one of those gentle April afternoons which cannot make up its mind whether to rain or shine. It was as though there were about her a continual light pattering. She was enchanting in her gracious kindness to everyone – even the meanest servants, who were devoted to her – yet elusive as a will o' the wisp in her restless, mercurial inconsistency. She was intent, she was indolent. She was resolved, she was undecided. She had a headache, had never felt better; she was sad, she was merry; she wished for this or that, she no longer needed it; she had forgot what it was that she had asked Anthony to do. Most of all, he had the feeling that she did not think of her life at Sheffield (or at Buxton, or at Wingfield, for they were continually moving from one place to another; boot-less activity which seemed all in accordance) as being her real life at all. She was like someone waiting for a ferry or a change of horses: she appeared for ever kicking her heels, unable to settle seriously to anything, 'passing time on', as Honsie would have said. Although she never lost her queenly self-possession, her charm and her natural, unforced composure, Anthony, as he got to know her, felt her to be ceaselessly fretting. 'Ah, if 'twould but rain,' she would say of a clear sky. And when it rained, 'Ah, if 'twould but cease this everlasting rain.' She was waiting for something to happen – whatever it might be – and until it did she could not be at peace.

"*Allons, allons gai, gaiement, ma mignonne,*
Allons, allons gai, gaiement, vous et moi, vous et moi.
Et j'y ferai un chapelet,
Pour ma mignonne et pour moi.
Gaiement, ma mignonne,
Allons, allons gai, gaiement, vous et moi."

The queen sighed, laid down her lute and again took up her needle, threaded with crimson. They were seated in the embrasure of her chamber, looking out over the sparse garden, the walls, the Loxley stream outside and the dry, hot moor beyond. All the windows stood wide in the heat and enervating sunlight. A faint breeze carried into the room the scent of pinks and stocks.

"Ah, mon Dieu!" said the queen. "Why can we not ride, and ride and ride?" She gestured towards the moor. "Midnight would have been ower yon top – Ye mind Midnight, Mary?"

"Well, madam."

"Did ye carry my message to the earl, Tony?"

"Aye, madam."

"And what said he?"

"He said he would dwell on it, madam."

"Aye, dwell and dwell and here we dwell. Take the lute, Tony. Some long tale to pass the time. What didst thou tell me thy nurse was called?"

"Honsie, madam. Her father was minstrel to Queen Katherine."

He took up the lute, fingered the strings and ran his thumb over a chord.

> "An outlandish knight from the north land came,
> And he came wooing of me;
> And he told me he'd take me to that northern land,
> And there he would marry me."

Screaming, the swifts darted high above the roofs. All other birds were silent in the heat, until from somewhere beyond sounded the 'whaup, whaup' of a swan's wings. They came closer and then faded in the distance.

> "He says, 'Unlight, my little Polly,
> Unlight, unlight' cries he,
> 'For six pretty maids have I drownèd here
> And thou the seventh shall be.'"

When he came to the parrot, he imitated its harsh, croaking voice. He did it well, and even Mary Seton was drawn to laugh.

"– To drive that old puss away."

He also laid down the lute and sat unregarding, his hands in his lap.

"Ye sing juist fine," said the queen. "Och, the heat! If I were only a witch, I'd make a charm for a cool rain. Come, Tony, sing again. No tale the noo. Sing of lads and lasses."

Tony paused a while, strumming, and thinking of Honsie sitting by his bed in the candlelight.

"Come all you tender girls
That flourish in your prime,
I bid you beware, keep your garden fair,
Let no man steal your thyme,
Let no man steal your thyme.

"I had a sprig of thyme,
It flourished night and day,
Till at length there came a false young man
And stole my thyme away.
And stole my thyme away.

"And now my thyme is gone,
And I can plant no new,
And every place where my thyme did grow
Is sad o'er-run with rue.
Is sad o'er-run with rue.

"O rue it is—"

201

"Och, stint ye, Tony!" cried the queen, spreading wide her beautiful, tapering hands. "D'ye mean to make me greet? Now my thyme is gone . . ." She broke off, then stood up and took one of his hands between both her own. "And yet my people are about me on every side. What would ye do for me, Tony, ye braw lad? Would ye fight for your Queen? Would ye hale her oot o' here if'n ye could?"

"Madam, if I live I will, and my troth on it."

"Ye're a grand wee fella. Ah, my head!" She rested her face in her hands. "Tony, will ye gang to the doctor and ask will he give ye some of the medicine for my headache?"

"Aye, madam." He took his cap and hastened across the sun-bright chamber to the door.

Anthony was barely eighteen when he married Margery Draycot. The betrothal – a short one – and wedding went as smoothly as could be imagined, for both families were favourably disposed. Anthony, for his part, felt that he was not only achieving what he had longed for during the past four years and more, but also that he was carrying out the intention for him of the Blessed Virgin Mary. In his prayers he felt the full tide of her approval and the happiest sense of fulfilling the will of God, both for himself and for Margery.

Margery was more than happy to find herself mistress of Dethick and, at nineteen, willing enough to defer to and take advice from Lady Foljambe, who in turn was well pleased to receive as a protégée this daughter of their dear friend, Sir Philip.

It was not long before Margery knew herself to be pregnant – sure proof to Anthony (if any were needed) of the blessedness of their union. Their joy was shared throughout the Babington household; but by none more deeply than Honsie.

Meanwhile, Anthony began the serious business of taking over the administration of the wide and prosperous Babington estates. The Babington family had been settled in Derbyshire since the eleventh century: but by the marriage, early in the fifteenth century, of Thomas Babington, fifth in descent, with

the heiress of Robert Dethick, of Dethick, the main branch
had become the principal family and largest landowner in
the county. Since then they had, by further marriages with
neighbouring heiresses, acquired additional property in the
adjoining counties. The Babington family were of great local
influence and importance. Anthony, as Honsie had told him
in the meadow, was called upon to become a gentleman of
standing and lord of all these estates. Although he was not of
age and therefore had not yet gained autonomous power over
his fortune, nevertheless with the approval of his stepfather
and Sir Philip he began to make his own decisions about
rents, employment and expenditure on upkeep. Assiduous to
a fault, like many young people in authority, he acquired the
reputation of a hard landlord, albeit a conscientious one.

When their daughter was born without trouble, a strong and
healthy baby, he and Margery were as delighted as any young
couple could be. Anthony devoted time to the baby, and would
often carry her with him about the house and in the grounds. He
even carried her once or twice on a quiet, slow-pacing horse,
but desisted in the face of Margery's anxiety.

The family, like that of Sir Philip, were on the county
list of recusants. The appointed fines for recusancy were
sometimes paid and sometimes not. This was the North,
where enforcement tended to be lax, and in any case it
was an embarrassing task to dun so exalted a family as the
Babingtons – a task which tended to get overlooked.

One soft May night of full moon, with a tawny owl calling
and a nightjar bubbling in the trees not far away, Anthony and
Margery were lying contentedly in bed together, after making
love. Neither yet felt disposed to sleep, and Anthony was
speaking of a stallion which he meant to buy, for stud, from
an acquaintance in Matlock. After a while, sensing Margery to
be a little preoccupied, he fell silent, turning on his side and
holding her hand with a feeling of comfort and satisfaction.

"Tony?" she said after a little.

"Mm."

"The faith. I have been thinking about the faith."

"Why curious about the faith? Is't not the very air we breathe?"

"Aye, we. But in this realm of England, Tony, and at the Court in London, thou knowest – ah, the very Queen's a heretic and her councillors too, and from this stems the heresy of the whole land."

"What of it? Our faith's no secret here. We stand well and we're no partners in the Queen's sin."

"Are we not, while we do nothing to right the wrong?"

"How should we right it? I am not the king."

"Yet at Court there is no lack of young Catholic gentlemen. If thou wert to join them, my Tony – a gentleman of thine ability and resources – what might not be accomplished?"

"Art thou counselling me to conspire in treason against the Queen?"

"Nay, I said naught of treason. I know not what I'm counselling. But Tony, thou shouldst know these men; they shouldst be thy friends. Thy star shines wider than Dethick and thy lands, broad though they are. There are Catholic gentlemen at Court: thou shouldst be among them. The outcome will declare itself, by God's grace."

"And thou?"

"I am ready to come with thee. Honsie will care for the babe, now she is weaned. Anthony, I that love thee, I long to see thee take thy true place in the world, a place of consequence and a place of hope for the true Church."

"Let me dwell on it, sweeting. Trust me, I'll not leave it out of mind."

Nor did he. A few weeks later, after much serious talk with Henry Foljambe and Sir Philip Draycot, Anthony and Margery set out for London. His initial intention was to study law, and at the age of nineteen he entered as a student at Lincoln's Inn.

Margery was soon proved right. Although Anthony grew tired of the law and fell away from Lincoln's Inn, it took him but a short time to build a full circle of acquaintance at Court. He was presented to the Queen, who spoke to him graciously, and told him she was glad to have heard well of him from the Earl of Shrewsbury. He leased a fine house at Deptford, whence it was an easy journey to Greenwich, and he also had other lodgings at Herne's Rents in Holborn, for ready access to

Whitehall. He entertained generously and became on friendly terms with many young gentlemen. Some of these were openly recusants, despite the growing suspicion and dislike in which Catholics were coming to be held; others conformed outwardly to the law concerning the Protestant church, but made no secret – among friends, at all events – of their Catholic sympathies.

It was in this company that he grew acquainted with Chidiock Tichborne, who was to become his closest friend and sympathiser. The Tichbornes were a Hampshire family of weight and standing. Though not so wealthy and illustrious as the Babingtons, they traced their descent from the twelfth-century court of Henry II, and were ardent Roman Catholics, making no secret of it.

Chidiock was a little under average height, wiry and dark-avised, thoughtful, with a swift-moving eagerness and ready wit which made his company the most stimulating and enjoyable Anthony had ever known. They would often sup together, sometimes playing and singing and at other whiles becoming engrossed in talk about the plight of the true Church and the need to reclaim England for the faith before it might be too late. It was at Chidiock's comfortable lodgings in Spitalfields that Anthony and Margery first heard motets and were transported by the inspired sorrow of Morley and Byrd. Chidiock himself was an accomplished musician. Often, at his suppers or at Anthony's, each guest in turn would be called upon to play or sing, with a frolicsome forfeit for anyone who defaulted.

Chidiock (as Anthony had not as yet) had travelled in France, whence he had returned with not a few holy relics and told Anthony of the Queen of Scots' supporters in Paris: Thomas Morgan, who had once been Lord Shrewsbury's secretary, and Charles Paget, the brother of Sir Philip Draycot's friend, Lord Paget of Staffordshire. "These are men thou shouldst know, Anthony," Chidiock would say. "They are in Queen Mary's confidence, and she sets store by them. Thou shouldst travel to Paris and talk with them."

"To what end?"

"To a glorious end," replied Chidiock. "But Anthony, it cannot be accomplished without the support of the King of Spain. That ought to be the purpose of any negotiation."

"Treason?"

Chidiock shrugged. "Where lies our true allegiance?"

"To the Queen."

"To which queen, Tony?"

Tony paused. "To Queen Mary."

"And how dost thou judge of her? Thou hast served her in person, hast thou not?"

"Aye. She is a most royal and sorrowful lady; a noble, gracious, Catholic queen imprisoned in a Protestant tower."

"Who holds her?"

"Queen Elizabeth. Thou wot'st well."

"Neither queen," said Chidiock, "is a stranger to imprisonment."

"But if the King of Spain were to land an army," said Anthony, "the first thing Queen Elizabeth would do would be to hale Queen Mary away to some unknown, secret dungeon – aye, and to kill her – if it came to killing."

"I have good horses, Tony, and I can ride fast. So canst thou. Thou hast loyal men, hast thou not, living not thirty miles from Sheffield? Might one not hope to outride the queen's men?"

Tony laughed. "My old nurse would say, 'Think on, lad.' I will, Chidiock. I'll think on."

They were going by water from Deptford to Greenwich; a crowd of gay young Catholic gentlemen, most with their girls, all looking to the wealthy, debonair Anthony as the head of their circle. It was early afternoon. They had eaten and drunk and were lying content in the June sunshine, the colours of their hats, doublets and hose showing up in rainbow brilliance against the grey, surrounding river.

Margery sat regally at the stern, in talk with Charles Tilney, a young man from Suffolk who was a gentleman pensioner of Queen Elizabeth. Arundel, Chidiock's girl, was lying enfolded in his right arm, her head on his shoulder. When Anthony tossed him the lute and told him to sing, he kissed her quickly on the lips and sat up, his back to a thwart.

The Outlandish Knight

"One morning in the month of May, down by a rolling river,
A jolly sailor he did stray, and there beheld a lover.
She carelessly along did stray, a-viewing of the daisies gay.
She sweetly sang her roundelay, just as the tide was flowing.

"Her dress it was as white as milk, and jewels did adorn her skin:
It was as soft as any silk, most like a lady of high kin.
Her cheeks were red, her eyes were brown, her hair in
    ringlets hanging down,
Her lovely brow without a frown, just as the tide was flowing.

"I made a bow and said: 'Fair maid, how camest thou here
    so early?
My heart by thee it is betrayed, and I could love thee dearly.
I am a sailor come from sea, if thou'lt accept my company
To walk and see the fishes play, just as the tide's a-flowing.'"

Anthony burst out laughing. "To be sure, I know what will
come to pass!"

"Nay, then, don't tell us, wilt thou?" replied Charles. "Sure
we should never guess it!"

"O it's there we walked and there we talked as we went down
    together;
The little lambs did skip and play, and pleasant was the weather.
So being fain we both sat down beneath a bough so fair
    hung down,
And what was done shall ne'er be known, just as the tide was
    flowing.

207

"Says she, 'My love, all's spent: no more: you've put me
    to purgation.
My jolly sailor I adore, sure he's my consolation.'
Says I, 'Dear heart, I've paid thee well, there's not one penny
    owing still
We'll stay to watch the waters rill, all as the tide's
    a-flowing.'"

"Fie!" cried Arundel, trying not to laugh, snatching the lute
and making a show of belabouring Chidiock with it. She turned
to Harriet Taylor, seated on the thwart nearby. "To think we
keep company with such rogues. He must do penance! Kneel,
Chidiock! Hold thy peace, thou knave . . ."

She gave him a blow with a cushion and each of the other
girls, as they took up the catch, did the same. Chidiock, having
graciously received his punishment, got up and clambered aft
to Anthony. He spoke quietly.

"Tony, I'll seek thee out this evening. There's news. News
of great import. Nay!" Seeing Anthony about to speak, he held
up his hand. "Not a word now. This evening, before supper,
and where we can be privy."

They were strolling in the garden, beside the borders bright
with honeysuckle, stocks, pansies, roses and marigolds. The
moths and bats were flitting and beyond the lawns the Thames
shone dully in the gathering dusk as the tide made to the
full.

Chidiock stooped, plucked a marigold and tucked it in
his ruff.

"The news is of great consequence to us all, Tony. To all
of the true faith."

Anthony said nothing, waiting.

"Hast thou heard of one Edmund Campion?"

"Aye: he was a great scholar of Oxford, was he not, but left
it because he would not abjure the faith? But that must have
been ten years ago. Is he not flown to Europe?"

"Thou knowest of the Society of Jesus?"

208

"Ignatius Loyola? The Jesuits?"

"The same. Father Campion has become a Jesuit. He and another, Father Parsons, have come secretly to England to work for the true faith. Father Campion was arrested at Dover, but the mayor released him and he is come to London. There is one George Gilbert here, who has formed an association among us to help the Jesuits. Tony, I have spoken with Gilbert, and he is to arrange for thee and me – all of us – to meet Father Campion and talk with him."

"Doth the Pope know of the Fathers' mission?"

"Aye doth he. He hath sent a message blessing the project and bestowing God's benediction upon the association. Thou'lt make one?"

"Chidiock, thou couldst not have brought me more welcome news, nor pressed me to any endeavour I would more willingly embrace. When are we to meet?"

Father Edmund Campion, smiling and gracious, clad as a priest of the Society of Jesus, sat with a glass of Anthony's best claret before him and benignly surveyed the two rows of eager young men looking towards him from either side of the table. He was some forty years of age, dark haired, with a lean, ascetic face and the look of man of scholarship. He had been speaking to them of his experiences at Douai, at Rome and lastly at Prague, where he had passed his novitiate and been ordained priest; and of how he had become a Jesuit. He had told them that he and Father Parsons were the first two Jesuits to be chosen to come to England. Now he invited them to question him.

"What are thy purposes, Father?" asked Anthony.

"To hear confessions and minister the sacraments to the faithful, as any priest must. Yet besides this, to rally and encourage those who have departed from the faith through persecution or through the constraints put upon the true Church by the English Government. Those who have lapsed are lost sheep: they must be sought and reconverted."

"But dost thou understand, Father," said Tilney, "that to have to do with such men must needs place thee in direst danger? Not all can be trusted."

"That is as may be, my son, and as God may dispose. My tasks are in no wise of a politic kind and I am devising nothing against the Queen. I am a priest and nothing else."

"Aye, *we* know that well enough, Father," said Chidiock. "Yet under the Act passed by Parliament nine years ago, it is treason to introduce or publish papal bulls, and they will say that thou art the emissary of the Pope."

"I am."

"And therefore, they will say, a traitor. Three years ago Father Cuthbert Mayne was put to death on no other grounds but those."

"We of the Society know this, my son. We are ready as Our Lord was ready. Yet we shall travel in disguise and dwell with friends, men of the faith prepared to receive and hide us. How long we last must be as God wills."

"I am lord of Dethick in Derbyshire," said Anthony. "Thou wilt be welcome there, Father, and safe in thy ministrations for many miles around. My people are all loyal to the faith."

"Thanks, my son. Now let us celebrate Mass and pray for God's blessing on thine association."

"And let us solemnly swear," said Chidiock, "to devote ourselves, our persons, abilities and wealth, to the conversion of all heretics in the realm."

Sir Francis Walsingham looked up at William Cecil, Lord Burleigh, across the piles of letters and papers stacked on his desk.

"This man Mendoza is no more to be trusted than was De Spes. To call either of them ambassadors of Spain is playing with words. De Spes was an enemy agent of Philip and so is Mendoza."

"Mendoza is worse, if anything," replied Burleigh, "for he is not only an agent of the King of Spain, but in league with the De Guises and for that matter with every papist in the world. He must have known of these Jesuits, yet he said nothing to us."

"Our country is like a sheep among wolves. Scotland is not

to be trusted. All that saves us from them is the squabbling and murdering of their nobles against one another. And if we turn our backs and look the other way, there lie France and Spain. We can only thank God for King William in the Netherlands."

"Aye, but who is it that doth lie at the very heart of all this trouble?"

"The Queen of Scots. While she lives she will be at the heart of one evil project after another. There will be endless Ridolfis. No doubt there is some plot brewing at this very moment."

Walsingham paused, then said with determination, "She must die."

"Aye, and so say we all, and so saith Parliament. Yet thou knowest that our Queen will not suffer it."

"Yet if Mary were to be detected in some plot; if proofs – written proofs – were evident and the Queen could not gainsay them—"

"Even then—"

"The Queen of Scots must be tricked – to use no choicer word – into compassing her own downfall. A plot must be contrived—"

"I would have thought there was barely need: they are two a penny."

"—must be contrived to which she gives her assent in writing."

"You will need agents."

"I have one at least. Solomon Aldred is a Catholic living in Rome. He is a useful man. He tells me that he has become acquainted with two men called Brackley and Gifford, who are ready to work for us. Gifford would be a particularly useful man. He is clever. He has studied under Allen at Douai and is presently at the English College in Rome. Now suppose this man – whom we would pay well, of course – were to come to England and actually contrive a plot on behalf of the Queen of Scots, to which we would be privy, and suppose the queen's letters to the conspirators were to come into our hands . . ."

It was a perfect evening in late July, 1581. The meadows of

Richard Adams

Dethick lay tranquil in the sunset, streaked by the long shadows of their trees. A herd of cows were making their unhurried way towards the milking shed, urged onward by a boy whose stylised cries – "hu-ick, hu-ick" – sounded almost like a kind of song as he moved back and forth behind them. Nearer the house a blackbird was singing, its slow, pause-broken phrases seeming to express the very nature of the peaceful scene.

Anthony sat in the bay window of the nursery, leaning over the sill as he looked out over his lands. Soon – in a year come October – he would be of age, and all would be his for himself alone to govern. He thought of the 'association' – his friends in London – and of his hopes for the Catholic cause. There would be enough money to further their ends. He would need to travel: to meet Queen Mary's adherents in Paris; to go to Rome. Glowing with confidence and loyalty, he imagined himself and his horsemen galloping to the gates of Sheffield Castle, of the gallant Queen joining them to meet King Philip's generals; and after that, what future for himself? "The Catholic Empire," he murmured aloud. "The Catholic Empire." Spain, France, England, the Americas; the Catholic embassy and trading centre in Cathay, where Spain and England would co-join as equals in peace and prosperity. The peace of God, purged of heresy.

Behind him, beside the cot where his daughter, the three-year-old Mary, lay calmly between lavender-scented sheets, Honsie was sitting like some angelic guard, invulnerable on behalf of her charge to all danger and assaults of the devil. She was singing a lullaby, so low that her gentle voice scarcely carried to Anthony in the window.

"First came in the little cat,
Kitty alone, Kitty alone.
First came in the little cat,
Kitty alone and I.

"First came in the little cat
With some butter and some fat,
Kitty alone, alone, alone and I.

"Next came in the little flea
Kitty alone, Kitty alone.
Next came in the little flea
Kitty alone and I . . ."

The door, which was slightly ajar, was silently opened by
Thomas, the butler, grey and stooping now but still a majestic
figure. With perfect tact he glanced first towards the child's
cot and then caught his master's eye. Anthony stood up and
went outside onto the landing.

"Sir, there is a young gentleman come, Mr Chidiock
Tichborne. Morris has taken his horse and I offered him hot
water and food, but he says his errand is urgent. He said he
has news of great import for you."

Anthony hastened downstairs. Chidiock, still cloaked and
booted, was sitting on a chest in the hall. He sprang up and
embraced Anthony, who led him into the library.

"Anthony, Father Campion has been taken by the Privy
Council. They are holding him as a traitor."

"Holy Mother of God! Tell me, Chidiock, all thou knowest.
Tell me the way of it."

"Thou hast heard nothing?"

"Nothing."

"He was betrayed some fourteen days ago, by one George
Elliott, in the house of a gentleman at a place called Lyford,
in Berkshire. They brought him to London by night. I myself
was roused by the ringing of bells. I got up and went out. They
were taking him to the Tower. All the people were hooting and

jeering. They'd made Father Campion ride at the head, with his elbows tied behind him and his hands tied in front—"

"Good God!"

"His feet were tied under his horse's belly and they'd stuck a paper in his hat saying 'Campion, the seditious Jesuit'."

"And what befell after?"

"It was a few days later that they sent him from the Tower to the Earl of Leicester. The earl treated him graciously and, as I heard, told him he had no fault to find with him, save that he was a papist. The queen herself, it seems, offered him his life and liberty, so that he would renounce his priesthood and become a Protestant. But he refused."

"So he is still in the Tower?"

"Aye. And will be brought to trial."

Tears stood in Anthony's eyes; he brushed them away.

"So there is no recourse but to prayer. Thou'rt a true friend, Chidiock, to have made this journey. Stay with us a while – as long as may be. I will be ready to return with thee to London. If there is anything we can do to help Father Campion—"

"I fear there is nothing, Tony. We can only pray."

The Privy Council gave authority for Campion to be tortured. He told little, although many Catholics were arrested in various parts of the country. While he remained in custody, they refused to confront him with those whom he was alleged to have accused.

However, they acceded to his request for a public disputation against a selected body of Protestant clergy. This took place in the chapel of the Tower. Anthony used his influence to gain admittance for himself and Chidiock.

Campion was put to stand in the centre, without access to books and without even a table to lean upon. He appeared to be almost on the point of collapse, terribly injured by the rack and his force of mind impaired. The disputation took the form of two three-hour sessions for each of four days. During these he was subjected to abuse and derision. However, he answered his adversaries so readily and patiently that most of the audience felt nothing but respect and admiration for him.

As a result of all he heard, the Earl of Arundel was converted to Catholicism.

Later, Campion was tortured again, but to little effect, except almost to kill him. An indictment was contrived against him, in which it was wrongly stated that he, Parsons and other priests had conspired to foster sedition and to dethrone the Queen. In court, his physical condition was such that he could not, without help, hold up his hand to plead. Although he answered his accusers so well that not only Anthony but many others felt sure of an acquittal, he was found guilty and condemned to death. (Years later Hallam, in his constitutional history, was to write: 'The prosecution was as unfairly conducted, and supported by as slender evidence, as any, perhaps, that can be found in our books.')

Anthony, Chidiock and several others of the association were present at his execution. From the hangman's cart Campion, although unable to stand unaided, answered for some time the taunts and jeering questions of Sir Francis Knollys and other gentlemen who had secured themselves seats of vantage. Finally, he was asked to pray for the Queen, and as he was doing so the noose was put round his neck, the cart was drawn away and the appointed barbarity commenced.

After the execution of Campion, Anthony returned to Dethick and lived in virtual seclusion, apart from visits from Chidiock and a few other members of the association. During this time, having come of age, he attained full control of the Dethick estates. Often, he received under his roof Jesuits and other Catholic priests, and helped them to continue on their clandestine journeys.

He grew firmly convinced that the Elizabethan government, in the hands of men like Burleigh and Walsingham – to say nothing of the queen herself – had become altogether evil, to be hated as Christ had hated Satan. He had grounds for his fear. At this time several Catholic estates fell forfeit to the Crown, following charges of harbouring the queen's enemies. The recusancy fines, now more severely enforced, bore heavily on ordinary, rank-and-file Catholics, so that increasing numbers left the Church. Anthony now believed that there was a real likelihood of Catholicism in England being altogether rooted up and destroyed.

What should he do? He was rich, influential, and held a position of authority. The priests advised him to help to bear the Church's hard lot with patience, to encourage his tenants and servants to hold fast to the faith and to help them by paying their fines. Yet with this he could not rest content. A truly good man, he felt, would play a more active part, would save his country from the roaring lions that walked about seeking whom they might devour.

Abroad were the powerful Catholic countries, France and Spain. Despite the Pope's ban of excommunication more than a dozen years ago, neither of these – no, not even Alva's troops close by in the Netherlands – had moved to enforce with arms the Pope's decree against the heretic English queen. De Spes, the former Spanish ambassador to England, had been expelled from the country for his part in Ridolfi's foolish plot, yet Spain had done nothing.

One day, news came to Dethick of the arrest of an English Catholic, Francis Throckmorton, who had been acting as intermediary between the Queen of Scots and Signor Mendoza, the Spanish ambassador in London. Under torture Throckmorton had told the names of the accomplices in his plot. All had been executed, although the queen, as before, had refused to proceed against Mary, implicated though she plainly was. Mendoza, like De Spes, had been expelled from the country. Yet still the Spanish monarchy took no action.

Six months later the Protestant King of Holland, William the Silent, was assassinated by a Catholic agent. To Anthony the regicide was a hero, and he himself a mere Jack o' Dreams.

He himself felt more and more the imminence of crisis. In answer to his prayers the Blessed Virgin assured him that he had a notable role to fulfil, if only he could summon the necessary courage and determination. He deliberated much with himself. His enterprise, he knew must – unlike the ill-judged and transparent plots of Ridolfi and Throckmorton – be well planned, concerted and deadly. The vital factor was help from abroad, and this would have to be negotiated. Letters were not to be relied upon; he would have to go himself. It would not be difficult for him to obtain permission to travel abroad.

Queen Mary had two agents in Paris. One was Thomas Morgan, who was in the service of Mary's ambassador, Archbishop James Beaton, having previously been secretary to the Earl of Shrewsbury. The second was Charles Paget, younger brother of that same Lord Paget of Derbyshire who was a friend of Sir Philip Draycot and of Anthony himself (and had been among the party when he sang 'King Herod and the Cock'). Anthony resolved to consult them both.

Like all Englishmen in Paris, he admired the city and took every opportunity of enjoying himself, of seeing the sights and of visiting and talking to the several distinguished people to whom he had been given letters of introduction. His meeting with Morgan and Paget took place one summer evening at Paget's lodgings. There was also present a certain Fontenay, a Scottish adherent of Mary of many years' standing. When Anthony had told them of his sympathies and that he had come purposely to talk with them about the affinity of France and of Spain towards a Catholic rising in England, Morgan replied at a tangent, by asking him whether he understood the business of ciphering. He himself was a cipher expert with many years' experience. Anthony, although an educated gentleman by any standards of the time, could not help feeling disinclination for the intellectual drudgery of coding and decoding. He was told, rather to his irritation, that however great his idealism, this accomplishment would be essential. He accepted it, and went on to speak at large of his own assessment of the situation.

"There are three elements, gentlemen, each necessary, each of the greatest importance. First, it is requisite that there should be an invasion of England by a Catholic army; as I suppose, upon the order of the King of Spain. I have considered where it should land. I believe that the port should be Newcastle or Hartlepool – at all events somewhere in the

217

north-east, where Catholic sympathies are strong and London is far away."

Paget nodded, saying nothing.

"Second, the Queen of Scots must be released with all possible speed, and that before the landing of the army. For we have to bear in mind that Queen Elizabeth will know of the invasion as soon as it sets sail – nay, even before that, it may well be – and will go about to put Queen Mary into some secret stronghold or even to kill her. I myself am ready, upon the instant of hearing from you, to lead sixty horsemen to Wingfield or wherever she may be held, to overpower the guards and hale her away to safety among our Catholic forces. The Catholics of England will certainly rise to support the invasion. They will number, as I surmise, some fifty thousand."

He paused, but none of his hearers made any comment.

With a certain hesitancy, Anthony continued. "In the third place, we must decide on our action against Queen Elizabeth. As you know, there hath been no lack of men prepared to kill her; yet I myself cannot but doubt whether this is conformable to the law of Christ. 'Thou shalt do no murder.'" He looked from one to the other.

Paget spoke. "Yet William the Silent was killed and the Pope did not condemn it. Catholic divines – de Mariana, Suarez, Mola – have written most convincingly that it is right and just to kill heretic rulers for the necessity of restoring the true Church and saving men's souls."

Still Anthony hesitated. At length he said, "I would not myself do it, but I do not lack companions who would undertake it."

"Doth the Queen of Scots know of thy design?" asked Morgan.

"Not yet. I am looking to ye, gentlemen, if ye approve it, to inform her."

"I will do so," said Fontenay. "But before all else, there is the matter of letters to be secretly delivered to the Queen. Beforetimes, we had means to get these to her, but those means have been cut off, and we need another way."

"We shall have these letters delivered to thee in London," said Paget to Anthony. "We have a man named Anthony Rolston, who will make himself known to thee; also there is one Mistress Bray who dwells at Sheffield."

"Dost thou judge me, then, a fit person to be the leader of the project to release Queen Mary?"

"Thou art the fittest man," said Fontenay, "that hath yet come in our way. These plans for an invasion will take time to prepare and propose, but meanwhile thou mayest expect to hear more from us."

Anthony, joined now by Chidiock, journeyed on to Rome; and here, in this greatest of all cities, where the true Church reigned supreme and secure as though Protestant heresy had never existed, there grew in their hearts such freedom, elevation and inspiration of soul that they were transported to a hitherto unimagined pinnacle of fervour. Merely to see the priests and cardinals walking at large on their affairs, receiving all honour, exercising their authority and pursuing their duties by indisputable right, was enough to cause both of them to dedicate themselves totally to the Holy Church and to give thanks to God who had called them to so sacred a task.

It was all of three years before Anthony returned to Dethick. To his wife he appeared preoccupied, and spent much time alone, either riding or walking. Though he was as loving as ever to her and to his little girl, it was plain that some great matter was on his mind. After only a few months at Dethick, he told Margery that important business compelled him to return to London and that he would take Honsie with him, for with regard to the business he had in hand, he said, he needed above all a discreet and trustworthy housekeeper, one who knew him well and could be relied upon to hear all and tell nothing. He hoped to return soon after midsummer.

Hi mihi sunt comites, quos ipsa pericula ducunt.

Anthony gazed at the portrait with pride and satisfaction. The painter had achieved excellent likenesses of himself and his comrades of the association. There he was in the centre, with Chidiock on his right and Tom Salisbury on his left. Habington, Tilney, Barnewell, Donn, John Charnock and the others were grouped around, some with their arms about one another's shoulders. His coat of arms was prominent in one corner. The painting made an excellent *pièce de résistance* to his supper room, catching the sunlight on this fine evening of mid-May. He had always liked these lodgings in Holborn – Herne's Rents, as they were known. With their three or four bedrooms, large dining-room and fully adequate servants' quarters, they were ideal for his purposes; readily accessible to his friends, big enough to entertain all of them together and to put up for the night any visitor who might need a bed.

Honsie admired the painting, but took no account of the hexameter.

"They're a fine bunch of lads, are thy friends, Master Tony, and it makes me glad that thou'rt in such good company at Court."

"We shall do well, Honsie, never fear."

"Yet thou'rt not telling me all, art thou? Oh, I can tell, Master Tony; after all these years. Come now, dear lad, tell me the secret of this painting. It wasn't for nothing but thy pleasure that it was made, was it?"

"Why, as to that, Honsie—"

There was a firm knock at the door – a knock that Honsie recognised.

"Oh, there now, that'll be young Master Tichborne. I'll go myself and open the door to him. Wilt thou have supper presently?"

"Aye, dear Honsie, presently. Let him in, take off his boots and give him a pair of soft slippers."

Chidiock stood admiring the painting. "Sure, 'tis an excellent piece of work, Tony, yet I must confess to some little doubt about the hexameter. Dost thou not think it a shade rash? Suppose our friend Sir Francis Walsingham were to learn of it, might he not reflect upon these *pericula*?"

Anthony felt in a mood to comply with any friend's wishes.

"Sure, then, Chidiock, I'll change it. Let's see. How wouldst thou fancy – er – '*Quorsum haec alio properantibus*'?"

And so it was agreed. The painting was remarked upon by several people who visited Anthony's lodgings. A description of it could hardly have failed to reach Sir Francis Walsingham.

It was a happy and rather boisterous supper party. All those present – the association – felt full of the glad confidence and immortality of youth and of friendship. There was much toasting of Queen Mary, of King Philip, of the Pope and the memory of the blessed Edmund Campion. Chidiock was pressed to sing, and to do so stood on his chair, pot in hand, surrounded by an encouraging audience.

"Oh, come all you good fellows that go out a-tippling,
I pray you give attention and list to my song.
I'll sing you a ditty of a jolly bold robber,
Stood seven feet high, in proportion as strong."

They cheered each verse and, as Chidiock continued the story of the encounter between the daunting robber and the resolute sailor, Anthony felt his spirits rise still higher. He himself, like the sailor, would be resolute and firm to encounter enemies. He would not fail his friends in his leadership; he would be prudent and circumspect as well as resolute.

At length he called them to order.

"Friends, I have much to impart to you. But it will be best if we do not consult together here. Walls have ears, they say. Let us take our cloaks and hats and repair outside into St Giles's Fields."

When they were all gathered close under the trees, Anthony told them of his meeting with Morgan and Paget in Paris, and of the triple design to give all possible help to a Spanish invasion, to free Queen Mary and to kill the queen. All were impressed and promised their willing support.

"But can we be sure of sufficient aid from the counties?" asked Tilney.

"The North and North-West will join us," replied Anthony. "Of that I am confident. My people in Derbyshire will rise as soon as may be required."

"The whole of North Wales will rise," said Tom Salisbury. "As you know, that's my country. In Denbigh they are Catholic almost to a man, and I have many friends."

"I will tell you now," said Henry Donn. "I can by no means be persuaded to be a queen-killer, but to deliver Queen Mary I pledge myself willingly."

"As soon as the project is launched," said Anthony, "you must ride to Wales, Tom, and raise the country. I myself will take sixty horsemen, ride to Chartley and rescue the Queen. I may have more than sixty, for they will be my own people from Dethick and nearby."

"How many altogether will rise, think you?" asked Charnock.

"I would say fifty thousand."

"But have they arms and armour?"

"The time will serve," replied Anthony. "Where there are resolute men, arms will not be lacking." Feeling a passing doubt on this score, he changed the subject. "I will confess to you that I myself have no desire to kill the queen. Yet it would seem that this must be done."

"I will do it," said Chidiock. "My conscience is easy. She is a heretic tyrant who has persecuted her people and cruelly slain our priests. Let there be but, let us say, six of us, and we can certainly prevail."

After some discussion – for there were others besides Anthony and Henry Donn who could not square their consciences with murder – four gentlemen pledged themselves with Chidiock.

"And are we to act presently, Anthony?" asked Robert

Barnewell. "Now that we are agreed, I think we should lose no time."

"Nay," answered Anthony, "we must await word from Paris."

"Why linger?" said Tilney; and several others took him up. "Why linger?" "Why linger, Tony?" "The more we linger, the more risk of discovery."

"The fleet," said Anthony firmly. "The Spanish fleet and soldiers are utterly requisite to us. Nay!" He held up his hand authoritatively. "We must await word from Mendoza in Paris — he who was formerly ambassador here — that the Spanish fleet is about to sail."

"But the queen and Burleigh will learn of that as soon as we, and they will act. We must forestall them."

"Tony, the Spanish will not sail until they know that Queen Mary is safe in our hands and Queen Elizabeth dead. We should not linger, but act at once."

"I tell you no!" repeated Anthony. "I am awaiting a messenger from Queen Mary's own man in Paris. He will come soon, have no fear."

After more talk, they returned to Herne's Rents and finished their evening merrily, for all the world like any young band of courtiers. In spite of the argument, there was not a man but trusted the confident, able and accomplished Anthony Babington.

It was shortly afterwards, one evening towards the end of May, that Anthony happened to be reading alone in his study at Herne's Rents when Honsie came to tell him that there was a stranger at the door seeking to see him.

"He gave me this, Master Tony."

It was a folded slip of paper. Anthony took it and read: 'Morgan and Paget desire me to have speech with thee.' He told Honsie to show the visitor in.

The person who entered looked to be in his early forties. He was dark, thin faced and spare, with a kind of intensity and feverish ardour in his expression, as though he were obsessed with some matter in which he was determined either to prevail or die. He refused food or drink, and sat down facing Anthony with a kind of tension, as though he could scarcely wait to speak.

"My name is John Ballard. I know the Spaniards in Paris. Thou hast thyself, Master Babington, spoken with Mendoza?" His voice was high and quick.

"Nay; but with Morgan and Paget I have."

"Mendoza has bidden me to inform thee that in his judgement there is none so fit as thyself to lead the English Catholics to our joint glorious victory."

Anthony felt a wave of exhilaration. Here was confirmation from a foreign power of the belief in himself, in his own comrades and in Paget and Morgan.

"I must ask more precisely, Master Ballard, who thou art and what are thy credentials."

"*Father* Ballard. I am a priest, trained at Rheims and close to Father Allen. I have been to Rome and am a friend of Rector Agazzari of the English College. Through him I obtained an interview with the Holy Father and procured his blessing upon our enterprise. I have been in England since last December, but have just now returned from Paget and Mendoza in Paris."

"And thy news for me?"

"Mendoza promises a French and Spanish invasion of England this summer. The Pope is the chief disposer. The invasion will be led by the Duc de Guise and the Prince of Parma, and the forces will number sixty thousand men. They have in readiness such forces and warlike preparations as the like was never seen in these parts of Christendom."

"It sounds too good to be true, Father. I would have thought that the home troubles of these princes were presently so great as to keep them from undertaking such an enterprise. And have they the ships?"

Ballard was about to speak, but Anthony went on swiftly.

"Besides, I think that their assistance would be small, notwithstanding the excommunication, so long as Queen Elizabeth doth live, and the state being so well settled." He thought best to test his visitor thoroughly.

"Nay, Master Babington. That difficulty will be taken away

by means already laid. The queen's life will be no hindrance. I have a companion, one John Savage of Derbyshire—"

"Of Derbyshire? I know the family, yet not thy John Savage himself."

"He is a soldier who has fought in the Low Countries. He is a man of desperate courage that will undertake anything."

"He will be welcome to us."

"I have two other comrades, Gilbert Gifford and Robin Poley. They are ready to join thee. I must also tell thee that Morgan has told Queen Mary of thee by secret letter. Thou mayest look to hear directly from her."

"From the Queen of Scots herself?"

"Aye. And I should make it plain to you, Master Babington, that there will arise for Englishmen the heavy matter of sheer preservation of their land and possessions. For the foreign soldiers will enter upon the country by right of conquest, without sparing any, excepting those English and Welsh who declare themselves as thine adherents. Those who would keep their lands must needs join thee."

"Of my support there shall be no question. But for all the Catholic landowners in England I cannot as yet speak."

"Master Babington, during the past six months I have travelled through every shire in England and spoken with the head of every honourable Catholic household. They are ready to rise upon the death of Elizabeth, as soon as Queen Mary is released and the Spanish force has landed."

"Arms?"

Ballard made an impatient gesture of dismissal. "Arms will be found." He rose, but still kept his glittering, fanatical eyes fixed upon Anthony's. "I must leave thee now, but we shall meet again, with Savage, Gifford and Poley." He made the sign of the cross. "God bless you, my son."

"Master Tony." Honsie, returning from showing Ballard out, stood beside Anthony's chair in the study. He looked up impatiently.

"Well, what now?"

"Master Tony, who is this man that just left thee?"

"Who is he?" Anthony rapped sharply on the desk. "That doesn't concern thee, Honsie. Prithee, let be."

"He is a bad man, Master Tony. I know it. I can tell. I dare be sworn, he is a cruel and evil man. Have thou no more to do with him, dear heart, else he will bring thee to ruin."

"Honsie, this is presumptuous. I could dismiss thee for this impertinence. Say no more about this matter, which doth not concern thee."

"Master Tony, thou knowest I've loved thee and attended thee all thy life. I love thee as I love myself. I know not what he came to tell thee, nor what may have been his business to thee. But I never heard nor saw a more evil man in all my days. I say again, he will bring thee naught but ruin. Dear master, go home to Dethick, now; and I will gladly go with thee."

"Honsie, thou wottest naught of what thou speakest. That man is a priest."

"A *priest*?" She stared at him, wide-eyed.

"Aye, a priest. And he came to talk with me on the realm's priestly business."

She stood silenced and dropped her gaze, but still stood wringing her hands. At length she said, "Is that indeed the truth thou tellest me, Master Tony? He is a priest?"

"Aye is he."

"Then I will say no more. Forgive me, Master Tony. All I said was spoken out of love for thee. There is none that loves thee more than I."

For a moment she embraced and kissed him, then left him to himself.

Anthony fell on his knees in passionate prayer.

"Anthony, we stand in a dilemma."

Four of them were conferring in the darkness of St Giles's Fields: Anthony, Chidiock, Tom Salisbury and Robert Barnewell. "On the one side, the Catholics of this land undergo ever more rigorous persecution. There is no Catholic whose life is not in the magistrates' hands. But on the other side, thou tellest me, we have it by messenger from Mendoza in Paris that this country is to be invaded and sacked; brought into servitude to foreigners. By September at latest."

"So in the case of an invasion we may expect the forfeiture of our estates," said Salisbury, "and the dishonour and desolation of our country."

"Yet in delaying the invasion," said Barnewell, "lies extreme hazard. As seemeth to me, we have worse enemies here. Here any Catholic is held a possible traitor. Toleration will never be admitted."

"Anthony," said Chidiock, "thou shouldst go to Paris: thou must needs have speech thyself with Mendoza."

"I will," said Anthony. "Father Ballard hath introduced to me one Robin Poley, who is our supporter. He is in the service of Sir Philip Sidney's wife, who is Sir Francis Walsingham's daughter. He will obtain me an interview."

It was towards the end of June when Anthony first spoke with Walsingham at Greenwich. He had already decided on his line, which was to offer to go abroad in the service of the Government, to convey information and to perform any diplomatic tasks which might be thought fit. Walsingham replied that this was a most generous offer and he would think it over. Anthony saw him again on 3rd July but, although he was politely received, he got no further with his request. He returned to Dethick, leaving Honsie in charge of his rooms at Herne's Rents.

To Master Anthony Babington, dwelling most in Derbyshire at a house of his own within two miles of Wingfield, as I doubt not thou knowest for that in this shire he hath many friends and kinsmen.

The boy, who was a stranger, stood fidgeting while Anthony read this curious address. He tipped him a groat and told Thomas that he was to wait in the kitchen. As soon as he was alone, he broke the seal.

My very good Friend, Albeit it be long since you heard from me, no more than I have done from you, against my will, yet would I not you should think, I have in the meanwhile, nor will ever be unmindful of the effectual affection you have shown heretofore towards all that concerneth me. I have understood that upon the ceasing of our intelligence there were addressed unto you both from France and Scotland some packets for me. I pray you, if any have come to your hands, and be yet in place, to deliver them unto the bearer hereof, who will make them to be safe conveyed to me, and I will pray God for your preservation.

Of June the twenty fifth, at Chartley.

Your assured good friend, MARIE R.

Anthony gave the boy the packets in his possession. Walking slowly up and down the library, it became clear to him that now there must indeed be no more lingering. The Queen had called him to her side. His course was clear. He must return to London forthwith.

Gilbert Gifford and Robin Poley stood facing Sir Francis Walsingham.

"You have shown yourselves good servants to the Queen," said Walsingham, "and you need have no doubt, my fine fellows, that you will be rewarded. You are sure that neither Ballard nor Babington suspect you?"

Gifford laughed. "Nay, nay, sir; be assured, we are the best of friends with them."

"Take care you remain so. Now read this copy of the Queen of Scots' letter to Anthony Babington, writ on the twenty-fifth of last month."

The two men did so. "Will you apprehend Babington and his accomplices now, sir?" asked Poley.

"Nay. You are to understand that we care not a straw for Babington and his friends, nor yet for Ballard. They are our dupes and them we may take at any time. It is the Queen of Scots whom we mean to draw on and then to expose for treason. The rest are small beer."

Walsingham's long, vulpine face gazed up at his two crea-
tures with a kind of sombre impatience.

"Your task, Poley, is by every means to urge Babington on,
and above all to ensure that he does not leave London – he,
Ballard and the rest. You must induce him to write again to
this evil queen: make him expose all to her, if you can. It is
her written agreement we need."

"You are sure, then, Sir Francis, of intercepting all her
letters, as well as those writ to her?"

"When her secretary has ciphered her letters, they are
wrapped in leather and thrust into one of the empty, outgo-
ing beer-barrels at Chartley." He chuckled mirthlessly. "The
brewer is an honest fellow. He is in our pay. They are
deciphered, brought to me, are copied and the originals then
returned to the barrels. She suspects nothing. Gifford, I wish
you to travel to Chartley. I will give you a letter to Sir Amyas
Paulet, who guards Queen Mary. He will tell you where to
find the honest brewer. You are to send to me with all speed
a faithful copy of Babington's next letter – and above all, of
Mary's reply. That last, I trust, will be the letter we need."

London 6th July, 1586
i.   Most mightie, most excellent, my dread sovereign lady
and Queen, unto whom I owe all fidelity and obedience.
ii. There was addressed to me from beyond the seas one
Ballard, a man of virtue and learning, and of singular zeal
to the Catholic cause and Your Majesty's service. This man
informed me of great preparation by the Christian princes,
your Majesty's allies, for the deliverance of our country from
the extreme and miserable state wherein it hath too long
remained.
iii. Which when I understood, my special desire was to
advise by what means with the hazard of my life and
friends in general I might do your sacred Majesty one good
day's service.
iv. These things are first to be advised in this great and
honourable action, upon the issue of which depend not only
the life of your most excellent Majesty, but also the honour

and weal of our country and the last hope ever to recover the faith of our forefathers.

[a]   First, assuring of invasion: [b] Sufficient strength in the invader; [c] ports to arrive at appointed, [d] with a strong party at every place to join with them and warrant their landing. [e] The deliverance of your Majesty. [f] The despatch of Elizabeth, the usurping Competitor. For the effectuating of all which it may please your Excellency to rely upon my service.

Your Majesty's most faithful subject and sworn servant,
Anthony Babington.

Chartley, 17th July, 1586.
        Trusty and well beloved,

According to the zeal and entire affection which I have known in you towards the common cause of religion and mine, having always made account of you as of a principal and right worthy member to be employed both in the one and the other: It hath been no less consolation unto me to understand your estate as I have done by your last, and to have found means to renew my intelligence with you.

For divers great and important considerations, I cannot but greatly praise and commend your common desire to prevent in time the designments of our enemies for the extirpation of our religion out of this Realm with the ruin of us all. For I have long ago shown unto the foreign Catholic princes, the longer that they and we delay to put hand on the matter, the greater leisure have our enemies to prevail and win advantage, and in the meantime the Catholics here remaining exposed to all sorts of persecution and cruelty do daily diminish in number and power. For mine own part I pray you to assure our principal friends that I shall always be ready and most willing to employ therein my life and all that I have in this world.

Now for to ground substantially this enterprise you must first examine deeply.

What forces you may raise amongst you all and what Captains you shall appoint in every shire.

Of what ports and havens you may assure yourselves,

as well in the north west as south to receive succour from the Low Countries, Spain and France.

What place do you esteem fittest and of greatest advantage to assemble the principal company of your forces at; and whether or which way you have to march.

What foreign forces you require, for how long paid, and munition and posts the fittest for their landing in this Realm.

What provision of money and armour you would ask.

By what means the six gentlemen deliberate to kill the queen,

And the manner also of my getting forth of this hold.

Upon which points having taken amongst you, my advice is that you impart the same with all diligence to Barnardine de Mendoza, ambassador for the King of Spain in France, who I may assure you will employ himself therein most willingly. I shall not fail to write unto him of the matter.

Whatever issue the matter taketh, I do and will think myself obliged, as long as I live, towards you for the offers you make to hazard yourself as you do for my delivery.

God almighty have you in protection.

Your most assured friend for ever

MARIE R.

Fail not to burn this present quickly.

Upon the outside of his copy of this letter, which he dealt with on the day following its date, Thomas Phelippes, Walsingham's cipher expert, temporarily resident at Chartley, endorsed the semblance of a gallows.

London, 3rd August 1586.

Honoured Majesty,

Your letters I received not until the 29th July. The cause was my absence from Lichfield contrary to promise. How dangerous the cause thereof was by my next letters shall be imparted. In the meantime Your Majesty may understand that one Mawde (that came out of France with Ballard, who came from Mendoza concerning this affair) is discovered to be for

231

this state. Ballard acquainted him with the cause of his coming, and hath employed him of late into Scotland with letters. By whose treachery unto what extreme danger my self have been, and the whole plot is like to be brought, and by what means we have in part prevented, and purpose by God's assistance to redress the rest, Your Majesty shall be my next informed.

Till when, my sovereign, for his sake that preserveth Your Majesty for our common good, dismay not, neither doubt of happy issue. It is God's cause, the Church's and Your Majesty's, an enterprise honourable before God and man, undertaken upon zeal and devotion, free from all ambition and temporal regard, and therefore no doubt will succeed happily. We have vowed and we will perform or die. What is holden of Your Majesty's propositions, together with our final determination, my next shall discover.

Having completed this letter, which he meant to cipher later, Anthony left it lying on the desk in his study, while he went to relieve himself. When he returned, after some ten minutes, he found Honsie bent intently over the desk. She started up and stood staring at him, her hands pressed to either side of her face.

"Master Tony!"

Before she could say more, he strode up to her and grasped her arm.

"Honsie, thou hadst no business to be reading this. Let it alone and get thee gone."

"Nay, that I won't, Master Tony. Tell me what this letter imports."

"Certainly not! Honsie, I tell thee—"

"Then *I'll* tell *thee*, Master Tony. This letter to the Queen of Scots doth bespeak nothing less than high treason. Th'art conspiring with her—"

"Honsie, leave the room!"

"Nay, that I won't, Master Tony. I'll not see thee taken and hanged for a traitor. Th'art to burn the letter and go back to

Dethick! Oh, if only I'd known of this before! Master Tony, hast thou considered? 'Tis mortal sin!"

"Honsie, say nothing to anyone. I am going out, and will return later."

Anthony and several of his friends were once more conferring in the open air near his lodgings. Chidiock, who had hurt his leg, was laid up and not among them. Anthony had expected Ballard, but they had been joined only by his friend John Savage, one of the six sworn to assassinate the queen.

Anthony had been speaking of once more seeking Walsingham's authority to travel abroad, and of the necessity of obtaining first-hand information from Mendoza about the coming invasion, when Charles Tilney appeared in the distance, pelting towards them, his hat clutched in one hand. When he reached them he was so breathless that he could scarcely speak.

"Tony! Ballard has been arrested!"

Anthony could find no words. They all stood dumbfounded, and it was Savage who spoke first.

"I will go now, at once, and kill the queen. There is naught else we can do. We must act immediately, before Ballard reveals everything under torture."

Anthony considered the matter quickly. "You are right. Come home with me now, and I will give you money to buy clothes to go to Court in." He looked round at them. "We must disperse at once. But I will send you word when to set out with me for Chartley. If you learn first that the queen is dead, come to me immediately."

Not long after Savage had left Herne's Rents, however, Robin Poley's man, a fellow named Scudamore, brought to Anthony a letter from Walsingham himself. Walsingham assured Babington that Ballard's arrest had been made not by himself but by an over-officious and notoriously anti-Catholic magistrate. He had given Scudamore orders to remain with Anthony; Scudamore possessed signed authority from Walsingham that Anthony was not to be taken into custody.

This relieved Anthony greatly. At the same time he felt it better not to remain at Herne's Rents, in case the officious magistrate's officers should come for him. He took Scudamore out to supper at a decent tavern not far away.

The food and wine were excellent and as they concluded supper Anthony, who now felt relaxed and cheerful, was speaking to Scudamore about the magnificence of the ruined Colosseum, when a man obviously not of the house brought in to Scudamore a note with a court seal. Scudamore glanced briefly at it, shrugged his shoulders and put it down on one side of his place. The messenger had already gone to the door when Scudamore turned his head, calling him back to tip him. It was in this moment that Anthony, glancing down at the half-folded note, read the words '—bington to be arrested forthwith, as soon . . .'

Clenching one hand under the table, Anthony finished to Scudamore his account of the Colosseum. Then, as casually as might be, and leaving his cloak, belt and sword where they hung on the back of his chair, he said he would go and pay the bill. As soon as he was out of the room he fled, running without stopping to the lodgings of Robert Gage and John Charnock at Westminster. Before midnight they were in hiding in the densest part of St John's Wood. Next day they were joined by Henry Donn and Robert Barnewell, to whom they had sent a note by Gage's servant.

It was the following morning. Honsie, who knew nothing except that Anthony had not come home all night, was giving one of the servants instructions about purchases in the local market, and was about to disburse the necessary money, when there came a heavy battering from outside. Telling the servant to accompany her, she went to the bolted door and called, "Who is there?"

"Open the door!" shouted a rough voice.

"And be quick about it!" added another, "or we'll break the damned door down."

Honsie, with a dreadful apprehension that this could only have to do with Anthony's night-long absence, went to an upstairs window and looked out. Below, before the door, stood a group of four or five coarse-looking men, all carrying clubs. She called down, "What do you want?"

"We want Mr Anthony Babington," replied one of them. "You'd best let us in presently. We have a search warrant from the Privy Council."

"Mr Babington isn't here," said Honsie. "He left yesterday."

"You let us in or else we'll force the door. I tell you, you silly bitch, we have a search warrant."

As Honsie still hesitated in wretched uncertainty, one of the men again began to batter on the door.

"Wait! Stop that!" she called. "I'll let you in."

They slouched through the door and followed her into the kitchen, where their leader spat on the floor and tapped her hand sharply with his club.

"What's your business with Mr Babington?" she asked, with the best air of authority that she could summon.

He laughed unpleasantly. "Our business? To arrest 'im for treason, that's our business." He turned to his men. "Search the house!"

They set about it, and it soon became plain from the shouts and other noise that they were smashing and damaging as wantonly as they pleased.

"Tell them to stop!" cried Honsie, at her wits' end. "I tell you again, Mr Babington isn't here! He left yesterday. Tell them to stop!"

"Where was 'e going?"

"I don't know."

"Where is 'e now?"

"I don't know."

"Oh, don't know, eh? Well, we'd better jog your memory, 'adn't we, sweetheart? Jim! Pete!"

He jerked his head. The two men gripped her arms on either

235

side. Honsie began to scream, and the man slapped her across the face.

"Where is 'e?"

"I tell you, I don't know." She wept, struggling.

"Course, we might take it into our 'eads to 'ave a bit of fun, mightn't we? Fine strappin' woman like you. Lay 'er across the table!"

Struggling, Honsie cried out, "I tell you I don't know where he is, and if I did I wouldn't tell the likes of you. And if you ravish me, I promise you the Queen herself shall hear of it. I have a friend among her maids."

"Oh, yes? A likely tale!" But all the same, they let her stand up.

"You're the 'ousekeeper, ain't yer?"

"Yes. Now go, all of you!"

"You just don't seem to understand, do yer, m'dear, that this is a matter of arrest for 'igh treason? Let 'er wash 'er face and put on 'er cloak. You must come with us, miss – madam – whatever you are. We're takin' you to the Captain."

Fifteen minutes later Honsie, distraught, trembling in every limb and supported by two of the men, found herself facing a trim and smartly dressed young man seated behind a narrow, polished table.

"What is your name?"

"Honor Godsell, sir."

"And are you a servant of Mr Anthony Babington?"

"I am his housekeeper, sir."

"Are you aware that there is a warrant for his arrest?"

"I wasn't aware of this, sir, until your men told me this morning."

"Where is Anthony Babington?"

"I don't know, sir. He left yesterday."

"Did he say where he was going?"

"No, sir. Not to me."

The young man paused, as though pondering. Then he said, "Do you expect him to return?"

"I don't know, sir, what to expect. He said nothing to me about when he would return."

236

"And was that common practice with him?"

"No, sir. It was very seldom that he went away without telling me where he was going and when he expected to come back."

"Well, you had better tell me what you know about this business. Were you a party to it? Did he confide in you about it? You are a Roman Catholic, I take it?"

"Yes, sir. But about what you call this business, I know nothing."

"And are you quite sure that you don't know where he is?"

"I'm quite sure, sir."

"Well now, I'll tell you what you're to do if you want to keep out of trouble. You're to go back where you were this morning and behave as if you knew nothing – and, of course, tell nobody anything. Two of my men will stay with you. You're to do all you can to make yourself and the place look as though nothing had happened. If Babington comes back – and it's quite possible that he will – you're to help my men to arrest him. Is that clear?"

"But money, sir. Mr Babington would have given me the housekeeping money today. I can't manage without."

He unlocked a drawer. "Here are twenty shillings. One of my men will keep them and spend from time to time as you ask him. You yourself are not to leave the place at all."

"And the other servants, sir?"

"Pay them what they have earned and dismiss them."

It was the tenth morning after the conspirators' flight. Filthy, famished, unshaven, racked with terror and by their lack of any plan of escape, Anthony and his wretched companions still lay in hiding. Barnwell had twice ventured out to buy bread in a nearby village, and had returned with the news that the whole country was up and that search was being pursued everywhere. Whatever might have become of John Savage, it was certain that he had not killed the Queen. Chidiock and Charles Tilney were already in custody, together with Ballard.

237

Driven by desperation and hunger, Anthony and his four friends at last set out for the house of a Catholic friend, Jerome Bellamy at Harrow. It was here that they – and Bellamy – were arrested and taken to the Tower.

News of the arrests soon spread over London and beyond, and did not fail to reach Honsie in Herne's Rents. The way in which she had been intimidated, and her powerlessness against it, had produced in her an unexpressed but fierce anger against the authorities who had compelled her to live as a virtual prisoner in what had been Master Tony's private dwelling – the dwelling which she had managed on his behalf and in which she had been a person of consequence. Apparently she had been required to do this in order to set a kind of trap for Master Tony in the event of his return. Now he had been arrested, therefore, there could no longer be any reason to detain her. She was not going to wait for any kind of official release handed down from on high. She would release herself forthwith.

Over the men who had been living in the premises with her she had already established a considerable ascendancy. For more than a week past they had stopped trying to order her about. They would not, of course, have admitted that they were afraid of her; but they were. They had handed all the money over to her; and when she told them to sweep the floor or clean the windows they did so. Now, when she said that all reason for her detention was obviously at an end, they were glad enough to accept what she said and obey her order to go home. She was half-expecting another visit from the men with clubs, but nothing happened, and after two days she felt sanguine.

Yet this brought her no relief. Master Tony was imprisoned and she had enough commonsense to feel sure that he would be found guilty and put to death. This in itself – the shameful execution of the child, the boy, the brilliant young man to whom she had been devoted all his life – plunged her into bitter grief and depression. A great part of this was due to her lack of any means to help or even to comfort him. She was acquainted, of course, with neighbours round about, some of whom she had come to regard as friends. Yet when she told them of her trouble and asked them for advice, they not only had none to give, but made it clear that they had no sympathy for an associate of conspirators and traitors, and only wanted her to keep away. Even so, it might have been possible to arrange a meeting with Anthony through the good offices of someone with power and standing, but Honsie had access to no one like this, and anyway lacked the address and manner to carry the necessary weight. Only one person showed her any goodwill; this was a kindly old soul called Granny Barlow, who rented to her, for a small payment, a room in her cottage; for Honsie had left Herne's Rents. Too many people knew that Anthony Babington had dwelt there, and there was no peace for his former housekeeper.

Underlying all was her anxiety over what to do now. Obviously she could not obtain another place in London; she was tainted with treason and conspiracy. Her one consuming wish was to go home to her mother in Derbyshire, but she had very little money and a great misgiving at the thought of being a penniless woman travelling alone. It was, she knew, about 130 miles to Derbyshire. How far was she likely to get?

This was her situation and state of mind when she learned that Ballard, Anthony and five others had been found guilty and sentenced to a cruel death; and were to be executed, a week from the date of the sentence, upon a scaffold specially erected in a field at the upper end of Holborn, close to the highway to St Giles.

Chidiock Tichborne was a young man of courage and fortitude, his faith staunch even in the face of the ghastly sentence pronounced upon him. "Thy will be done," he prayed continually; and "deliver me from doing evil in the time of trial." Yet he could not keep himself from reflecting continually upon the waste of his young life; upon the waste of all their lives. The plot had been a charade. Sir Francis Walsingham had fomented it; had known all from the very beginning. Gifford had been a spy, Poley had been a spy, Mawde had been a spy. At Tichborne's examination the Privy Councillors had shown him decoded copies of Queen Mary's letters and of Anthony's to her. There was not even a question of torturing them (though Ballard had been tortured). The Privy Council had been fully informed ever since May and there was no more to be known.

Chidiock, as he waited in the Tower, determined to occupy his mind before he went mad. They had left him the money he had had on him. He called for the gaoler and bribed him for pen, ink and paper. He spent two days in composing and revising his poem. This is what he wrote:

> My prime of youth is but a frost of cares;
> My feast of joy is but a dish of pain,
> My crop of corn is but a field of tares,
> And all my good is but vain hope of gain.
> The day is past, and yet I saw no sun,
> And now I live, and now my life is done.
>
> My tale was heard and yet it was not told,
> My fruit is fallen and yet my leaves are green,
> My youth is spent and yet I am not old,
> I saw the world and yet I was not seen;
> My thread is cut and yet it is not spun,
> And now I live, and now my life is done.
>
> I sought my death and found it in my womb,
> I looked for life and saw it was a shade,
> I trod the earth and knew it was my tomb,
> And now I die, and now I was but made;
> My glass is full, and now my glass is run,
> And now I live, and now my life is done.

The grinding and scraping of the hurdles along the dirty September road could not be heard above the jeering shouts of the crowd. The worn-out old nags dragging them went slowly, continually beaten on by the guards, jerking them over protruding stones, tugging them sluggishly through patches of thicker filth. From windows above and from the roadsides, the prisoners were pelted with mud, with stones, with offal or anything that came to hand. Their ankles and wrists were tied to the bars with rope, and most had been chafed until they were bleeding. Henry Donn had a long, oozing scar down one side of his face, where a stripped shin bone had struck him.

The seven conspirators were drawn in single file, one behind the other. They made a narrow procession up the line of the kennel, leaving space on either side for spectators to run forward to spit on them and to shout curses. One man ran at Robert Barnewell with a club, but a guard pushed him back. "Nay, goodman, they're not to be injured – not yet."

The distance from the Tower was about two miles – an hour's journey – out of the city by Aldersgate and over the Fleet river to the village of St Giles's Fields. Here the scaffold had been set up. The spot had been chosen as being close to where the conspirators had been accustomed to meet and confer. It stood a good seven feet high, a little above the heads of the huge crowd filling Holborn as far as could be seen. As the first of the hurdles was observed approaching, roars and yells broke out. "Traitors!" "Papists!" "Execution!" "Long live the Queen!" There were scuffles and brawls as knots of the spectators tried to push their way closer. Those thronging the windows leaned forward, waving black cloths and old sheets daubed with red.

At the foot of the scaffold the horses were halted and tethered to the supporting posts. One by one, the conspirators were cut free and dragged up the wooden steps, exposed to the crowd's view. As each appeared his name was called out by a herald.

"John Ballard, the seditious priest!" There were shouts and missiles; a stone struck Ballard on the shoulder.

"Anthony Babington of Derbyshire, traitor to the Queen!"

Next, Chidiock limped forward to Anthony's side and for a moment took his arm. "Today we shall be with Him in Paradise." Anthony made no reply save to grip his hand. Somehow he had retained his hat, which was still on his head. He clasped his hands and prayed silently, remaining standing the while. This was remarked by an eye-witness as 'a sign of his former pride, his hat on his head as if he had been but a beholder'.

241

The scaffold had been carefully constructed and equipped. The gallows itself was of stout oak, the crossbar planed smooth and fitted into the uprights by dovetailing. Below stood a broad, heavy bench – a butcher's bench – on which lay an axe, two weighty cleavers and a pointed knife about seven inches long, with a serrated edge. Behind this stood the two executioners, bare-armed, in leather aprons and stained, greasy breeches. To one side stood a brazier of coal and beside it lay a pile of sacks, two great bags of sawdust and a wooden block some fifteen inches high.

All seven of the conspirators were plainly light-headed and faint, from lack of food, from terror and from the sight of these preparations, but mostly from the mass of sheer hatred and malevolence beating upon them from all sides. They seemed drowning in hatred. Among the crowd there was not to be seen one wife nor child, not one sweetheart nor friend to call out a word of comfort or encouragement. Who would dare to endanger their lives among this frenzied mob baying for blood, or – if they were of the better sort – to prejudice irretrievably their social positions and prospects by identifying themselves with these despicable traitors to the Queen? The Queen herself felt so deep a loathing of them that she had asked the Privy Council whether there were not some more cruel death by which they could be executed. The Privy Council had advised against this, on the grounds that worse might only have the effect of arousing public sympathy. So the sentences had been confirmed. 'To be hanged until half-dead; then to be cut down; their privities to be cut off; to be disembowelled alive and seeing; then quartered.'

The conspirators were to be executed one by one, Ballard being the first. Nothing was done to smother his half-choked screams. The blood – the huge tide of blood – reached Anthony's feet where he stood on the edge of the scaffold.

Thereupon, in the half-silence that followed the display of Ballard's head and the cry of "So perish all the Queen's enemies!" a voice – a woman's voice – broke out from the crowd below, at which Anthony started and looked about him as though suddenly awoken from sleep. After a moment he stared incredulously, like a man seeing a vision.

For it was Honsie down there in the sweaty, stinking crowd; Honsie pushing and elbowing her way towards him, pulling this man and that by the shoulder and all the time crying aloud, "Be of good cheer, Master Tony! Be of good cheer! I will pray for thee!"

They were cuffing her, knocking her about. A red-faced man had her by the hair and was dragging her backwards. Yet still she cried, "Be of good cheer, Master Tony! Thy sins are forgiven! Our Blessed Lady waits for thee!" The man struck her on the mouth with his open hand.

Suddenly a big young fellow, muscled like a blacksmith, stepped forward to Honsie's side. "Let her alone!"

"What for?" retorted the red-faced man.

With a huge fist the young man knocked him down. "That's what for!" Then he glared at them all, put one arm round Honsie and shook the other in the air. "Anyone wants the other fist he knows how to get it! I says let her alone!"

They fell back from around him, and he gently led Honsie to the foot of the scaffold where Anthony was standing. "Easy, now, missus! 'Ere we are, then. Don't you be afeared, now! What's thy name, good soul?"

"Honor Godsell," she answered. "I'm Honor Godsell."

Anthony, turning and looking down, saw the tears falling from her eyes. Yet her voice was steady, as she called yet again, "May thy true Queen bless thee, Master Tony! May Our Lord and His Holy Mother comfort thee and be with thee! I am with thee! Hail, Mary, full of grace . . ." Several around her took it up.

Then he was dragged away and the rope was put round his neck.

"*Parce mihi, Domine!*" he cried, and said no more.

Yet through all that followed, until he lost consciousness, he could hear Honsie's voice clear among the rest – "Be of good cheer, Master Tony! Thy Lord loveth thee! Be of good cheer!"

As his body was quartered by heavy blows of the cleaver, jets of blood spurted across the scaffold, covering those immediately below with a red spray. The smell of blood filled the air, mingling with the stench of the crowd. A thin, red mist hung over the platform, like the surrounding clamour grown palpable. Those closest to the bodies breathed this mist, coughing it from their lungs. The raucous din seemed no longer to be made up of intelligible words, but had become a snarling roar, like the baying of beasts over a kill. Gaping mouths drivelled and salivated. The executioners licked the blood off their bare arms. One of the onlookers had wet himself, and stood cursing as the piss steamed and dripped from his breeches. Another, who was standing behind a woman, had her by the shoulders and was rubbing himself against her, seeming no more aware than an animal, his eyes fixed in an unseeing stare. The crowd, scarcely conscious of one another, were still united by a single, burning ardour, a frenzy for more agony, more blood, more death.

Honsie had fainted, falling heavily over her protector's arm. Stooping, he lifted her bodily, turned and began to push his way back out of the crowd. It was hard going, for none paid him attention, except for one man who swore at him and spat in his face. Having at last thrust his way clear, he carried Honsie well away from the throng and laid her down on a grassy bank beside the road. After some moments her eyes opened and she raised her head, trying to look about her. Before she could speak he said again, "Easy, missus; easy now!" She seemed about to cry out, but he put a hand gently over her mouth.

"No need to take on, missus. You'm safe here; I shan't go away. Just 'e bide now and take it easy."

She struggled up yet again. "Master Tony! Master Tony!" Once more he restrained her. She fell back, and he slid one arm behind her head.

"You can't do no more for 'im now, missus. You done foine; done everything 'e could. Just 'e rest easy now!"

Two men were approaching and he gestured to them to turn away.

"Bide till 'e feels better, ma'am. I'll see 'e home. Got far to go, 'ave 'e?"

"No," she whispered. "No, not far."

Suddenly, the distant noise of the crowd splintered into

renewed shouts and yells. Shivering, she stopped her ears and again began to weep, sobbing convulsively and pressing her face against his shoulder. Murmuring, he stroked her hair and at length she became calmer.

"Best come on, now. Us don't want t'ang about 'ere, do us? Folks come starin'. You just lean on me, now. I'll get 'e home. Where do 'e live?"

She told him. At that moment a cart could be seen approaching from a side road. As it came closer he called to the driver, who nodded, drew up and extended one arm to help Honsie to clamber up beside him. The young man followed.

"She bin taken bad, y'see." The carter nodded and jerked his head in the direction whence they had come.

"Ah. Reckon no bloody wonder."

They went on in silence until Honsie, with a hand laid on his shoulder, asked him to stop, pressing dry lips to his rough cheek and smiling by way of thanks.

As they walked on in the soft September sunshine, she began gradually to recover herself. But her hand was trembling so much that she could not fit her key into the lock. He took it from her, opened the door and gently led her to the nearest chair. She tried to speak, but could only stammer and stumble. He took her hand and, as she fell silent, seated himself beside her.

"Anthony Babington," he asked, "you were 'is friend? I seen that."

"I looked after him all his life from a baby," she answered. "I was in his service all his life."

"But they didn't never arrest 'e? Didn't ask 'e – to tell – to tell 'en about the plot an' that?"

She shook her head. "I'm only a servant; and anyway they knew all they needed to know already." She paused, and then added, "They'd known for weeks."

"Then why didn't 'en arrest Mr Babington – well, before—"

"They were waiting for the true queen – Queen Mary – the queen they've imprisoned – they were waiting until they had clear evidence that she was in the plot."

"And was she?"

"Oh, yes."

"But 'ow did 'en find out?"

"I don't know. But they did; and it was only when they had that – what they really wanted – that they went after Master Anthony and his friends."

"Not you, though. But you're a Catholic, of course?"

"Of course; and you?"

He smiled. "Of course, Miss Honor Godsell. I'm Jack Hulton, by the way. I reckon 'e ought to eat summat now. Is there anythin' in the 'ouse?"

As they were eating, she asked him, "Where do you live? You're not married, are you?"

He laughed. "Married? No; I only come nineteen a month back. My father works on Lord Hillmount's land, 'tween Hungerford and Newbury. I used to work there too, but I wanted to get away, see a bit of the world, like, do summat different. I bin lookin' for work, but now I seen a bit of London I don't go much on it. I don't reckon it'll suit me, but all same I'm not goin' 'ome, everybody laughin'."

"So you're all on your own here, then?"

"Ah." He laughed again. "No work, no money. Ennit real?"

"I'm going home," she said. "To Durbyshire."

"Durbyshire? Where's that, then?"

She told him about her life at Dethick, about the great Babington estates that embraced virtually the whole county, and about her honourable service during Anthony's boyhood. "Master Anthony married Miss Margery Draycot about eight years ago. They had a little girl, but – she died – oh, only a short time back. But I've heard tell," she ended, "that if anyone's convicted of high treason, everything – their land, their houses – it's all forfeit to the Crown. Master Anthony's father's been dead these fifteen years, but then his mother, her that was Lady Darcy, she married Mr Foljambe and they're both still living at Dethick. Master Anthony's two younger brothers, Master Francis and Master George – perhaps they'll be allowed to keep Dethick, I can't say. But whatever happens, the ordinary folk, the farmers, the labourers and servants and that, they'll still be there. I've only been away about a year and a half. If I can only get back home I can live with my mother

246

at Matlock. She's a widow, you see; my father died when I was only twenty. She'd be glad to see me come home, and I could stay with her until I got a place in some household."

"Reckon 'e could?"

"I'm sure of that. If I stay here I'll starve, no danger. No one's going to employ a woman who was in the service of Anthony Babington."

"But they'd take 'e on in Durbyshire?"

"Oh, yes. If I can only get there an' go an' see Miss Margery, she'll certainly help me. Up there, you see, most everyone's Catholic – Mr and Mrs Foljambe and all the big, important people; they all know me. I was reckoned a good servant."

"'Ow do 'e mean to get back there, then?"

"I don't know, Jack. I've still got a few things – presents that Master Anthony gave me. I've had to sell a lot of them. When the rest have gone, I'll have no money – only one or two changes of clothes, that's all." She wiped her eyes.

He paused, then said very deliberately, "Would 'e care for me to come along with 'e to Durbyshire?"

"Oh, Jack, do you really mean it? Oh, I'd be so glad if only you'd come. You'd certainly get good employment up there, you know, a big, strong young fellow like you, with experience on the land. And I'd be more than glad to have a man along o' me, making a journey like that. Woman on her own, asking for trouble, that'd be."

"Well, I done 'e one good turn today. Reckon it won't hurt me to do 'e another, Miss Godsell. I got a few shillings left in my pocket. Shall us start tomorrow, when 'e've had a chance to wash that poor lad's blood off'n our clothes? Ah, that's if only us can get hold of some soap and water."

There is no need to recount in detail the journey made by Jack and Honsie from London to Matlock. It lasted the best part of five weeks, for they had continually to stop in one place or another, working in order to make enough money for the most frugal of livings. Sometimes they ate turnips stolen from the fields. Once or twice they were taken short distances by friendly carters or tranters, but most of the 130 miles they walked. Not infrequently they were exposed to rain and frost, and often counted themselves lucky to find shelter in a barn or a loft. Once Honsie became feverish and lay for four days in the house of a kindly old clergyman while Jack worked for him. Through all these hardships he showed himself staunch and supportive, and encouraged Honsie with cheerfulness and confidence.

They reached Matlock on a wet afternoon in late October. For some moments Honsie's mother did not recognise her, thin, muddy and tattered, for she had supposed that her daughter must have shared the fate of the conspirators, or been murdered by some of the bloody-minded heretics in London who had hated Anthony Babington. Her joy and relief knew no bounds.

Throughout the neighbourhood, Honsie and Jack were treated as honestly as she had anticipated. Mrs Foljambe readily received her back into service, while the Head Forester was glad to take on the sturdy Jack, who settled down and did very well.

Yet Honsie was mistaken in her expectation of true warmth and kindness from her former friends and associates. Although the majority of the tenants on the Babington estates were either open or clandestine Catholics, none felt any sympathy or esteem for Anthony. He was a traitor who had discredited them, who had brought them down to the lowest level of suspicion and the harshest recusancy laws which they had suffered since Elizabeth's accession. The cruel execution of Queen Mary and the declared enmity of Catholic Spain were laid at his door. Everyone wanted to be disassociated from him and his criminal band of conspirators. Besides, they added for good measure, he had been a harsh and relentless landlord. There were those who wondered how much Honor Godsell, his lifelong servant, might have had to do with the plot.

Honsie prayed for his soul night and morning. After a time her natural diligence and humility made her friends among the other servants, and these came to believe her tearful insistence that she had tried, as best she could in her position, to dissuade Master Anthony and to warn him against those who had destroyed him. It was the wicked Ballard, she told them, who had played the chief part in leading him on to his downfall.

The Outlandish Knight

As the years went by she became once more a trusted and privileged servant, much relied upon by the housekeeper, especially as a friend and adviser of the young and inexperienced. She lived on well into King James's reign, and in old age would sit knotting by the fire or out in the summer sunshine, the very exemplar of kindly serenity. At her neck she wore a fine gold chain, the gift of her Master long ago. But that provenance was her secret and known to no one else.

Lady Susan Perris, the seventeenth-century diarist, was a guest at Dethick in 1608. She mentions 'Godsell' as a servant who struck her favourably, and, among a few trifling details, records a song which took her fancy when she heard Honor sing it to 'some of the children'.

Go from my window my love my dove
Go from my window my dear
For the wind is in the west and the cuckoo's in his nest
And you can't have a lodging here

Go from my window my love my dove
Go from my window my dear
O the weather is warm, it will never do thee harm
And you can't have a lodging here

Go from my window my love my dove
Go from my window my dear
The wind is blowing high and the ship is lying by
And you can't have a harbouring here.